Tales of
WULFGARD
Volume 1

A collection of Wulfgard stories by
Justin R. R. Stebbins *and*
Maegan A. Stebbins

ISBN: 0-9727341-9-8
ISBN-13: 978-0-9727341-9-6

Cover design and all illustrations by Justin R. Stebbins

Visit us online at:
www.wulfgard.net

Special Thanks

To all of our patrons and supporters, especially the following:

Our Family
Ajestice
Alex
Caleb Blanchet
Matthew Blanchet
Jared Buniel
Jonathan Davis
Jack Mitchell
Ryan J.
Jan Lingenfelder
Nicholas Randall
Kyle "Ambad" Smith
Valerie "Coop"

CONTENTS

Speak No Evil
Whisper's Tale

by Justin R. R. Stebbins

Part 1: Seen and Not Heard

She knew the City like the back of her hand. It had many names, but to her it was just the City. She lived in the poor section, the "Outer Ring," or Iron Ring. The buildings were actually newer than in the wealthier sections, yet they looked older, black and scarred and in disrepair. Their dark windows yawned like the eyes of skulls. She knew their long faces like the faces of old friends.

She sat atop one now, gazing down from the edge of the roof at the men and women walking below. She knew many of *their* faces too, though only a few knew her. Seldom did she walk among them, for she preferred to live above. There below sat the homeless men on the street corners, begging for a pittance. There roved the band of young hooligans, out to cause trouble. There marched the pair of watchmen – just two men to cover so many streets. They would never notice her.

At length she spotted a mark: a traveling merchant, obviously new in town. From the furtive way he glanced at every alley, she doubted he would soon return to the City once he had left it behind. Good.

She ran to the corner of the roof, slipped over the edge, and plunged into the deep shadows of the alley below, like a diver into a pool of darkness. Climbing the side of a building was as easy to her as running along the ground. She saw handholds quickly, jumped to them without fear, and she always landed on her feet. Some of her friends called her reckless... but then, she currently only had one friend.

When her soft shoes – more like foot-wrappings, really – landed on the ground, she whispered into the shadows: "*Shade!*"

"'m 'ere," a boy murmured back, emerging from a dark doorway that led nowhere.

"Double around," the girl said, pointing. "I'll trip the mark."

He shrugged. "A'right."

He disappeared. Now alone in the quiet alley, the girl began taking deep breaths, working herself up, watching her narrow view of the dimly-lit main street. There were few streetlamps in the Iron Ring, and the moon was overcast.

She heard the mark whistling. The sound of it echoed around her. It was a nervous sound. She imagined herself as an alley cat and pictured the mark as a dim-witted bird, strutting helplessly past her hiding spot. Some people called her Alleycat. It was one of her many nicknames, since she didn't have a real one.

She pounced. It was the simplest of attacks: she charged headlong, barreling into the merchant and knocking him to the pavement. He had been carrying a package under his arm. Now it lay in a distant corner, next to some stairs.

The merchant, after getting back to his feet, glanced back at the package, and then at the girl in front of him. She lay on the ground, nursing a thin, pale arm, trying to look hurt. The mark looked at her with pity… for a second too long. From the corner of her eye, the girl saw the boy search the man's dropped bag, rummaging through its contents.

"Are you alright?" the mark asked, reaching down to help her. He was a slightly corpulent man, with a thick, light-brown mustache and clean clothes.

She nodded at him, saying nothing, looking up with her big green eyes. Those great green eyes, staring out from the little girl's pale face, framed by her dark cloth head-wrapping… got 'em every time. The man looked distraught, as if he'd stepped on a baby.

He helped the girl back to her feet and said, "Let me look at your arm. It's alright; I'm a physician."

She let him hold up her soft little arm and feel of the elbow. There was, of course, nothing wrong with it. She knew how to fall without injury. It was a lesson she'd learned from falling many, many times. Every time she rose up a little in the City, she knew she would soon fall back down.

"What were you running from?" the mark asked.

She looked back at the alley, green eyes wide with fright. Then she moved her feet, nervously and clumsily, tripping over herself so that the man had to catch her. She let him support her, while she went through his pockets.

"Easy there!" the mark said, standing her upright again. "Just wait a moment, and I'll get my bag. I can help you get back to wherever –"

The moment the mark went back and lifted up his dropped bag, he noticed the difference in weight. He quickly glanced back to the girl – but she was gone. He checked his pockets, confirming his suspicions. Then he spat out a furious curse, scooped up his bag, and ran toward the dark alley from which the girl had come.

He ran in so fast that he nearly bumped into a second child, this one a boy. He was a poor boy with messy brown hair and a scar on his lip, but not a total vagabond. His clothing marked him as part of the merchant middle class, not unlike the mark himself.

"Outta m' way, if y' please," said the boy, mixing rudeness and courtesy in a way that left the merchant babbling for an appropriate response.

It took the man so long to find his tongue that the boy had slid past him and nearly out into the street before the merchant called at him: "Wait! Where's the girl?"

"That's who I'm chasin' after!" shouted the boy, waving his arms angrily. "She took my stuff! Did you see 'er?"

The mark's anger rose even more, and he eyed the boy warily. "Yes. I thought she went down here…"

The boy shook his head and gave a final dismissive wave of his arms before dashing off down the pavement. The disgruntled merchant chased after him, but once he reached the street, the boy was gone. Much as the mark had expected. Taking a deep breath and letting it out in a half-sigh, half-curse, he tossed his empty bag aimlessly away and stomped down the middle of the road, hands buried deep in his bare pockets.

"That poor dumb cully," said the boy. "Should we go find the bag?"

The girl leaned out over the rooftop, looking both ways down the street, her long black ponytail dangling. The faces of the city buildings looked back at her, impassive. The mark had long since been swallowed by them, as he made his way along the twisting grey road to wherever he was going. Visitors to the City often left poorer than they had come, unwillingly providing for those who lived here.

"Whisper?" the boy prompted.

She looked back at him, with a thin smile beneath her great green eyes. "No, let the City have it. What was in it?"

Shade dug around through the various hiding places on his person. He was known among the vagabonds for his well-tailored clothes, old and worn now though they were. They also knew he was a "knuckle" – the word used on the street for a young pickpocket. For a few years, Shade had worked at a cleaner's, where he'd learned how to wash and sew. But then some of the other urchin boys had teased him, saying he did a woman's work, calling him "Needle-boy." So, a few days later, he'd put on the best tunic, vest, and trousers he could find at the cleaner's, grabbed an armful of any other valuables he could carry, and fled to another part of the City.

Whisper didn't know his real name. He'd asked her to call him "Shade," probably because it sounded tough, but the name Needle-boy was not inaccurate. Using his skill at needlework, he had sewn hidden pockets into nearly every part of his outfit, allowing him to ferret away valuables so they seemed to just disappear. He'd taught Whisper some of what he knew, but only reluctantly. He didn't like to tell the story of how he'd done a woman's work. Whisper never brought it up again.

Suddenly, Whisper's ears – covered though they were by the dark shawl wrapped over her head – perked up, and she looked away at the other rooftops. Where most of the inner city was decorated by tall pillars and beauteous domes, the Iron Ring had many flat rooftops, almost like the tops of castles, with stairs leading up to them. But Whisper and Shade never frequented those. They were currently sitting on a low-sloping, shingled roof with no easy access.

"What is it?" Shade asked.

"Were you followed?" Whisper hissed.

His light blue eyes went wide, but he repressed his fear with anger and said, "No! 'Course not! I mean, there was one fella watchin' me from across the street, but I gave 'im the slip. No one ever *climbs* up after us."

Whisper sank down low, watching a loose pile of wood on the neighboring roof, where she had seen something glint in the shadows. *A pair of eyes*, her instincts said. And she trusted her instincts.

"We need to go," she whispered.

Shade crouched down with her, stuffing the loot back into his pockets. "Where?"

She saw a man emerge from behind the wood pile. He was clad all in dark leather, with a black hooded cloak, and mask of dark red cloth over his mouth. She spotted a dagger sheathed at his side, just before he started running toward the edge of the roof... running as if to jump across.

Whisper leapt to her feet, pulling Shade up with her.

"*Scowre!*" she cried. That was thieves' slang for: *run*.

They made the jump to the next roof easily. That was what *she* had trained *Shade* how to do. When she'd met him about a year ago, he'd only been a decent climber. Now his skills were almost a match for hers, though he never came close to her sheer effortless grace.

They sped from building to building, sliding down one roof, leaping to the next, climbing up the stonework, changing direction... and yet, every time Whisper looked back, she would catch a glimpse of the shadow that followed them. Her heart was in her throat now. Never before had she encountered such a relentless pursuer. She had crossed the Night Watchmen from time to time, but they gave up quickly, and never had even one of them tried to follow her up a building, much less from roof to roof.

Shade stopped, putting his hands on his knees and gasping for breath. Whisper grabbed his sleeve and tried to pull him along, but he wouldn't budge. He looked like he might pass out. She thought about leaving him behind. It wouldn't be the first time, and many friends had abandoned her the same way. But for some reason, she liked Shade more than those others. Something about the way he carried himself, the way he always fixed his messy hair down so it shadowed his blue eyes, but they always shone through regardless...

She stayed beside him, muttering a curse. But she didn't have to regret the decision for long, and she quickly realized they never could have escaped. For in the blink of an eye, there appeared not just one hooded figure, but two. The second man rose up in front of them, vaulting onto the roof as easily as Whisper had ever done, even though he was nearly twice her height.

She saw the first hooded man drop down behind them, a pair of dark eyes glinting beneath his hood. He spoke with a voice like sandpaper on gravel: *"Don't try to run again."*

"Easy," said the second man, his voice much softer. "We're not guards; we won't hurt you. My name's Camron. What are yours?"

The two kids exchanged glances. Camron removed his mask and cowl, revealing his face. It was a handsome face. He had youthful features, sand-colored hair, and friendly light-brown eyes. He looked at the two of them with great wonder, as if he were truly interested to learn their names. Everything about his demeanor and voice spoke of warmth and kindness.

Whisper didn't trust him one bit.

But Shade answered: "I'm Shade, and she's Whisper."

"Ah, so you've chosen your own names," said Camron. "That's good. It speaks of independence. My friend and I are all about independence. We've set up a home for orphans of the city, where you can have food, beds, shelter… all without any priests or soldiers watching your every move. We'll even help train you on how to avoid them."

Shade glanced at Whisper, who seemed afraid to speak, as she often was. He asked, "What if we say no?"

This time the dark-eyed man behind them answered, in his gritty voice: "You can't. You can either come with us awake and blindfolded, or out cold."

"See," said the sandy-haired man, "we want to keep this place a secret. We can't have you telling anyone about it. But if you don't like it, we'll take you right back. I promise."

"*Let's run*," Whisper whispered to Shade. "*We can make it.*"

"I think we should go with 'em," the boy replied.

"Dammit, Shade!"

With that, the girl took off. She managed to make it all the way to the edge of the roof before, in a few great strides, the dark-eyed man caught up to her, grabbing her by the legs. She fell on her face, and her shawl was shaken loose, freeing long black ponytail… and her ears. She looked back at the two men with terror in her wide green eyes. She even saw Shade staring at her ears again, like he *always* did, *every* time. She wanted to slap him.

"A child of the Alfar," Camron muttered. "Unexpected…"

Whisper had never heard the word "Alfar" before. "Elf" was the one most people used – or "fairy" or "nymph" or "sprite." She wasn't quite sure what "Alfar" meant, except that her long, pointed ears marked her as one.

As a small child, the priestesses who had cared for her had always treated her kindly, even with something approaching awe.

But most people from outside the Temple of Artemis looked upon her with great suspicion. When she showed her ears, she could hear them muttering about dark magic and curses, saw them making holy signs to ward off evil, keeping their distance...

She remembered when the Temple Knights had come for her. She'd overheard the priestesses talking to them, saying they were to take her back to the elves. She still wasn't sure why she'd fled: fear of the unknown, anger at the priestesses for throwing her out, for trying to control her life...

Whatever the reason, she had covered up her ears and left through a window, never to return. The City was her home, and although life was hard sometimes, she felt free on the rooftops, looking down over the familiar streets. It was the only home she knew.

These were her last conscious thoughts before the dark-eyed man held a cloth up to her face, and her world went black.

When Whisper awoke, she wondered if she had somehow been transported to an elven kingdom, for standing above her was the first elf she had ever seen outside of her own reflection. The elf woman's features were severe yet perfect, with pale skin, high cheekbones, and brows that gracefully arched over her pale blue eyes. Her long, smooth hair was such a pale blond that it looked nearly white. She had it braided to proudly reveal her elven ears, which were slightly shorter than Whisper's, yet as pointed as arrowheads.

Whisper stared in amazement, but she quickly noticed the elf's dark leather armor, similar in design to that of the two men who had attacked her and Shade on the rooftops. This elf also wore a long cloak of the same shade of deep red as the other men's masks.

"She's coming around now," said a cold voice, and Whisper turned her head to see the dark-eyed man looking down at her with utter indifference.

"Good," said the elf woman, her voice like silk. "Finally, you bring back someone worth saving, Hanan."

Whisper heard Camron's voice somewhere in the room: "You think she nearly got away just because she's an elf? Her friend kept up with her, and he's just a mortal boy."

The elf woman huffed dismissively. "Yes, perhaps he'll be the next great Hanan al-Saffah... for the pittance of decades his lifespan allows."

Camron cleared his throat. "Not in front of the children, Seona."

The elf scoffed and stomped away. Whisper found herself wanting desperately for the elf woman to stay, wanting to ask her about the 'Alfar'... but when she tried to call out to her, the elf was gone before Whisper could summon her voice. The dark-eyed man, Hanan al-Saffah, left as well, through the same door. Perhaps they were going to hunt down more children.

Whisper sat up and looked around. The long room was full of beds, each bearing two sleeping figures of her own size... "children," as Camron had called them, though in fact most were in their teens. Whisper was unsure of her own exact age. She only knew that her friends seem to grow much faster than her, leaving her behind one by one, year after year, as they moved on to what they called adulthood.

"Alright, everyone!" Camron shouted, clapping his hands and beaming his friendly smile. "It's time to meet the Mother!"

He led them all into what Whisper assumed was the main hall of the building. It was a great, square, unadorned stone box lit by torches on the otherwise bare walls. The ceiling above was wood, supported by crisscrossing beams from which dangled a few loose ropes. Otherwise, the room was featureless. There were no windows, no decorations, and the only bit of furniture in the room was a cushioned chair resting atop a wooden stage. In the chair sat an old woman who could only be the Mother.

Her hair was stark white, tied into a tight bun, and though her face was wrinkled and gaunt, she sat straight as a pike shaft, clad in smooth, spotless blood-red robes. A pair of black-gloved hands extended from the robes' loose sleeves, tapping their thin fingers together under the old woman's chin as her pale blue eyes roved the faces of the two dozen or so children. Her gaze landed on Whisper and stayed there for several seconds. Whisper returned the stare without flinching. The old woman nodded, as if in approval, and then continued her survey of the room.

A rod appeared in her hand – Whisper wasn't sure if it was a riding crop or a sap – and she slammed it on the arm of her chair. The sound echoed through the great stone box of a room, and the crowd fell silent, staring. She motioned for them to sit, and they did. Whisper crossed her legs on the cold, slick wooden floor.

The old woman pointed to two boys, one with each hand, and said, "Take these two away. They are troublemakers, nothing more. See them back to where they came from."

"What?!" one of the boys cried out. "We ain't done nothin'!"

"Yes, you have," said the Mother. "You have spoken without permission. The next child to do so will also be sent away."

"And trust me," said Camron, who was standing behind the crowd, his hands behind his back and a smile on his face, "you don't want to be sent away. The fun hasn't even started yet."

He said this without a trace of sarcasm, as if something truly enjoyable were about to begin, yet Whisper did not like it at all. She looked around at the great blank walls. There was no telling where they were. They could be high in a castle, or deep underground...

Once Camron and another leather-clad man had seen out the two rejected boys, the Mother went on: "Listen well, all of you, for I will never repeat myself. You have been selected for very special training. We will feed you, clothe you, give you beds, and we will teach you. You will work tirelessly, day and night, learning to move unseen, unhindered, and unopposed through any obstacles. You will learn how to fight, steal, and kill. If any of you are not interested in the life I have just described, raise your hand now, and we will send you back to your former one on the streets. You will never see us again. But you must speak now, for this will be your only chance to leave of your own choice."

Whisper looked at the wide-eyed children around her. All of them seemed fascinated. None were quick to reject the Mother's offer. None except Whisper. She hated this place, this oppressive room, these strange people... She felt at home on the rooftops of the City, beneath the open sky. Life on the streets had been hard at first, when she was truly a child, and it was still hard sometimes, but... it was home. She felt a sort of freedom there. Not like here, boxed in by huge blank walls.

Yet she sat there, clenching and unclenching her fist, unwilling to raise her hand. Would these people really take her back? She didn't trust them. Where were they really taking those who left? Also, though she hated to admit it, she wanted to see the beautiful elf woman again, to speak with her...

And so, for one reason or another, not a single hand was raised. The Mother nodded again, though it looked less like approval this time. To Whisper, it looked more like: *"So be it."*

Part 2: The Messengers

She wasn't sure how long she stayed there – weeks, maybe months – living and training with the other orphans in the Box. That was what she called it in her mind: the Box. She still had never seen a window or a door to the outside world. One room contained stairs leading down several floors, but there were none leading up. There was only a trap door on the roof far above, and none of the instructors ever opened it.

Her first task had been in the room below: a labyrinth full of obstacles and traps. The children were sent into the maze to find a golden key. Whisper had immediately observed that the walls of the labyrinth didn't reach all the way to the ceiling. Several others noticed this as well, but none of them could even hope to jump high enough to reach the edge, at least a dozen feet above.

Whisper did it almost without thinking. She found the widest corridor in the maze, ran toward the wall, ran a few steps right up the side of it, and grabbed the top. Then she pulled herself up. The upper edge wasn't even six inches wide, but she balanced on it easily, running lightly along and searching each corridor below. It wasn't long before she spotted the key, retrieved it, and returned, without ever facing a trap.

Her instructors had mixed reactions.

There were only five of them, the strange men and women in the dark leather and red cloaks. The leader was the Mother, who merely gave another of her mysterious nods when Whisper returned from the test. Whisper sensed that she was satisfied. The next in rank of importance seemed to be the dark-eyed man, Hanan al-Saffah. Everyone spoke of him with great respect. He just looked at Whisper with cold contempt. Camron, of course, smiled and laughed, congratulating her on her ingenuity. There was also another man, but Whisper saw little of him, and he never took off his mask.

And then, of course, there was Seona, the female elf. When Whisper beat the maze test, Seona just smiled smugly, looking around at the others to rub Whisper's victory in their faces. Even this expression could not diminish her otherworldly beauty. Whisper ached to ask her about her people, the 'Alfar,' but as usual, she couldn't summon the courage to speak.

She continued to curse herself about that, for she hadn't seen the elf since then. And she didn't even know how long it had been – several months, possibly. There were no real days or nights in the Box, with no sun or moon or stars to be seen. But over the course of her time there, she had learned much, while also impressing her instructors with the skills she already possessed.

It was not a bad life, for a life in a great prison cell. At least no one would run her out of it, and she had plenty of food. Her bond with Shade had grown, though she continued to keep her distance from the other children as much as possible. She had also grown to like Camron, the kindly instructor who was always smiling. Though she had thought his kindness insincere at first, his continued good treatment of herself and the other students eventually won her over.

Not so with the dark-eyed man, Hanan al-Saffah. There was something in his eyes that made a chill run down Whisper's spine, like the touch of the bony finger of death. Today, he was to teach them more combat techniques. The children always carried blunt wooden knives now, tucked in their belts or shoes if they had any, or else on a bit of string slung around their neck or waist. The instructors had taught them how to use the daggers to 'silence' watchmen, even ones wearing armor. At first, Whisper had found it a little unsettling, but she had been abused by the city watch on many occasions, and had more than once wished she could defend herself.

"I hate Hanan," Whisper said to Shade as they headed toward the main room for their training.

"Yeah..." Shade replied, with a shrug, "but I can deal with him. The others are great. Camron's been showin' me how to throw knives so the pointy end hits instead of the back! That's a lot better than learning how to *sew*."

"You've stolen a day's meal with your sewn pockets," Whisper said quietly. "I don't know how throwing a knife is going to get you a day's meal..."

Shade didn't seem to hear her; he just went on: "It's great here, isn't it? I think I've eaten more this week than I've eaten the whole rest of my life, and they say if we finish our training we get to go to their *real* base, where there's food fit for kings!"

"They won't tell us who they're training us to fight..." Whisper muttered.

"Camron said they fight who they're paid to fight, like mer... mernecerries... merc'n'ries. You know, sell-swords. It's like being a soldier, but working for yourself and not some fat rich king!"

At length, they joined the rest of the children seated in the great Box, waiting for lessons to begin. The only instructor present was al-Saffah. He sat cross-legged on the raised platform, at the feet of the Mother's chair, watching them with his sunken eyes. The room was utterly silent, until one boy, whose continued good performance in the combat trials had perhaps bolstered his courage, spoke up.

"Are you from the Far South?" he asked Hanan. "I knew a merchant from a place called Desrit once. I liked him. He sold dates. Used to give me a free one to eat every day."

Al-Saffah let the echoes of the boy's voice die awkwardly in the vast Box, before he finally deigned to look down at him and reply: "The place is called *Deshret*. And I am no seller of dates."

After another long moment of silence, Hanan at last leapt softly down from the platform. With a wave of his hands, he instructed the children to form a ring, leaving the central space open. This was where he would train them to fight.

"Today, we're going to do something different," he said, his voice as flat and emotionless as ever. "When we finally send you out on a real task, in the real world, you will usually work in pairs. You should know your partner well. Everyone, choose your partner now."

Whisper and Shade exchanged glances. They were already sitting together, so they simply didn't move. The others knew not to ask them. They were well-known to be a team.

Once everyone had selected a partner and settled down again, Hanan's unsettling eyes locked straight onto Whisper, and he said, "You two. Step forward."

For a second, Whisper sat frozen, hoping he'd meant someone else. But Shade quickly stood, glancing down at her with slight annoyance on his face. She swallowed her fear and joined him in the ring.

Hanan glanced between the two of them. "You two are friends."

It was more of a statement than a question, but they both nodded.

"I'm sure you each think you know the other quite well. You think you know your friend's strengths and weaknesses. But you'll find you still have a lot to learn. Draw your daggers. The two of you will fight until one delivers a killing blow."

Whisper's eyes went wide. She reluctantly reached for her wooden blade, but Shade had already drawn his and was turning to face her. He gave her a shrug and dropped into a defensive position.

Whisper kept her eyes on Shade, for she didn't want to meet Hanan's dark gaze, even as she asked him: "But why would we need to know how to fight each other?"

"To learn," replied Hanan, "and because I told you to. Now *fight.*"

Shade immediately made a clumsy attempt at a surprise attack, which Whisper dodged almost by reflex. Shade didn't relent. He continued stabbing and slashing, swinging wildly at her, as she ducked under and sidestepped and leapt away from each attack. He only grew more furious as she led him around the ring. It was slightly terrifying, but Whisper kept her cool, stepping always lightly away, as if it were a dance.

At last, Shade slowed down, panting for breath. Whisper suddenly realized she could beat him easily. All she had to do was keep avoiding his attacks, and he would tire himself out. Then she could move in with ease and defeat him with one or two quick strikes. But one look at Shade's blazing blue eyes made her hesitate. His eyes were overflowing with pride and determination. He did *not* want to lose. If she humiliated him here in front of everyone, he might never forgive her.

She had to let him win but make it look like he'd really beaten her. She moved in for a clumsy lunge, which he blocked with a swipe of his arm. He used the opening to stab at her with his wooden blade, but she rolled away. Once back on her feet, she dropped into a defensive pose, waiting for him to resume the attack.

"Enough of this farce," said Hanan al-Saffah.

He waded into the ring, grabbing Shade from behind. In the blink of an eye, the boy was disarmed and face-down on the floor. Then Hanan advanced on Whisper, wielding Shade's wooden knife. He took a stab at her, which she dodged while trying to strike his throat. He ducked under her attack and slashed open her stomach. Then he grabbed her arm, twisting it painfully, and pinned her to the ground.

"Had this been a real dagger, your guts would be spilled over the floor," he said, driving his knee into her back. "You went straight for my throat, I noticed. That was smart. You should have been that smart with your little friend, instead of trying to let the blundering fool beat you."

He grabbed her ponytail in his fist and jerked her head back, stretching out her long, pale throat, over which he ran the wooden blade. Then the knife went up to her ears. She felt the cold wood run along each one, all the way to the pointed tip.

"Do you know how I would kill you, girl? First, I would cut off these ears and show them to you. Then I might slit your throat, all the way from the stub of one ear to the other. Or perhaps I would strangle you." Here he threw down the wooden knife, and she felt his black-gloved fingers caress her neck. "I usually prefer to leave a clean body, so that whoever finds it wonders if you are only sleeping… until they draw close enough to see the truth. Perhaps I'd leave one ear for them to find. I'd keep the other as a memento."

Whisper had been trying not to scream, but she could take it no longer. She felt the squeal of a frightened girl rising in her throat – a sound she hadn't made in years – and she fought to choke it back. Only a little squeak escaped.

But that was enough to rouse Shade into action. He charged in to defend her, scooping up the wooden knife she'd dropped and raising it to stab Hanan. But al-Saffah quickly and violently twisted Whisper, bringing her in the way of the attack. Shade looked shocked as his wooden blade struck her in the collarbone, causing her to wince.

"Look at that," Hanan said matter-of-factly. "Your little boyfriend just killed you. And now I will kill him."

Hanan shoved Whisper to the floor and kicked Shade in the gut. The boy doubled over in pain, coughing and sputtering. Whisper gasped for air as she scrambled back to her feet, looking for a weapon...

And then a familiar old woman's voice came from the direction of the raised platform, calmly saying a single word: *"Stop."*

At the Mother's command, Hanan dropped his training dagger and let it clatter to the floor. Whisper looked around at all the staring faces, especially Shade's. Thankfully, he didn't look angry with her for trying to let him win. His eyes only showed fear and pity.

The Mother said, "Is this how you treat your students when I am not present, Hanan? Some of these children are your future brothers and sisters."

"You clearly haven't met my *real* sister," Hanan said, and left it at that.

The Mother seemed to pretend not to hear that response. "Bring Whisper and Shade to my quarters. It is time."

Hanan didn't have to say anything; Whisper and Shade were eager to follow the old woman and escape more of al-Saffah's brand of training. The Mother led them out of the main "Box" and into the stairwell. Whisper had been to the floor below, which contained the labyrinth used for many of the training exercises, but the Mother led them even lower, down another flight of stairs. They entered a narrow hallway lined with closed doors.

Whisper got the distinct impression that they were now deep underground. There was no way to be sure, as there were still no windows anywhere. It was probably just her imagination, but she started breathing shallow anyway, as if they might run out of air. She hated being underground.

The Mother unlocked one of the doors and waved them inside.

The room was nicely furnished, compared to the ones above. It contained a long mahogany table surrounded by tall-backed chairs. There were even some pictures on the walls: paintings of noble men and women, some clad in very exotic clothing. A great iron-bound chest sat at the far end of the room, bound with a heavy lock.

"The paintings are Camron's," the Mother said, with a wave of a black-gloved hand. "He fancies himself an artist. So does Hanan, but in another way. He views killing as an art."

"The highest art," said Hanan al-Saffah, who had slipped into the room behind them.

"Did we fail?" asked Shade, trying to mask the shame and fear from his voice.

"Quite the contrary, actually," said the Mother, with a thin smile. "We are going to welcome you into the family... right after you perform one essential task."

Whisper said, "You want us to kill someone."

Hanan al-Saffah gave a guttural chuckle. "Clever girl."

Just then, the other instructors entered the room. None of them sat down in the chairs. They just gathered around the two children, smiling. Camron leaned against a wall. Seona perched herself on the corner of the table, one long leg dangling as she twirled a knife expertly between her fingers.

"Now what," said Camron, as he munched an apple, "makes you think we want you to kill someone?"

Whisper didn't return their smiles. "You're training us to break into houses, climb walls, avoid guards, sneak up on people..."

"And kill them," the Mother finished for her. "Yes, you've worked it out. It's very simple really. On occasion, an individual is marked for death. Some of us like to say they're marked by the gods, or by fate, but I don't care for such mysticism. They are marked by men. Let us say, for example, that a young girl stands to inherit a kingdom. A rival family with claim to her crown threatens to go to war over it. Thousands will die in the conflict, thousands more will suffer. The noble girl's family does not care, even if the common folk riot, clamoring for them to relent and give the throne to their rivals. So, to avoid all of that needless destruction... someone comes to us."

Whisper stared into the old woman's eyes, not speaking. Shade glanced between the two pairs of eyes – the bright green and pale blue. Neither the girl or the old woman flinched. The silence was only broken when Camron took another bite of his apple. The Mother looked annoyed. Suddenly, one of her arms shot up, and a dagger flew out of her seemingly empty hand, straight into Camron's apple. The fruit was launched out of his fingers and pinned to the wall by the blade.

"Don't eat in the council room," said the Mother.

"So," Shade said, "you... want us to kill the girl?"

The Mother laughed, leaning back in her chair. "No, child, I don't want you to kill anyone *yet*. And everything I just told you was hypothetical – made up. We *were* hired to kill a young girl from a very wealthy family," and here she drew out and unfurled a small scroll, "but we do not know *why*. This is the contract, but it states no reasons. We are only messengers. We do not ask what the message is, what it means, what purpose it serves. We merely deliver it: the silent message of death."

"We can't read anyway..." Shade said.

The Mother smiled. "Well, that is something else we'll have to fix."

"This is the girl," said Camron, presenting a small painting – clearly by his own hand – of a child in a white dress, with blue ribbons in her blonde locks. "She lives in a manor at the corner of Gold Way and Wallshadow, overlooking the slums from the heights of the Bronze Ring."

The Mother nodded. "As I said, we don't expect you to do the deed. You are not yet ready. A job so delicate can only be trusted to professionals."

Camron smiled. "We can make her death completely painless, like falling asleep."

"It will be beautiful," said Hanan al-Saffah, his dark eyes staring into nothingness as he pictured the scene, "a life snuffed out in the greenest spring of youthful innocence. Her father will return to find her asleep in her room, without a mark on her body. Only when he tries to wake her will he find the blade. It won't be in *her*, of course. That would be crude and ugly. Perhaps in a bedpost, or in the mattress beside her. He will notice it after. He will get the Message."

"'Tis a sad thing," said Camron, "but it must be done."

"The sadder the work of art," said Hanan, "the more poignant. This will be a masterpiece."

Whisper felt horrified at this exchange, but the words of the elf woman, Seona, stung her the most: "Youthful innocence... *pfah*. Six years old or sixty; what's the difference? Mortals are all children, next to the Alfar, passing like leaves in autumn."

The room fell silent then. Camron and Hanan were exchanging glances, shaking their heads at Seona's comment, but the elf ignored them, keeping her frosty-haired head pointed high. Whisper found that she was shaking all over, whether with fear or anger, or nausea, she wasn't sure. She saw to her relief that Shade was trembling as well.

"All you will need to do," the mother clarified at length, "is open a door. You will not witness the deed. You will simply open a door, to let us in. But we'll give you more details about that later. For now, I'll let you get some rest. Tomorrow, your real work begins."

The old woman left then, and the others filed out behind her, leaving the two children standing there in a daze. Hanan and Camron were the last to go, but they paused when they heard Whisper speak softly.

"I can't believe you'd murder a child," she said.

Camron realized the comment was for him. He paused and turned back, looking at them with his usual kindly smile, which Whisper now saw as condescending.

"I understand how you feel right now," he said, "but it's not really all that bad."

He sighed, looking at the doorway and at the room around them. Then he seemed to make up his mind about something and took a painting down off the wall. He crouched down on his toes in front of them and held up the picture. It was an image of an old man dressed in fine clothing, his face pale and worn with wrinkles.

"This is my father," Camron said. "Of course, he never really dressed like this. I grew up in a little town near the wild northern border of the Empire – a place called Eloh. Some people say 'Ay-loh,' but all the locals call it 'Ee-loh.' Anyway, my father was a miner. He worked his hands to the bone every day for us, but we barely saw him even once a month. He was pale, bent, stunted, and half-blind from working in the cramped mining tunnels. He never went out when the sun was shining. He died at age thirty. I barely knew him... and I swore I would never live like him."

"So, you became an assassin?" Shade asked.

"Oh, it's never that simple. I started stealing, a lot like you... and then *they* found me, a lot like you. It's just a job – a *good* job. Your partners watch your back, it pays well, and you can do what you want. I've discovered that my true passion is art, and now I'm free to pursue it. This is one I painted of my father as he should have lived, if all things were equal..."

His voice trailed off there. At length he stood up, replaced the picture, and headed for the door. As he left, he looked back at them one last time.

"Don't worry," he said. "It gets easier."

Once he had gone, Hanan – who had been standing in the corner silently – approached the table. Whisper felt a chill as she looked up at him. Shade massaged a bruise from the recent fight. He looked angry at Hanan, and yet... strangely respectful. The look made Whisper feel sick.

"Weak men like Camron try to justify what we do," said Hanan al-Saffah, looking down at them, "even if only in a small way. They still try to deny that our profession is evil, according to the silly concepts of 'good' and 'evil' defined by those in power. An impossible task. You'll find the job much easier, and more enjoyable, if you abandon these outdated misgivings, and just embrace it. Good and evil are not real. *Death* is."

With that, he swept from the room like a retreating shadow on the wall. When he was gone, Whisper turned away from Shade, leaning against the table and staring at the floor. Shade reached out to comfort her, but hesitated and let his hand drop. He slumped down in a chair, silently thinking.

For a few moments, the world was deathly quiet. There didn't seem to be a sound that could permeate the walls of the Box. The City itself could be burning outside, and they would never hear of it. If they were even in the City...

Eventually, Shade shrugged, slid out of the chair, and stood.

"I don' know," he said, his voice full of that familiar false confidence and bravado. "Maybe Camron's right. Stupid rich mort, sleepin' every day on her feather bed while we sleep on rags in the gutter... The wench prob'ly has it coming."

Whisper's head shot up, and her green eyes, glistening with tears, looked daggers at him. Without a word, she stormed out of the room, slamming the heavy door behind her.

Through the halls she ran, up the stairs to the main floor. She slowed down then, to avoid drawing attention, as she slipped through the other kids and headed for the sleeping quarters. Once there, she threw herself down on her bed and hid under the sheet, trying to block out the world.

Only one thought kept repeating in her mind: *She had to escape.*

Part 3: Keeping Quiet

Whisper didn't come out from beneath her covers until all the other students had gone to bed and the room had fallen quiet. Now she poked her head out into utter blackness and silence, broken only by a few snores. More than ever, she felt trapped. The walls seemed closer than before, the room smaller. She felt she was being suffocated in this horrible box, this school for murderers.

She had to get out.

It was time to put her new training – and her natural talents – to the test. First, she waited and listened. Surely some of the assassins would be watching the children. But if they were, she couldn't detect them. After a few minutes, she slid out of her covers and dropped quietly to the floor. Crawling on all fours, she moved between the beds, trying to remain invisible as she headed for a door to the main room.

Fortunately, there were no actual doors on the openings, so she was able to slip right out. Now the main "box" yawned before her: a great void, lit only by some stray candlelight trickling in from the sleeping quarters. The torches on the tall stone walls sat dead. For several minutes, she waited quietly, her eyes and pointed ears adjusting to the gloom. Yet once again, she caught neither sight nor sound of any watching assassins. All she heard was the faint squeaking of mice on the rafters up above.

The rafters. They crisscrossed the ceiling above, some tied with ropes, the ends of which dangled over the children's heads every day. Whisper wasn't sure if she could reach one, but she had to try. It would not be as easy as running up the wall in the maze. But once she was up there, perhaps she could find a way into the upper rooms, where they were never allowed. Perhaps she could find a way out...

For a minute or two, she searched the walls for the best location, finally settling on a rope that dangled high above a torch mount. The sconce was too high for her to reach on her tiptoes, but she was able to do it with a running start, like she'd done in the maze. She ran two steps straight up the side of the wall and then caught the torch and hauled herself up.

Now perched precariously on her toes atop the narrow bit of metal, she carefully stood, scanning the wall for handholds. The stonework was nearly perfect, as smooth as any she had ever seen. But she could handle it. First, she leaned against the wall and took off her shoes. Then she pressed her toes into a shallow crevice, taking great care, testing her body weight before she continued.

It didn't take her long. One foot, one hand, and another and another, and soon she could see the shadow of the rope dangling just overhead. She reached out and grabbed it, keeping her feet on the wall as she climbed. It was almost like walking vertically. Now she could see the rafter clearly. A rat sat atop it, staring at her with tiny black eyes. She hated rats. But it scurried away when she put her arm up around the beam.

She hauled herself up. There it was: the hole in the ceiling that the rats were using to come and go. It was just above the point where the rafter connected with the stone wall. Lying on her back on the wooden beam, Whisper put both her feet on the plank above – the one with the hole – and pushed.

To her surprise, it snapped immediately, the sound echoing through the room. She caught the broken board and set it down on the rafter, before it could plummet to the floor far below. Her position had surely been announced already, but she didn't want to make any *more* noise. She didn't like noise.

Up she went, through the hole and into the room above.

Moonlight. This room had windows, looking out over the City below. She ran to one and gazed out, taking a deep breath of the free air. Never before had she felt so glad to see those filthy grey streets and the long faces of the dark, narrow buildings of the Iron

Ring. Yet she knew she couldn't look for long. The assassins might be headed her way now, investigating the sound she'd made.

Turning her eyes back to the room itself, she quickly saw it was a storage area. There were crates and chests everywhere, and one very well-crafted writing desk with a chair. Whisper only saw one entrance, which she quickly moved to barricade. Putting her shoulder against one of the large crates, she pushed with all her might, sliding it slowly in front of the door to block it. Hopefully that would delay them reaching her.

The boxes were very heavy. Looking around the room again, she spotted a long knife atop one crate and used it to pry a box open. Inside were yet more knives, but these were unlike any she'd ever seen.

They were solid black, from the tip of the blade to the end of the hilt. Each dagger was a solid metal object, its "blade" pointed but the edges dull, with no binding or decoration on the hilt. They were symbols, not weapons. She knew exactly what they were.

These were the daggers of the Silent Messengers.

She had suspected, but refused to believe. The Silent Messengers were legendary, so much so that Whisper had thought them merely a myth and put them out of her mind. Stories said they were a cult of assassins originating from the deserts of the far South.

Over time, their influence had spread throughout the West, for there was always someone in need of their services. They were famous for slipping into a target's home completely without warning, leaving no trace of their presence... except for a single, signature black dagger near – or in – the body of their victim.

Some people called the dagger 'the Message,' but the dagger itself wasn't actually the message they delivered at the behest of their employers. It was something utterly silent, yet louder than words. The true message was death.

Whisper quickly pried open more boxes, finding yet more weapons inside, along with many other things: food, candles and scrolls, lengths of rope...

Then her eyes landed atop the writing desk. There upon it lay the very same contract she had seen once before, in the black-gloved hands of the Mother. She couldn't read it, of course, but she recognized it instantly: the contract hiring the Messengers to kill a little girl who was probably fast asleep right now, blissfully unaware that someone had signed her death warrant. The sight of the scroll made Whisper sick, but it also steeled her resolve. She rolled it up and took it with her.

She also took nearly everything else she could carry. She strapped a quiver of arrows to her back, took a bow and a long leather whip, some food, and a pair of tall black boots to replace her shoes. To her surprise, she found some that fit her. Finally, she took a long black cloak and pulled the hood up, tightening it over her head to cover her ears. She left the obsidian daggers where they lay.

And then, without another look back, she slid out of a window and into the night.

Returning to the rooftops of the City felt like going home after a long and harrowing journey. She took a deep breath, filling her lungs with the putrid urban air – putrid, but free. She could go anywhere she liked, and she knew just where she would go first. What was it Camron had said?

She lives in a manor at the corner of Gold Way and Wallshadow, overlooking the slums from the heights of the Bronze Ring.

Whisper started moving in that direction. She knew most parts of the city like the back of her hand, and on the rooftops she could travel faster than anyone walking or even riding the streets. Besides, it was easy to find the way to the Bronze Ring. Each circular district of the City, moving inward, was elevated higher than the previous one. The Bronze Ring loomed so far above that the city's designers had even built bridges right over the breadth of the Iron Ring, so the wealthy merchants and noble patricians would never have to pass through its squalid streets.

The Gold Way was one such bridge boulevard, stretching all the way eventually to the City's innermost Gold Ring. Wallshadow was a road that ran right along the edge of the wall separating Iron from Bronze. Whisper could see them even now, the silhouettes of wall and bridge standing out against the starry sky. As she drew closer, she could make out the upper floors and pointed towers of the great manor where the Messengers' target must live. They overlooked the slums quite literally.

Whisper's large eyes widened, her pupils fully adjusted to the darkness, able to make out every detail of the distant house high above. A window was open. She silently thanked whatever gods might be, for making her job easier. She knew of only one way to send a message to the family inside... a much friendlier message than the one the assassins wanted to send.

She brought out the contract, the one for the little girl's death. Then she drew an arrow and wrapped the scroll around the shaft, tying it tight with a bit of string. Finally, she put the arrow to her bowstring and drew it back. She was no expert archer, but she had experimented with bows and arrows before. After all, her early childhood had been spent in a Temple of Artemis, the goddess of the hunt.

The well-lit open window was a stationary target, at least – but it looked miles away from where she stood. There was no wind, for which she was thankful. Aiming high, she tried to imagine the flight of the arrow... and then she let it go. It sailed straight up toward the window, fell slightly, and hit it on the edge, bouncing right into the house.

Whisper let out her breath. At least that had worked. She could only hope some servant would find the arrow with the contract and would take it back to the master of the house, or someone else who could respond appropriately. It was the best she could do for the girl and her family.

Now Whisper had to worry about herself.

Out of the corner of her eye, she saw them. Most would not have noticed, but her every keen Elven sense was on high alert for just such a sight: a dark figure, moving through the shadows of her rooftop domain. The figure was many buildings behind her, on a lower roof, but she knew there would be more. The assassins were following her, and they would catch her eventually.

She had to go somewhere safe, but where?

There was but one real answer to that question. Whisper's eyes turned away from the Bronze Ring, roving in the opposite direction: the outer wall, the edge of the City. There were many watchtowers along the wall, and she knew just which ones were well-garrisoned. The main tower of the City Watch – the *Vigiles*, as they were officially called – was just where one would expect it: at the main gates. She could see the pointed towers of the great barbican from here, decorated with the mostly crimson flags of the Achaean Empire, Coronaria, and the First Legion, among others.

She headed in that direction, running and leaping and climbing, all while keeping her eyes on every shadow for movement. Yet she knew her plan was shaky. Even if she begged the watchmen to help her, they would probably just chase her away. Street urchins were always playing pranks on the watch, and they didn't care enough to risk their already difficult job on the word of a dirty little orphan. Whisper almost wished she'd taken one of the Silent Messenger daggers, though even then they might not believe her. They might even arrest her for questioning.

At length, she arrived. She found herself gazing down at the city's great Southwestern Gate. Though perhaps 'gazing down' was not the best way to put it, for though she stood on a rooftop, the towers of the gate fortress still loomed far above her. She could see lights in the towers' arrow-slit windows, and far below, the Watch patrols kept arriving and departing like clockwork. Most of the guardsmen wore full suits of mail, with short swords and steel helmets, axes and halberds. The assassins with their leather and daggers would stand no chance against them in a real fight. At least, she hoped they wouldn't.

But how to get their attention?

She was just beginning to ponder this question when she heard the slightest sound behind her. It was soft – so soft that it would have been inaudible to most ears. Even Whisper almost dismissed it. But at the last fraction of a second, she whirled... and the assassin's knife cut a hole in her cloak, barely missing her skin.

She didn't turn to fight, or even look long enough to identify her assailant. She simply fled, right over the edge of the roof. Somehow, operating almost purely on instinct, she made her way down safely. She first landed on the neck of a gargoyle, then leapt off to grab a flagpole sticking horizontally out of the wall, twirling around it, and finally dropped down into the branches of one of the few trees that decorated the street near the gates.

Just then, she saw a cart passing by. It must have been a merchant who had just entered through the main gate, for his wagon was loaded down with boxes of goods. On a whim, Whisper ran gracefully along one of the old tree's long limbs, and then leapt right into the back of the cart. The driver didn't even have time to turn and face her before she had grabbed him by the shoulders and shoved him down onto his side. Then she stood up, planted a foot on his hindquarters, and pushed him right out of his seat and onto the pavement below.

"Stop! Thief! Help! Guards!"

Whisper ignored the merchant's shouting as she sat down and looked for the horse's reins. Yet even with the reins in her hands, she had no idea how to make the animal speed up. In fact, she hadn't the slightest idea how to drive a cart or ride a horse at all. But she did have a whip.

"Sorry about this," she said to the unheeding beast as she uncoiled the whip from her belt.

It only took one crack, and she was nearly thrown out of the cart as the steed whinnied loudly and took off at a gallop. She pulled hard on the reins, trying with all her might to steer the horse toward the assassins' hideout. It took all her concentration to try to drive the animal in the right direction while clinging desperately to the bouncing cart; she couldn't bring herself to glance over her shoulder to see if any guards or assassins were giving chase.

Fortunately, the old tower where the assassins had made their dwelling was not far from the southwestern gate. It was decrepit, abandoned – a relic, perhaps, of older times, when the walls to the City had been shorter and the Empire half its current size. As she drew close to its shadow, she turned around and, with all her strength, pushed one of the merchant's wooden crates out of the back of the cart. Then she pushed another, and another, and at last she fell right out of the wagon along with the last one.

The fall nearly knocked the wind out of her. She stood up, gasping for breath, smelling the rich aroma of smashed fruit coming from the boxes she'd dumped. Looking back the way she'd come, Whisper saw the rushing horde of guards. To her eyes, they looked like a charging army, all clad in glinting steel and red and white tabards. Behind them, further down the street, she could just make out a few men on horseback coming to help.

That was her cue to run. Again operating on instinct, she grabbed the first visible handholds on the wall of the assassins' tower and started her ascent. Luckily, the stones of the old building were uneven and easy to climb. She was more than halfway up by the time the guards with bows and arrows arrived.

The first arrow startled her, bouncing off the wall right beside her head. The second actually imbedded itself in a crack between two stones, where it stuck tight, quivering before her eyes. She could hardly believe that they would actually shoot at her. Perhaps they couldn't see she was just a little girl, because of the long black cloak and quiver of arrows. Or perhaps she wasn't as little anymore as she still thought. Or perhaps they just didn't care.

But the gods must have been looking out for her that day, for none of the arrows struck true. The closest one lodged itself in her cloak and dangled there, upsetting her balance slightly, but she paid it no heed as she finally reached the window at the top of the tower and hauled herself inside.

In she tumbled, rolling along the floor, and then she jumped to her feet, dagger drawn. But to her surprise, there was no one inside. The storage room at the top of the tower seemed to be exactly as she'd left it.

Still, Whisper wanted the guards to follow her inside. So she grabbed one of the black Messenger daggers and prepared to drop it out the window, hoping they would recognize it. Then she paused. With sudden fury, she put the dagger back into its crate and picked up the entire box instead. With a great groan of effort, she lifted it to the window and dumped them all out, dropping the box behind them.

The crash of the cascade of metal daggers died away amidst the clamor of the guardsmen shouting and moving about in their armor. Whisper dared a peek over the edge to see one of the mounted knights taking charge. A guardsman handed him a dagger, and he shouted some orders, so loud that she could hear.

"The Silent Messengers!" he said. "Open those doors! We'll tear this place to the ground!"

The soldiers gripped the iron rings to fling the doors wide and found that there was no lock, no bar blocking their way. The doors swung out quite easily on their hinges. But they were not expecting what waited within.

"There's no door, sir!" cried a watchman. "Nothin' behind 'em but stone walls! All the doors are fake!"

The knight paused, perhaps feeling a twinge of fear as he stared at all that blank stonework, and then said, "Captain, send a runner to inform the First Legion! We need a battering ram! Inform everyone you can – even the Paladins! We'll purge this Assassin scum from our city!"

Whisper withdrew back into the tower, almost smiling now. Her job here was done. She could leave, and let the Watch and the Legion handle the rest. And yet, something compelled her to stay. Was she worried for the fate of the children in the tower? Or did she just desire closure? A part of her wanted to put an arrow through some of the Messengers herself, at least through the Mother... and Hanan al-Saffah, that monster.

Almost against her own will, she found herself crouching on the floor, finding the same hole through which she had climbed earlier that night. She slid down onto the rafter again and listened. Immediately, she could hear the voices below. The children were all out in the main room, in the Box. And at least some of the assassins were there as well. Lying on her back on the rafter, Whisper drew out an arrow and nocked it to her bowstring, then peered down as cautiously as she could.

"You have all failed," the she-elf assassin Seona was telling the assembled children. "Do you realize that? We're leaving now, and you will never see us again. You will die wondering who we might have been, what your life might have been like had we selected you. But we will be like a memory of a dream to you... something that was real one moment and gone the next, never to return."

Camron stood beside her on the raised platform, smiling down at the children. "But don't fret. Some dreams are not meant to be. In truth, only one or two of you, if any, would have passed our final trials. Some of you would have died. Perhaps a few of you will try to seek us out again. Perhaps one will show enough promise that we might reveal ourselves to you. But it's better not to chase dreams. Far better for most of you to live your lives as if this had never happened. I, for one, wish you good fortune."

Whisper looked at the faces of the children. A few were angry, but most were confused or even sad. A few had tears in their eyes. And there was Shade, looking utterly distraught, as if the sun might never rise again. Whisper felt disgusted at how easily this cult had brainwashed him, and all the others. So, settling herself into the most secure position she could manage, her back nearly flat against the low rafter, she turned sideways, drew back her arrow, and sighted down the shaft.

She aimed first at Camron... but she couldn't shoot. There he was, smiling his smile of twisted benevolence, of willful ignorance of the evils he was committing. She couldn't put an arrow through that smile. So, she moved her sights to Seona, the tall and regal *Alfar*. There she stood, her hair and face so fair, her features as cold and beautiful as the finest marble statue. Whisper's kindred – the only other elf she had ever known. She could not shoot her either.

Why did it have to be them? Why couldn't it have been al-Saffah? She could have put an arrow through one of his black eyes as easily as breathing. But as she lay there imagining it, she felt another sensation grip her: fear. What if she missed? If Hanan showed himself, and she gave away her position to him, he would hunt for her. He would make her feel as helpless as she had felt when he'd interrupted her fight with Shade... when he had pinned her to the floor and hurt her. And that hadn't been the first time he'd done it. He'd hurt other kids too, put fear into all of them...

Whisper cursed herself. Perhaps she was brainwashed too.

Suddenly, the voices of the assassins and the children were all drowned out by the reverberating boom of a battering ram against the building's stone wall. Whisper held on tight as the rafter began to shake beneath her. Dust and debris tumbled from the ceiling. Some of the children screamed.

Whisper heard the voice of the Mother coming from the next room, out of sight: "Seona! Camron! Time to leave."

The assassins ran to join her, heading into the room with the stairs leading below, and closed the doors on the children behind them. The kids started to panic, their voices echoing off the shaking walls of the stone chamber.

Whisper decided it was time for her to leave too. There was nothing she could do for the children below. The Messengers would no doubt close off whatever secret escape route they'd used, and there were no other exits. She could try to help some of the kids up to the rafters with the ropes, but it would be slow and dangerous. The soldiers would breach the wall soon. She just hoped they would treat the poor urchins well.

So, Whisper climbed back up through the hole and out into the night.

She watched from a distant rooftop as the First Imperial Legion smashed through the wall of the assassins' lair and found the children inside. The orphans were quickly herded out and led down the street, to be taken... somewhere. Probably to temple orphanages, like the Temple of Artemis where Whisper had been raised.

Whisper kept an eye out for Shade, but he apparently slipped away and disappeared so quickly that she never spotted him. He had no intention of being taken to a temple... or a prison.

Instead, he joined her on the rooftops.

It was daybreak by the time he found her. The sun's first rays were barely visible in the sky, yet had not touched the city itself, which still lay in the shadow of its great walls. Whisper was looking up at the fading stars when she heard Shade's signature footsteps.

"I'm glad you made it out," she said, but when she turned around, she saw that Shade was furious.

"You should be," he snapped, stamping his foot and pointing at her, his blue eyes ablaze, "because it's *all your fault!*"

Whisper's eyes went wide with shock. "What?"

"You ruined everything!" he went on, walking in circles and running his hands through his hair. "I heard them say it! They had to leave and collapse the tunnel behind them because *you* led the city watch there! And the Legion!"

The surprise on Whisper's face began to fade, giving way to anger.

In a low voice she said, "They were *murderers.*"

"You're so *stupid!*" Shade whined. "Do you like this life, scraping food out of gutters and praying a guard isn't looking? They were gonna teach us to do everything they could do! No one would be able to stop us!"

"They ran like cowards when the Legion came," Whisper said, almost with a touch of pride.

"Well, go off and join the Legion then! Go murder people for the Empire, under the centurion's whip! I'm sure they'd be happy to take a skinny little elf pixie girl!" Shade paused then, as if immediately regretting the insult.

He was silent for a moment before he added, in his usual low mumble, "Or else you could come with me, y'know, an' help me find 'em. The Silent Messengers, that is. They might still take us back; Camron said so. I heard one of 'em mention a base in Whitehorn east of here..."

At that, Whisper stood up, ran toward Shade, and shoved him to the ground. He looked up at her with a confused expression, rather than the angry one she had expected. But she did not relent.

"Fine!" she shouted, her namesake quiet tone suddenly gone. "Go then! Go find your cult of kidnappers and murderers; see if I care! But if I ever see them back in my city, I'll *kill* them. And that includes you, if you join them. If you go after them then I never want to see you again!"

Shade fell silent. He stuck out his lower jaw, hauled himself slowly to his feet, and brushed off his clothes. Then he stuck his hands in his pockets and made a big show of rolling his shoulders, as if trying to shrug nonchalantly. Whisper didn't buy it for a minute. He was a terrible liar.

"Alright," he said, rubbing his nose with the back of his hand, "you won't."

For a second or two he stood there, waiting for her to snap back at him, or to take back what she'd said. But she just stared at him, her green eyes narrow, cold and impassive, burning bright in the fiery light of the morning sunrise. For some reason, Shade suddenly thought she looked more like an elf than ever, standing there proudly in her new dark leather, with her black cloak and bow and arrows. She almost looked like Seona.

So, Shade swallowed hard.

"G'bye, Whisper," he mumbled, and then he turned around and walked away, slipping off the rooftop and climbing down out of sight.

Whisper stood for a while, gazing out at the long shadows of the City, its rooftops glowing orange in the morning light. She never saw where Shade went. She wondered if she would ever see him again...

Then she heard something land with a sad, soft little sound on the roof shingles beside her. She looked down to see a small lock of golden hair, bound by a blue ribbon. The edge of it looked like it had been cut off roughly, as if by a dull blade.

A chill ran over Whisper's entire body. She'd seen hair and ribbons like that before: in the portrait Camron had painted of the little girl they'd been hired to kill. The one Whisper had tried to save.

Failed to save.

Inhaling sharply, Whisper jumped back and looked up. There stood Hanan al-Saffah, looming on a rooftop above, the wind blowing his deep crimson cloak as he gazed down at her, his sunken eyes revealing no emotion. Without a word, he turned to leave. Whisper tried to shout at him as tears clouded her vision, but the words caught in her throat.

She climbed up the building after him, but when she reached the top, the roof was bare. She did a quick search of the nearby buildings, hoping to confront the Assassin again, even if she had no hope of defeating him. But he was gone.

Whisper slept the day away in various old haunts of hers, in coarse beds on rooftops and in abandoned corners of the City. Whenever she found she couldn't sleep well, she moved on to her next hideout and tried again. This continued until the evening, when she decided it was time to go to work. No one would be providing her meals that night, or any night in the foreseeable future. She would have to steal them on her own, like always. But that was okay, she told herself. She was good at it.

And so she went out, and she found enough food to be content. And then she made her way to the top of the tallest tower she could reach, just to look down. She looked down at the First

Legion still tearing apart the old Assassin tower – cutting it out of her City like a cancer. Even if she hadn't saved the noble girl, at least she'd helped to run the Messengers out of town... for now.

Breathing a heavy sigh, she continued watching the tall, thin buildings that crowded the narrow streets of the Iron Ring. Their long faces were the faces of old friends – her only friends. They were impassive friends, made of wood and stone, uncaring. They were not looking out for her.

But she was looking out for them.

A Wolf in Sheep's Clothing
Chris's Tale

by Maegan A. Stebbins

Darkness. With the shutters closed tightly against the cool autumn weather, not even the light of the rising sun found its way into the small peasant cottage. So the exceptionally small bedroom remained shrouded in shadow, and the figure sleeping beneath the meager, tattered covers on the meager, tattered bed – the only object furnishing the small room – did not stir.

The door slowly creaked open, and in stepped a tall, strong Northwoman with long, golden-brown hair fixed in an intricate braid. As she entered, just enough light streamed in through the door from the living room for her to see that her son still rested sound asleep. She smiled and shook her head.

Helga didn't bother trying to be quiet as she approached one of the two windows on either side of her son's bed, as even her thick boots made little sound upon the soft dirt floor. She unceremoniously opened the shutters of one window and then the other. A breath of the fresh fall air blew into the room, and her son groaned in annoyance. He pulled the covers up over his head and rolled away from the light. Helga turned about and yanked the blanket right back off, but his head was still shoved beneath his straw-stuffed pillow.

"Chris," she said, shaking him gently by the shoulder, "time to get up. Your father needs your help."

"I'm sick of this farm," Chrisanthos mumbled in reply.

Helga merely snorted and removed the pillow from his head, prompting him to turn over and meet her gaze. The ray of sun from the window lit up his features, and he squinted his bright blue eyes.

His eyes were striking and his features handsome, but the first thing anyone ever noticed about Chris was his hair... his shockingly white hair. There was no way a man so young should have hair so white. Yet he was not an albino: his eyelashes were dark and his skin no paler than normal for men of the North. If it wasn't for that accursed hair, nothing would betray what he really was.

For a long moment, Helga merely looked into her son's blue eyes. Not one day passed that she didn't wonder if she and her Achaean husband were doing the right thing by choosing to protect their only son, their eldest child. Every time she looked into those eyes, every time she saw his white hair, she wondered... Was harboring Chris and secluding him from society the right thing to do?

Upon first seeing that their son had been born with white hair, Helga and her family had initially reacted with panic. They feared the family had been cursed by the gods. They'd heard that such signs were markers of foul magic, that children like him should be cast out, for the good of everyone around them...

But their own son – they couldn't do it. *She* couldn't do it.

"Alright, alright, I'm up," said Chris, stretching and leaping to his feet.

Shaking away her dark thoughts, Helga focused upon what really mattered: the young man before her. Her heart swelled with pride just to look at him. He was handsome, lean, strong, and even taller than his father. And Helga knew just what a golden heart he had. He was the best son she could ask for, aside from that one great flaw: the taint that ruined everything.

She tried not to think about the life he might have led, if only he were normal. Helga wished he could leave the farm as he so desperately desired and find a better life for himself... but it was too dangerous. They had sometimes tried shaving the boy's hair – which was why it was currently a mess of somewhat short, unkempt spikes – but he hated it. It upset him, and the more upset and the angrier he grew, especially in an unfamiliar environment with unfamiliar people...

Well, she tried not to think of what might happen.

"Mother," Chris said again, and Helga returned to reality. He frowned. "You do this almost every morning."

She laughed. "I'm sorry, Chris," she said, walking around the bed and pulling him into a hug, giving him a kiss on the head. "I was just thinking."

"Like I said, same thing every morning," Chris fussed as the two left his room and entered into the large kitchen and living area.

It was the only room in their small, wooden home other than a second bedroom. "It's me, isn't it?"

Helga blew out a sigh. She was about to respond when the door to the house burst open and in ran a little girl with long, golden-blonde hair just like her mother's. The girl, Sophie, beamed a great big smile that sparkled in her blue eyes as she ran over and embraced her brother, though she was not quite able to reach his waist.

"Good morning, sleepyhead!" she chirped.

"Morning, Sophie," answered Chris, patting her on the head but shooting their mother a suspicious glance.

Helga merely shrugged it off with a smile, setting to work in the kitchen while speaking to them over her shoulder. "Sophie, come here."

Sophie smiled up at Chris one more time before promptly doing as she was told and heading over to her mother.

"Chris," Helga said, looking back at him again, "you go on outside and see if you can help your father."

"Yes, mother," he replied obediently.

The moment Chris stepped outdoors, a blast of fresh, crisp Northrim air gusted into his face. This was the only life he had ever known: the small home at his back; the little stable just across from the house; and to either side of him, the narrow, dirt road.

To his right, to the east, the path eventually led all the way to Rimegard, one of the only great bastions of Imperial civilization this far into the wild lands of Northrim. To his left, it ended abruptly in the fields and pastures of the all too humble family farm.

A mid-sized, tawny white dog suddenly trotted up to him, happily lolling his pink tongue. Chris scratched the dog behind his pointed ears, making him wag his curled-up tail in delight.

"Hey, Watcher," said Chris. "What's Father being fussy about now?"

"Glad you made him happy," said a gruff voice, and Chris looked up to see his father approaching. And, just as Chris expected, he looked very grim. "He certainly wasn't too cheerful earlier."

George stood around average height for an Achaean – a couple of inches shorter than Chris, who had the advantage of some Northern blood. Chris's father had been born and bred a farmer, and he looked it, with his rough, strong physique and fair skin bronzed from the sun. A pair of earth-green eyes shone out from the dirt on his face, which matched his dark hair.

"What's wrong now?" asked Chris, crouching to pet Watcher some more.

"We lost the last of the cows," George said sternly, his expression like stone. The dirt collected in the deep creases of worry on his face made him look all the worse. "We're running low on livestock, son, and, well... all the crops – you know. They're gone."

Chris swallowed hard. He knew his father was trying to go easy on him by not rubbing it in his face some more, but he wasn't sure if that made him feel better or worse. *He* was the reason their crops were gone. He could barely even remember what happened, just that something had upset him... and then the entire field had frozen solid in a gust of frigid air. Now his family only had livestock – and, every night, something picked off more and more of them.

"All we have left is the sheep," George finished after an uneasy pause. It was only then that Chris paid attention to the fact that his father was holding his long, rough-hewn shepherd's crook. "Ten sheep."

"That's not much of a farm," Chris murmured.

"It's not much at all," answered George, placing a large, strong hand on Chris's shoulder, "but it's all we got until we can replant the fields. I need your help keeping watch over those sheep, alright?"

"What's killing the animals?" asked Chris, rising to his feet. Watcher sat on his haunches between the two of them, staring up curiously. "Wolves?"

"Probably," George sighed. "They're a real problem, especially up here in Northrim." He shook his head, a little smile suddenly playing on his face. "But I wasn't about to stay in the Empire, not with Helga up here."

Chris laughed. "You *still* haven't told me that story, Dad. I'm not your 'boy' anymore, I'm a man, and I still don't even know how you and Mom got together. I mean, you were born in the Empire, and like you said, this is Northrim."

Giving a short laugh, George replied, "There's more and more Empire in Northrim every year. But I'm afraid I'm gonna have to delay that story again. Come on, let's go check on the sheep."

The rest of the day passed with little incident. They counted the sheep – all ten were alive and well – and finished up the other chores. They cleaned up the house, took care of their only horse, and of course, Chris also played with Sophie and Watcher. With so little of the farm left, Chris found he spent more and more time with his sister. As much as he knew that losing the farm was bad, he couldn't help but cherish the fact that it was earning him more time to relax with Sophie.

Even if, every day, he wondered what the real world was like. The real world – away from this one little farm, the only 'world' he'd ever known.

As the sun began to sink once more, leaving a beautiful red sunset behind, Chris led Sophie toward the stable. The moment they arrived, he grinned down at her, backed up a few paces, ran, and leapt up to grab hold of the roof. Sophie stared.

"Chris," she said, suddenly trying not to snicker as he pulled himself up onto the roof and turned to look back at her, "Dad told you not to do things like that!"

He just laughed, waving his hand dismissively. "Or else what?"

"You could hurt yourself…"

"Come on, it's easy," Chris replied. "Come here, I'll help you up."

Sophie hesitated as she watched Chris jump down off the roof again, landing in a graceful crouch. It wasn't like he had much else to do out here, so he'd been practicing. Satisfied with himself, he smiled encouragingly at her again, beckoning her over as he stood just underneath the edge of the roof.

"Are you going to play a trick on me again?" she asked hesitantly, fidgeting a little.

Chris laughed, but when Sophie kept staring at him, it quickly faded into a frown. "Why would I do that?"

"That's what you *do*."

"Oh come on, Sophie," Chris said dismissively. "Look, I promise it's not a trick. Okay?"

"You *promise*," she echoed with great emphasis.

"I *promise*," Chris repeated again. Finally, Sophie came over. "Don't be scared. This is gonna be fun," he encouraged with another smile, picking her up and holding her so high she could reach the roof on her own. But she refused to grab hold.

"What's the matter?" he asked. "Just pull yourself up."

"What if I fall?" she whimpered. "It's such a long way…"

"It's really not," Chris muttered with a snort. Still, he placed her on his shoulders instead. "In that case, let's go for a ride," he said.

'Going for a ride' meant riding on Chris's shoulders and he went at whatever speed Sophie requested – though he often ran around like a maniac, partially to try to scare her and partially because that was the most fun. Sophie wasn't allowed to ride their horse yet, and she was always jealous of Chris when he got to gallop the horse around the farm, so he substituted as her steed.

"But this one is going to be a little different," Chris finished with a mischievous little smile.

"Uh oh," said Sophie, sliding down his shoulders onto his back and clinging onto him as if for dear life.

"Here we go," he said, repeating his same maneuver: backing up a few steps, running, and leaping up to grasp the roof. The moment his feet left the ground, he felt Sophie tighten her grip. Probably a good thing, but it didn't matter either way, as it only took a second for him to haul himself onto the roof.

"Told you there's nothing to it," he said, grinning over his shoulder at her. He helped her off his back and took her hand, leading her further up onto the rooftop. There, he stopped, taking a seat while Sophie sat down beside him.

The moment she did, she gasped at what she saw: the beautiful sunset far on the horizon, turning the clouds pink and purple with glowing, golden outlines. Chris smiled and wrapped an arm around his little sister, hugging her close while they watched the day fade away. *Yet another day gone*, Chris thought, despite his best efforts to fight it.

"Sophie," he said hesitantly after a long while, "what's it like at Rimegard?"

"Big," Sophie answered. "Big and loud. And all the people smell bad, too. Or maybe it's the horses... I dunno. Anyway, a lot of them give Dad funny looks when we ride into town."

Chris gave a laugh. "So you don't like it?"

"Not really. The farm's nicer." She looked at him. "And you're here. Nobody plays with me in the big city."

"Not even people in the villages outside the walls? Not the other kids?"

Sophie pouted some. "No." She paused, studying him for a moment. "Don't be sad they won't let you go into town, Chris. It's really boring there, anyway." Turning to the sunset again, she said as firmly as someone her age could, "It's a lot nicer here."

He snorted, shaking his head. "Sure, I'll bet it is..."

"Sophie! Chris!" called Helga, stepping out from the house. "Come on inside, it's getting late!"

"We're coming!" answered Chris, though he didn't rush himself. Helga had already gone back inside and closed the door, so Chris just sat there a moment longer, watching the twilight start to fade. A few minutes passed before he even noticed that Sophie had dozed off, her head leaning against his chest.

"Chris!" barked George in a far less pleasant tone than Helga had used as he stuck his head out the door. "Get Sophie in here – neither one of you should stay out at night!"

Chris said nothing as he gently lifted Sophie into his arms, carefully making his way toward the side of the roof in a crouch and then jumping off. He hit the ground a little harder than he expected, and Sophie briefly woke up with a start.

"Sorry," he said with a sheepish grin, carrying her toward the house.

She didn't even seem to care. "Your hands are cold," she mumbled, half asleep. Chris grimaced and felt stupid, repositioning one of his hands so that his fingers touched Sophie's clothes instead of her bare arm. He knew Sophie didn't mean anything by it, but he couldn't help but feel a little hurt.

"It's time for bed," he said quietly, in an effort to make sure those weren't Sophie's last words to him before they both went to sleep.

"But Dad snores so loud..." Sophie mumbled sleepily, not realizing George stood near the doorway that Chris now approached. Chris just grinned at him as he stepped inside, and George rolled his eyes.

"I know he does," Chris whispered he carried Sophie into their parents' bedroom. Behind them, George shut the door to the house and bolted it tight. Helga took Sophie from Chris and tucked her into the small bed in their room, smiling at him.

"Good night," she whispered.

"Night," answered Chris, feeling a little dejected as he moseyed off to his own room, picking up the candle Helga had left out for him.

He was worried about the farm – and he kept returning to the thought that this was all his fault. If not for him, they would have fields to harvest. At least the fields would've been safe from whatever was killing the livestock.

That worried him, too. Whatever it was, it left no trace, no paw-prints or anything. The cattle would just disappear. They were lucky if they even found any hints of a devoured corpse somewhere far away from the herd.

A dull pain arose in the pit of his stomach at the thought of losing the sheep, too. As he closed the door and the window shutters, setting the candle on the floor alongside his bed while he slid into it, these worries weighed heavily on his mind.

He leaned down to blow out the candle, but as he held onto the head of the bed with one hand, the wood creaked and popped from sudden cold. Where he touched it, fingers of ice spread in small, ferned patterns that danced in the flickering candlelight.

Instantly, he retracted his hand, snorting in frustration. When he finally blew out the candle, he wondered for a second if he had seen his own breath as a cloud of frost just before the light went out.

Chris couldn't sleep. He lay awake, tossing and turning beneath his covers that kept freezing slightly wherever he touched them, collecting thin layers of ice. Eventually, Chris kicked them off entirely, sitting up and curling into a ball, resting his chin on his knees. After a moment, he felt his way about in the dark, eventually finding the window and gently pushing open the shutters, careful not to make too much noise.

The wood creaked only slightly as he moved it, and then beautiful moonlight spilled into the room. The moon, almost full, stared down at the farm and bathed everything in its silvery-blue glow, so bright Chris could see almost as if it was daylight. The sudden urge to sneak outside almost overwhelmed him. The night was perfect to play and set up tricks for his family to find. That never got old. He had to entertain himself *somehow*, after all.

Barking. Loud, fast – and scared. It was Watcher.

Chris tensed, all thought of mischief gone. From here, he couldn't even make out the sheep in the pasture. For too long, he stood there dumbstruck, heart racing as he wondered what he should do.

Leaving the shutters open so he had enough light to see, Chris scrambled over to the door – and the moment he left his room, the door to the other bedroom burst open.

George halted his charge for the door outside when he saw Chris, meeting his gaze. He opened his mouth to speak when a new sound snatched their breath away.

Scratching.

Something began scratching loudly at the door to the house. It sounded frantic.

George and Chris reacted at the same moment, barreling toward the door, though Chris nearly tripped over himself. Helga tentatively approached the doorway to their bedroom, a terrified Sophie in her arms.

Watcher's high-pitched whining erupted from the other side of the door. The dog never stopped scratching.

George reached up and took hold of the bolt – and stopped.

"Dad!" Chris blurted out at his father's hesitation.

For a second longer, George didn't move. Just when Chris moved to do it himself, George unlocked the door and threw it open.

Watcher stood on the other side, as expected, but there was no sign of trouble otherwise. The dog, however, wasted no time – he instantly bolted into the house, tail between his legs, whimpering all the while, ears laid flat in a panic.

"Watcher!" Sophie cried, and she and Helga tried to comfort the dog, which turned circles in pure, confused fear. Chris stared in bewilderment. Watcher *never* acted like this.

"Worthless dog..." George muttered. "Come on, Chris," he urged, giving his son a strong tug on the arm. He didn't wait for Chris to catch up before disappearing outside – after removing the wood-axe from above the doorway.

"Be careful!" Helga called after both of them as Chris, without hesitation, followed in his father's footsteps, armed only with an old shovel he picked up from near the door.

The night was cold, and the breath of Northrim blew upon them, whispering through the tall grasses of the pasture. George led the way a short distance down into a hollow where the sheep were kept. Forest surrounded the hollow on all sides except in the direction of the farmhouse. Far from the best location, even with the fence they built, but it was the only one they had.

As they approached, Chris paused and turned aside, running off the path and up onto his favorite knoll overlooking the pasture. From here, he could see – and count – all the sheep. Several white blobs, so pale they almost seemed to glow in the bright moonlight, dotted the pasture.

He counted nine.

Something stole away his breath for a moment just before he set off at a run after his father once more. George was already making his way into the pasture, looking over all the sheep and making sure the remaining ones were unhurt. The sheep bleated in terror, scattering as George neared.

"Nine!" Chris shouted as he passed by the fence. He heard George swear.

"There are no holes in the fence," George muttered quickly as he exited the pasture again, rejoining Chris. "There's no sign of anything being dragged..." he drifted off, his eyes darting all across the pasture. "Look for blood," he suddenly ordered, vaulting over the fence and searching for blood among the sheep.

Eyes on the ground, Chris began to circle all around the fence, scanning this way and that for any sign of blood – or even the slightest hint that something walked on the grass. For several minutes, though it felt like hours, the two searched – until finally George called out.

"Found some blood," he declared, sounding disgusted. Chris rose to his feet from where he had begun to move along the ground in a crouch, desperate to find something.

"What's it look like?" Chris asked hesitantly.

George stood and blew out a heavy sigh, hands on his hips as he kept staring down at the ground. From where he was, Chris couldn't see what he was looking at so hard. "It wasn't dragged," George said, barely lifting his voice enough for Chris to hear him. He paused. At length, he muttered again, "It wasn't dragged..."

"But... wait, how does that even work?" Chris asked at length. "You mean it was *carried?* It can't be a *person* doing all this – the cow fence was broken that time, and the whole cow was just gone..."

"I know, I know," George interrupted, holding up a hand for him to stop. He sighed again and motioned Chris toward the farmhouse. "We need to get back. I don't know what's going on, but gods know it isn't safe to be out here this late."

The remainder of the night passed with little sleep for anyone. Watcher stayed indoors, having refused to go back outside. Everyone knew it was impossible to sleep now, but Helga ordered Chris and Sophie back to bed anyway. There, Chris continued his routine of tossing and turning for the rest of the night, his accursed magic chilling his room below a reasonable temperature.

When at last the sun rose, Chris got up in an instant, rushing out of his room. George was apparently already up, to Chris's surprise, though it seemed Helga and Sophie were still in bed.

"Good morning," said George, scarcely glancing at Chris as he pulled on his heavy boots and went over to the door, unbolting it and stepping outside without a word. Chris frowned, glancing at Watcher – who simply looked back at him while lying in the floor – and then at the closed door to his parents' and Sophie's bedroom.

Chris heard the large door to the stable creak open. Wasting no time, he ran outside, shutting the door behind him. Silently, George hitched the family's chestnut horse to the cart they had built from scratch several years ago, before Sophie was born.

"Where are you going?" asked Chris, stopping in his tracks once he saw the cart.

"To Rimegard," George said flatly. "I'm going to buy some supplies and some better equipment for trapping – maybe even try to get some help with whatever it is that's killing our animals." Once he was done rigging up the cart, George went over to the stable and snatched up a shepherd's crook.

Chris watched him work. "Do Mother and Sophie know you're leaving?"

"They do," said George.

"Then..." he began hesitantly, "no one's going with you?"

George paused for a moment before finally turning about and approaching Chris, stopping to stand directly before him and look into his eyes. "You can't go with me, son."

Drawing in a sharp breath, Chris just straightened up, defiantly looking back into his father's eyes. "I could go *instead* of you," he answered. "I want to help – and I've been cooped up here all my life..."

"Chrisanthos," George interjected, placing a heavy hand on Chris's shoulder and squeezing it tightly, "I need you on the farm right now." He released his shoulder, taking Chris's wrist instead and shoving the shepherd's crook into his hand. "You need to look after what little we have left. Understand me?"

Chris stared at him for a moment longer before finally sighing and leaning on the staff placed in his hands. "Alright, fine," he grumbled.

George just nodded, turning about and climbing up into the cart. "Take good care of the ladies... and the sheep."

Without even waiting for a response, George set the horse off at a trot. The cart rattled down the rough, dirt road, and Chris kept leaning on the staff, watching his father steadily ride away. The horse and cart had almost disappeared over the hilly terrain when, suddenly, the door to the house opened at his back.

"Dad left?" asked Sophie. After her, Watcher wandered out of the house, tentatively sniffing the air as if making sure whatever had scared him was really gone.

Chris just nodded, glancing up at the large, rough crook made into the end of the staff. "Looks like I'm in charge of... stuff."

Sophie clearly noticed the worry in his tone, and she came forward to tug on his free arm. "Don't worry, I can play with Watcher while you work," she said with a smile.

He managed a laugh. "Thanks, Sophie." Looking up, he saw Helga watching them from the doorway.

"If you need any help, Chris," Helga said, "remember I'm not some weak Imperial woman."

"You'd never say that if Dad was around," remarked Sophie.

Helga just smiled through the worry in her eyes and shrugged as she turned to go back indoors. "Actually, I think that's why he married me," she replied over her shoulder.

Somehow, against all odds, Chris and Sophie both laughed. The two exchanged one last look before Sophie chased after Watcher, and Chris wandered off in the direction of the sheep pasture.

The day dragged on, and almost all the while, Chris merely sat atop his favorite knoll and watched the sheep in the pasture. Occasionally he dozed off for a few minutes, leaning against his staff or lying back in the cool grass, but it never lasted long.

Sometime in the afternoon, a worried Sophie drifted over to him. From the look on her face, she was upset and getting worse by the minute. Chris sat upright.

"Sophie?" he said as she neared. "What's wrong?"

"I can't find Watcher," she mumbled, looking at the ground a moment longer before slowly drawing her eyes up to his. Chris opened his mouth to speak, but Sophie abruptly sat down next to him.

"I'm scared," she said. The words made his insides twist.

"I know," Chris replied, hugging her close. "But it's gonna be alright... and I'm sure Watcher's fine. You know how he likes to run off sometimes."

"He doesn't stay gone all day."

"Well, when did he leave?"

"I came when Mother called, and when I went back out to play, he was gone."

Chris paused for a moment before rubbing her shoulder and saying, "He'll turn up. I know he will."

Sophie said nothing.

Glancing up at the sky, desperately hoping for something else to talk about, Chris looked at the position of the sun. "Almost time for supper," he said, trying his best to sound cheerful. "You wanna go on back to the house and tell Mother I'll be there in a bit?"

Sighing, Sophie replied sadly, "Okay."

Chris watched as she shuffled off home. He frowned, thinking about Watcher. If whatever was attacking the sheep had frightened him so badly before, why would he suddenly run off? To their knowledge, this mysterious beast had never struck during the day before – yet Watcher had disappeared fairly early on a bright, beautiful day. It didn't make any sense.

Rising, Chris looked out across the sheep one last time before making his way up toward the house. He might not have gotten much sleep last night, but he was about to get even less.

Even if it was the last thing he did, he would keep those sheep safe tonight.

After eating a decent supper and spending some quality time with his mother and little sister, Chris told Helga of his decision to stay awake and watch over the sheep.

She said morosely, "You're old enough to make your own decisions, Chris. I won't try to stop you, but I'm not sure this is the smartest thing to do. You're worth much more than any sheep we might lose tonight."

"Come on, Mom," answered Chris, "they're all we have left. Father entrusted me to protect them." His expression hardened. "And maybe if *I'm* there, it won't come at all."

"I just want you to remember one thing," Helga said gravely, taking both of Chris's hands into her own. She paused for a moment, looking into his eyes, much like George had – but her gaze seemed even harder. "You have your magic, Chris. I know you say you can't control it, but it's still in you. If you need it... just *try*."

Chris swallowed hard. He nodded, not sure what to say. They all tried to never talk about his magic.

Helga offered a smile, kissing him on the cheek. "Be safe."

With that, Helga and Sophie disappeared into their bedroom. Chris exchanged rather uneasy smiles with them one last time before snatching up his shepherd's crook that stood propped by the doorway. Trying his best to remain quiet, he slipped outside, closing the door behind him. He wished he could bolt it shut, but he knew Helga would probably be along to do that once Sophie was in bed.

Resting atop the knoll once more, Chris let his gaze wander across the sheep, quickly counting them. Nine still remained.

He tensed, almost wishing that one had already been taken while he was gone so he wouldn't have to be here when it happened. The sun was now set, and a beautiful moon stared down at him. The gale that blew down from the north was cold as ice, yet somehow it felt good to Chris. He took a deep breath of the crisp Northrim air, the chill soothing his nerves.

Seconds dragged into minutes, minutes dragged into hours, and yet... no sign of danger. Chris kept shifting about, one minute leaning on his staff and the next minute lying down flat on the cool earth. As he lay down yet again, his eyelids steadily dropped. He resisted the urge to sleep for only a few moments before he dozed off.

Then, Sophie's scream pierced the night.

Chris jumped to his feet in an instant, holding his staff in a death grip. The scream came from the woods off to his left, and he barreled toward them at top speed. The thought of why Sophie was out this late – and how she snuck out of the house – never even entered his mind.

"*Sophie!*" he yelled as he ran. Her small shape scrambled out of the woods as fast as her little legs could carry her. The moment she stepped out into the large pasture, she collapsed onto her knees, and Chris also collapsed right before her.

"Chris!" she wailed, grabbing fistfuls of his shirt and burying her face, wet with tears, in his chest. "A monster! A huge, scary *monster!*"

"What? Where?" Chris blurted out, embracing her, staff still in one hand. "What're you even *doing* out here, Sophie!?"

"I was trying to find Watcher," she moaned. "We need to run – I think— I think it might be after me!"

No more time for questions. Chris wrapped one arm around Sophie, who still clung to his chest, and quickly lifted her up. He paused only long enough to glance over the woods, lit partially by moonlight filtering through the branches of the black pines... but he saw nothing.

"Alright," he breathed shakily, backing away from the woods, "let's get you home—"

It leapt.

A figure of muscle and grey fur suddenly sprang – seemingly from thin air – out of a hiding place at the edge of the forest. Chris barely caught a glimpse of it before it landed on him. All three of them toppled to the ground in a heap.

Sophie screamed again. The beast growled. And Chris reacted.

He had no idea what this thing was or what was going on, but he *reacted*. Almost the instant the monster tackled them, the instant it was about to tear both him and Sophie apart, a mighty wind as strong as a cyclone and as frigid as Skadi's own breath struck the beast at full force, sending it flying right back into the woods as abruptly as it came. Claws still rent Chris's flesh even as the gale threw it off, leaving hot blood behind.

Whatever it was, Chris still heard it moving – and snarling. That impact would've knocked a man unconscious – or maybe cracked open his skull and killed him instantly. But this beast wasn't even affected.

They hadn't a second to waste.

Leaping to his feet, Sophie still clutching him in white-knuckled terror, Chris took off toward the house. Behind them, the creature moved again, stepping out into the moonlight.

One quick look over his shoulder and Chris saw it. That brief glimpse was all he needed.

The monster stood a little taller than the average man, portions of its body covered in grey fur and with bulging muscles from head to toe, its fingers ending in long, dark claws. Its humanlike ears were pointed, its face distorted and bestial, its eyes a bright orange-yellow. Aside from these wolfish features, the monster looked remarkably like a man...

A man with about a third of a wolf's attributes – but all of the animal's ferocity.

It broke into a run – too fast. Faster than any man could ever dream of running, carrying itself on bare, clawed but humanoid feet. The monster bared its long, sharp teeth in a hungry, gut-wrenching snarl.

"Sophie," Chris blurted as he paused just long enough to set her on the ground, "run!"

"Chris—!" she cried, but he immediately cut her off.

"*RUN!*" he roared, just before wheeling about to face the wolf-man that charged toward him.

Mustering every ounce of his courage, Chris stood his ground, raising his staff and gripping it with both hands. He stared right into the beast's eyes. Nearer and nearer it came – but he kept meeting its terrifying, unearthly stare. He tried to challenge it, tried to draw it to him, to keep it away from his little sister.

The monster stopped in its tracks, teeth bared and growls rumbling in its throat. It hesitated for only a moment – long enough to meet Chris's stare and send a surge of fear coursing cold through his veins – before it leapt again.

But this time it didn't leap to tackle. It swung one hand in an arc, which Chris narrowly caught on his staff. Before he even had time to think, the long claws of the monster's second hand raked across Chris's right arm, leaving deep trails of blood and pain. Chris cried out and stumbled back, but the wolf-man did not relent.

It attacked again. Deadly claws rushed down upon him – and Chris could do nothing to defend against the assault, blinded already by pain. Those claws tore him to shreds, rending his flesh, tearing apart his arms, his chest, his stomach—

In wild desperation, he swung his staff about to strike the beast, but it merely raised an arm and received the blow without even a flinch.

Again the wolf-man lunged, this time tackling Chris off his feet. His world was pain, pain worse than he had ever imagined. Deep, freely bleeding gashes crisscrossed every inch of his upper body. The monster atop him pinned him to the ground, its fanged maw agape. Through the haze of agony that blurred his vision, Chris barely made out its eyes locked onto his vulnerable throat.

It lunged. Somehow, Chris narrowly managed to squirm just enough to avoid the creature tearing his throat out – and, instead, he felt the monster's sharp teeth sink into his left shoulder, immense fangs easily piercing his soft flesh.

Chris screamed. A fresh flood of pain and terror rushed into him. His heart raced so hard it pounded against his ribs like an animal trying to escape a cage. Desperation flooded his very being, his life flashing before his eyes. But with this knowledge that he was about to die came a surge of inexplicable power.

Everything happened at once.

Another unforgiving gust of wind, so cold it carried flakes of snow and ice, blew hard upon the monster. Any man, it would have blinded and chilled to the bone. In every direction, the grass around them swiftly froze solid.

Tendrils of ice froze formed on the wolf-man's hands, which still pinned Chris's wrists to the ground. The ice crept steadily up the creature, threatening to freeze its entire body solid within moments.

The monster tore away from Chris in an instant, ripping apart much of his flesh and sending hot blood spurting from his mangled shoulder. Chris cried out again, pinching his eyes shut and losing sight of what little he could see through tears of pain and impending death. Wind whistled in his ears...

And he scarcely made out the sound of the wolf-man – alarmingly, still very much alive and unhurt – making a hasty retreat.

Then, everything slowly began to fade. The wind died down, the few sounds Chris heard grew distant and indiscernible... and everything fell away into silence and blackness.

Helga kept running, wood-axe in hand. Sophie had arrived at the door screaming and crying, and she wasted not a moment with explanations other than one simple fact: a monster was trying to kill Chris.

As Helga neared the pasture, there was no mistaking the frost that glistened brightly under the moonlight. A field of ice spread out over the earth, and at its center lay a human figure sprawled out on the ground. But the shimmering frozen grass around him was tainted dark by something else...

Helga saw another humanoid figure quickly retreating into the woods, but she did not even pause to glance at it. She never stopped running. It felt as though the farther she went and the harder she ran, the farther away Chris's motionless form became.

Then, at long last, she reached him.

Helga paused in shock. The darkness around Chris was blood. He was *covered* in it. His clothing was torn to ribbons, and his flesh had suffered the same fate. An enormous bite – bloody and hideous – marred his left shoulder.

His chest scarcely moved. Even from here, Helga could hear his ragged breathing.

Carelessly throwing aside her axe, Helga went over to him, crushing the frozen grass underfoot. An impressive layer of ice and frost covered even the ground itself, like she had crossed over into some Far Northern frozen wasteland. It was so thick that she had to be careful to keep her balance.

Helga knelt near Chris, gently touching his less wounded shoulder. He flinched and moaned.

"It's alright, Chris," she whispered, very carefully taking him up in her arms, though he groaned in pain and delirium all the while. "I'm here. You're safe now. We're going home."

He was heavy, but she was strong. She put one boot down hard in the ice so it cracked, and then did the same with the next, until she was back on solid earth. She kept speaking softly to him during the entire walk back to the house, though whether he even heard any of her words, she couldn't be sure. As she approached the door, she halted, about to kick the door open when she recalled that Sophie remained inside, terrified.

"Sophie," she called, trying her best to maintain a calm tone, "honey, open the door. Everything's going to be alright now."

The door was pulled open in an instant, but Sophie gasped in horror at the sight of the bloody and wounded Chris in their mother's arms. Tears instantly welled up in her eyes, and she broke into wild sobbing.

"He'll be fine," said Helga as she rushed into the house. "Shut the door and bolt it. Do it quickly."

Though Sophie could barely function, she did as ordered while Helga laid Chris out on the table in the center of the room. Silently, she gathered some cloth, a knife, an ointment she had made herself from herbs, and other supplies, bringing them all back to the table and setting to work cleaning and bandaging Chris's wounds as best she knew how.

A blood red sunrise loomed on the horizon as George returned home. To his surprise, he did not see Chris, Sophie, or even Watcher anywhere. He knew it was early, but even so, he'd expected them to hear the rickety old cart rolling up.

Even after stabling the horse and putting everything away, there was still no sign of his family. George frowned, rubbing the rough stubble on his chin as quickly went to the house, knocking on the door.

At first, only silence met him. Anxiously, he waited.

Finally, someone threw the bolt back, and the door creaked slowly open.

Helga stood on the other side, looking tired and haggard. She forced a smile, but George saw something in her eyes... She was afraid.

"George," she said, stepping back a little so he could come in, her smile rapidly fading, "I have something to tell you."

Sophie suddenly burst out of Chris's room, interrupting Helga as she leapt up to hug George. Fear stuck his words in George's throat even as he picked his daughter up and wrapped his arms around her.

"Watcher... disappeared yesterday," Helga began hesitantly. "Chris watched over the sheep last night instead, and..."

"And a monster attacked," Sophie cut in very quietly, still hugging her father. "It tried to eat me, but Chris kept me safe. I didn't see it. He told me to run, so I did."

"I don't know what it was," Helga sighed, "but it injured Chris very badly. Thank the gods he's still alive – he's actually doing incredibly well, especially after the condition he was in last night. I..." she drifted off there, averting her gaze. George realized what she left unspoken: she had feared Chris was dead. Helga had to pause to recompose herself before adding, "I think it must be because... you know."

"His magic," George concluded for her. "Is he in his room?"

Helga nodded. "He's not talking much yet, but you might get a word or two out of him."

"Sophie," said George, setting her on the floor, "stay with your mother for a minute."

Sophie looked at him almost suspiciously before stepping over to Helga as if to confirm that she would follow his orders. George went immediately to Chris's room, and he shivered the moment he stepped inside. The air here bore a slight chill... George could only guess Chris was still scared.

"Chris?" he said, quietly stepping over to the bed. Chris was lying on his back beneath his usual meager covers, and George glanced over the thick coating of bandages that his son now wore. Blood stained them all. Some were completely soaked in it. Judging from the condition of the wounds Chris had sustained – to his chest, in particular – George was truly amazed that his son still lived at all.

Slowly, groggily, Chris managed to force his eyes open, though they threatened to fall shut again any second. George couldn't help but notice that his impossibly blue eyes seemed somehow even brighter than before – unnaturally so. They were so vibrant they almost seemed to glow, now more than ever. They would glow when his magic lashed out, but... this was different, somehow. He felt sure of it.

"Hey, Dad," Chris murmured with a crooked smile.

Oddly enough, George couldn't help but cough out a short laugh, from relief if nothing else. "Good gods, son," he said, kneeling by Chris's bed, "I never meant for you to risk your life over some damn sheep."

"Not just sheep," Chris mumbled, shifting slightly and apparently regretting it, for he grimaced and went still. "Sophie..."

George nodded. "She told me you saved her."

Chris said nothing.

"That was very brave," George said quietly, lightly touching his son's right shoulder, given that the bandages on his left shoulder and arm had some of the darkest bloodstains. "I'm proud of you."

Chris drew in a sharp breath.

"Chris," George added quietly, "I want you to know... I've always loved you. I know sometimes I don't know how to show it, and I know I—" he blew out a sigh, pausing again before continuing, "I know I've said things... bad things, about you and your... condition. Your magic." He knelt lower to look Chris in his strange eyes, which blazed out from beneath tired, drooping lids. "I'm sorry."

Chris just managed another crooked smile. "I know," he groaned, his eyes slowly falling shut again.

George was just about to leave the room when he heard Chris almost whisper: "You're acting like I'm gonna die." Hesitantly, George turned to look at his son again – but his eyes were still closed, even as he spoke, and his voice sounded rough and forced. "Am I?"

"No," George said as encouragingly as he could. "Helga told me you're pulling through just fine. Very well, in fact."

Chris blew out a long breath, and George barely heard him say, "Good... I don't really wanna die."

George said nothing, smiling a little as he quietly stepped back out, pulling the door to Chris's room shut as he left.

How strange it was that the gods would curse his family with this magic taint – and then turn around and make that same curse save the lives of both his son and daughter.

Fate certainly worked in strange ways.

By noon, Chris was fully awake and showing remarkable strength. Though his wounds were healing rapidly, such great blood loss prevented him from moving around much during the first day. Since he was still fairly weak, Helga commanded that he remain near the house if he got out of bed at all – which was something she didn't actually expect him to be doing for several days. But somehow, he did.

George reported that all nine sheep were still in the field, something he seemed to believe was a miracle. After hearing Helga's description of the magic she saw left behind from whatever Chris did, George began to hope that the beast was run off for good.

The next day passed peacefully. Chris rested and played with Sophie, George set up a few traps around the edges of the pasture, and life went about as it always had – barring the fact that Chris was unable to climb about and play all his usual tricks.

On the second night after the attack, Helga removed Chris's bandages to replace them with clean ones again. But nearly all of his wounds were healed. Even the bite-marks on his shoulder were mostly closed, though the fangs were obviously going to leave nasty scars.

She stared. This made no sense. No one – *no one* – healed from wounds like that, not this fast. Not half this fast. Now that hideous scar on his shoulder was not the only permanent effect that worried her.

Gently, Helga touched a part of the wound where the skin looked healed. "Does this still hurt?" she asked.

"Burns a little," Chris muttered.

Helga swallowed hard and hoped Chris wouldn't notice how pale she must be getting.

What was *it that bit him? The creature he described...* No. It couldn't have been.

The skin wasn't broken anymore, and the bite-marks didn't look swollen. Why it was burning, she could only wonder, but she rubbed a bit of her herbal ointment on it anyway just in case. Perhaps it was an effect of this unnaturally fast healing.

He'll be fine, she told herself. *Chris is a special boy, with magic beyond man or beast.* No curse would hold him. It wouldn't.

"Well, you're almost free of these bandages already," she said cheerfully, smiling as she left the room. "Good night."

"See you tomorrow," Chris replied, returning her smile.

As she closed the door, Chris leaned back in bed. Somehow, he felt wonderfully alert. He could hear an owl hooting far away outside, he could smell the fresh, tangy scent of pine carried all the way from the forest, and he could see every detail of his room in the light of the full moon that shone through his still half-open shutters...

He felt *amazing.* He'd never felt better in his life.

But the moment he closed his eyes, all the pleasant sensations melted away into the pain, blood, fear, growling, and screaming of the monster attack. Chris opened his eyes again with a gasp and a start, thrashing about and sitting upright for a moment before finally allowing himself to sink back down onto his pillow.

Sleep felt like an impossibility.

For a moment, he merely lay there, trying to clear his mind. What *had* that thing been? Would he ever know? He hoped he wouldn't. Slowly, he began to drift to sleep...

And then all he felt was pain.

So much pain, pain that made the monster mauling him feel like a scrape. His shoulder burned like fire. His head felt as if it would split in half. Every inch of his body screamed with unspeakable agony. He shook uncontrollably, so hard he convulsed.

And then it started.

His skin began to crawl. His fingertips hurt, his heart pounded in his too-tight chest— every inch of his skin felt like it was being torn apart.

He screamed.

Every second, it got worse. His eyes burned. Tears flowed down his face. His pinched his eyes shut, trying to pretend this wasn't happening, trying to pretend this was a nightmare – trying to pretend, hoping with all his might, that whatever was happening would end.

But it didn't end.

Somehow, it only got worse. All Chris could do was writhe and scream, crying out as his muscles swelled, his bones creaked, cartilage popping. He *changed*. His teeth grew, feeling too large for his mouth – until his mouth too started growing, elongating, his entire skull altering— his legs contorted, his world nothing but pain...

And every fear, every thought, every desperate scream and plead for help filling his heart, his mind, his soul, all of them became something else. All of them were buried.

All he felt, all he knew, was darkness – and hunger.

Chris's screams didn't stop.

George flew from the bed, almost falling over himself in a mad scramble of limbs before he managed to stand. Still those blood-curdling cries rang through the house. Sophie had already started to cry and to scream, herself. Helga went to her immediately, taking her up in her arms. While their daughter buried her face in her mother's shoulder, screaming and crying in uncontrollable fright, George's gaze met his wife's.

So she had thought the same thing. They had both known, though neither had wanted to say it out loud. George could see it in her eyes.

"Stay here," he ordered firmly as he opened the door to their bedroom, hesitantly approaching Chris's chambers.

The door stood shut. Frigid air seeped through the top and bottom of the doorway and between the cracks of the wood. Fingers of frost reached across the ground and ceiling alike, steadily branching out. Chris never stopped screaming.

In all his life, George had never heard someone in so much pain. Or so afraid.

George hesitated, turning about and fetching his wood-axe before daring to approach Chris's room a second time. The moment he reached toward the doorhandle, cold air wafting between the cracks made his blood run ever colder.

Then, just as he prepared to open the door, Chris stopped screaming.

Utter stillness invaded the house. A tense, unnatural stillness, as if Chris's agony had frightened away every earthly creature that had previously been sounding its call. Even as far away as the forest, George couldn't hear a single sound. No distant owls, no sheep, nothing. The night itself had been silenced.

"Chris?" George called after a long and uneasy pause, trembling with fear. At length, he repeated, *"Chris?"*

No response. Setting his jaw and steeling himself, George suddenly threw open the door.

A draft of arctic air met him immediately, making him shiver. The entirety of Chris's room was frozen solid. Icicles hung from the ceiling like stalactites in a cave, and the wooden walls had been split in several places by the expanding ice. The air was full of a frosty mist, and George could see his own breath.

"Chris?" he hesitantly said again to the unwelcoming cold and dark.

Then it leapt.

Springing from the shadows, a great beast tore out of Chris's room and nearly tackled George to the ground – and it could have. But it hadn't been aiming for him.

Whatever it was, it was huge. It had the head, legs, and tail of a wolf, but the torso, arms, and hands of a man – even if its fingers were tipped with long, sharp claws of ebony black. Stark white, scraggly fur covered great sections of its body.

And there it stood, in the middle of the room, so enormous its leanly muscular, lanky form barely fit under the ceiling. But it froze, turning to stare at him with its impossibly blue wolf eyes.

It was a monster.

George's first instinct was to strike. He did this without hesitation. Scrambling to act, he charged the beast, swinging wildly with his axe. The monster dodged his blow, taking a step back and snapping its jaws at the empty air near him, its ears flat against its head.

"George, wait!" Helga cried, but it was too late.

George swung again. The white beast tried to retreat another step, but its back hit the wall – and George's axe sliced a gash across the monster's chest. It snarled then—

And it lashed out with its claws, far quicker than George could ever have hoped to move. The blow sent George flying across the room onto his back, blood spattering the floor.

They had no time. George struggled to stand again, trying to fight through the pain.

"Helga!" he shouted. "Take Sophie and run! Go to Rimegard – go *now!*"

to know that is not the case. I am not holding you back – I am holding you in reserve."

Septimus suppressed a laugh. "In reserve for what? In case my six older brothers all suddenly catch the plague?"

"Do not be so quick to scoff at the idea. I know I've told you this many times, but you seem to easily forget: I too was seventh in line to inherit this place, my name and titles. I lost two brothers to war, three to disease or accident, and one to assassination. At least two of your brothers are utter fools and may not outlive my horse. Indeed, I hope they do not. They would only drag down the family name. But you, my son, would *not* drag it down. Not at all – of that I am confident. So... bide your time. Educate yourself and improve your skills. And eventually, your day will come."

Plutarch took another sip of wine, looking his father in the eyes. "And what if I don't want to be your... contingency plan?"

Lord Titus gave a thin smile. "Of course you do. You want power – it's plain in your eyes – and this is the surest way to get it. And in the meantime, during your studies, maybe you can help us conquer another house through marriage instead of the sword. Maybe you can seduce the only daughter of some wealthy old family like Beltizar or Olgovic. I hear you're good at that."

"A waste of my talents," muttered Septimus Plutarch, looking into his empty glass.

"The gods give each of us certain tools," Titus replied, with an air of finality as he opened the door and head back out into the hall. "We must use what we are given."

With that, he closed the door behind him, leaving Septimus alone with his green wine and his thoughts.

Their daughter watched everything, saw everything. They had no choice. No time to think, to feel, to talk – they had to act.

Helga covered Sophie's eyes, tightened her hold, and ran out of the house. She ran right past the monster with its attention focused on him – she ran right to the door and unbolted it and barreled outside in one swift motion.

Even from here, George heard her muttering prayers to every god she could name as she carried their daughter away into the night.

Once they left, George arose with renewed confidence, fighting through his pain. He would do it. He would slay this beast and protect his farm and family once and for all. Now standing straight, George gripped his axe and looked at the beast.

The monster stood its ground, glancing at the open doorway, its ears laid flat and its bright blue eyes watching George's every move. The white wolf-monster whined, like a pathetic trapped animal – George wasn't sure why, he had barely even nicked it – and held its head low, but George did not let the malformed beast back away.

He ran forward, axe held high...

But the man-wolf did not let him swing it again.

The last thing that George saw were the beast's blazing eyes. Its strangely familiar eyes... so blue they almost seemed to glow.

Helga kept running. She and George both had only one goal: to protect Sophie. And, as much as she wanted to stand alongside her husband and fight the monster, she knew that they stood no chance. She knew George had chosen for her and Sophie to live, rather than himself.

She would make sure his sacrifice was not in vain.

"*Mom!?*" Sophie shrieked.

"No time," Helga answered as she led the unbridled and unsaddled horse from the stables, placing Sophie on its back. The girl instinctively clutched the horse's mane in fear, looking down at how far off the ground she was. Behind them, Helga heard George's scream cut short – and the growling of the monster.

"Sophie, listen to me," Helga said gravely. Sophie's blue eyes, wide as saucers, stared at her in unthinkable horror. "Whatever happens, you *do not* let go of this horse until you reach town, until someone helps you. Do you understand me?"

"M-mother…"

"*Do you understand?*" Helga insisted.

"Yes," Sophie blurted, but she sobbed wildly. "Mom—!"

Helga gave her no time. She slapped the horse's hindquarters with all her strength and shouted, "*Go!* Go to Rimegard, and don't stop until you get there!"

Sophie kept crying, screaming something into the wind that Helga scarcely even understood – but Sophie did not release the horse, clinging desperately as it ran with all haste toward the outlying towns surrounding the enormous, walled city of Rimegard. For half a second, Helga stood and watched the horse run.

She knew the horse could have carried them both, but she would slow them down. In case the beast came out of the house for them, she wanted to be absolutely sure that at least Sophie survived. Helga thought to remain behind and distract the beast if necessary, to do everything she had to for Sophie, and she turned to face her fate—

But the monster did not come out. Only silence answered.

There was nothing she could do. Trying not to look back, following the path of the horse that had carried her daughter to safety, Helga started running.

Cold.

Chris awoke with a start. Running water gurgled somewhere nearby and the fresh morning scents of the thick, black forest of pines filled his nostrils. His wounds didn't ache as badly as they had yesterday, though when he moved, he flinched at the protesting of a few remaining gashes.

But... where was he?

Cautiously, he sat up and surveyed his surroundings. He was fairly deep in the woods somewhere, beside a fast-running stream. How he came to be here and what in Midgard he was *doing* here, he had no clue. He'd fallen asleep at home, safe and sound. Last thing he remembered, he had just bid his mother good night.

He looked down. His clothes were torn to shreds. He wore little more than a pair of tattered breeches. *Very* tattered.

For a long moment, Chris sat there, confused. Did he have some kind of episode? Was he a sleep-walker?

Eventually, he silenced all those questions and got to his feet. Gradually he began to recognize landmarks – these were the woods near the farmhouse. As he found the right direction for home, his mind raced, trying to figure out what was happening. Nothing seemed wrong – he wasn't hurt, there was no sign of man or beast anywhere around him. It was a beautiful day, he felt strong and almost fully healed...

Then, as he emerged from the forest, he saw his home upon the hill – with at least a dozen figures standing around it. They were *tall* figures, silhouetted in the dim light of the new morning. Strangers.

Chris stopped in his tracks, staring at them from afar for a few initial seconds of shock. What if they were bandits? He broke into a wild, frightened run, charging down one knoll and up another to reach home.

As he neared, all of the rough, ragged peasant men – more than ten of them; he didn't have time to count – turned to regard him. They were gathered in a group around something on the ground, standing so thick about it that Chris couldn't see what was so interesting.

They all stared at him. Chris stared right back.

"What's going on?" he finally demanded, standing his ground and quickly shifting his glare among their rugged faces. "Where are my parents? Where's my little sister!?"

The men continued to stare. They all carried tools or weapons – pitchforks, shovels, axes, hammers. He remembered the stories his father used to tell to keep him from sneaking off... stories about bandits and mobs of magic-fearing villagers, burning those they suspected of witchcraft – like young men with stark white hair.

"What in the gods' names *is* he?" asked one man, glancing at his fellows when he dared to take his eyes off Chris.

"He's a demon!" declared another, clutching his pitchfork with trembling hands. "He'll curse us!"

"George doesn't have a son," murmured a third.

At the mention of his father's name, Chris rounded on the man who spoke it. "What do you know about my father?" he snapped.

Then, some of the men who had gathered together began to disperse. Chris looked at them, frustrated at the bewildered silence and the frightened, angry stares. And then he looked past them, at whatever they'd gathered around...

It was a mangled corpse, stained in blood, its flesh torn asunder. But Chris recognized him.

It was George. It was his father.

Something horrifyingly familiar happened then. It was the same thing that had happened the night that monster had attacked him and Sophie, and he had felt overcome by fear that he and his sister might die.

Magic.

A great surge of emotion welled up inside of him. With it came a great surge of power. Snow and frigid air blew from nowhere, blinding all the strangers as they shouted in fear and surprise, covering their faces against the biting gale.

"Kill him! Kill the witch-boy!" shouted one man, rushing for Chris as best he could manage against the wind.

Chris saw stains of blood on the man's shirt – George's blood. Had they killed him?

They'd *killed his father.*

Anger. It filled him, blinded him, so great he barely noticed the incredible pain that surged into his limbs. Something *else* was happening to him, something different, but he didn't know what.

His mind pushed it aside, buried it in his rage. These men had killed his father.

"Kill the monster!" someone shouted again.

And all at once, the mob raised their weapons and rushed him.

Obeying some natural instinct – perhaps to surrender or to ward them off – Chris raised his hands. A light flashed, a blinding light, so bright Chris wanted to close his eyes... but he didn't. He watched as the explosion of raw magical energy erupted from his fingertips. It sent the entire crowd of peasants flying backward, toppling over one another.

The magic was wild and uncontrolled. The foremost men were nearly vaporized, the skin blasted from their bodies, leaving only strange, twisted corpses behind. Others were alight in magic blue flame, their flesh scarred in bizarre patterns. And yet more were frozen to solid ice, toppling to the ground as stiff as statues, sickening cracking sounds splitting the air as they fell.

Chris was lost in a storm of emotions – a storm he couldn't control. Couldn't stop. But the storm in him took shape, formed in the real world, and it was this storm that slaughtered the men around his house...

The men, he thought, who had come in the night and slain his family. Something told him that had happened. An uncontrollable instinct, just like his magical reaction. He couldn't reason with it, couldn't stop it. He could only watch it happen.

But he didn't have to watch long. In an instant, it ended.

Everything stopped, falling to silence. Chris collapsed on his hands and knees, gasping for breath, every ounce of his energy drained. Whatever had started happening to him also stopped, that strange pain that had slowly but steadily grown. All at once, it faded.

What had he *done?*

Chris tried not to look at the destruction he'd caused, so he didn't see if any of the men got away. And when he finally did gaze out at the field of snow and ice and death, he couldn't bear to count the corpses. He couldn't even bear to look at them. He didn't want to acknowledge that, somehow, he had caused... this. He had caused so much death.

Shakily, Chris got to his feet. Somehow, he made himself cross over the snow-covered ground and approach the brutalized corpse of his father. It had left a trail of blood behind when the men had dragged it out of the house.

But upon reaching the body, Chris's strength left him again. He collapsed once more into the snow, weeping like a child. He clutched George's hand, almost curling into a ball as he sobbed and gasped, closing his eyes, tears streaming down his face.

Then, finally, Chris lifted himself up. He searched the house for any sign of Helga and Sophie, but he found nothing – save more blood left behind from whatever had happened.

"Mom! Sophie!" he shouted, but there was no response.

He ran back outside, trying to look around without seeing the twisted bodies of the villagers and of his father.

"Mom! Sophie!" he cried again, this time charging into the stable. His entrance frightened several mules, donkeys, and even a horse – none of which were their family steed. They must've belonged to the strangers outside. Some had saddles on their backs.

But Helga and Sophie were not there.

Chris swallowed hard. He had no idea what was going on. He had no idea why, how, when— he even had no idea *where* these men had come from. It would have been easier for him to believe that the monster from two nights ago had come and killed his parents, rather than these strangers from nowhere.

But there was no monster, just like there was no Sophie and no Helga.

There was also no sign of the family horse. For a while, Chris paced in the stable, carefully looking over every new animal there, making sure none of them was that old horse he knew so well. But no, he was right. That horse was gone.

Who were these men? Had they come, killed his father, kidnapped his mother and little sister, stolen their family horse, and taken them away? Why had they left so many men behind?

At length, Chris told himself that it didn't matter. All that mattered were the facts: his father was dead, his mother and sister were gone, and now, he was a murderer. But if those men had killed his father – which was the only thing that made sense – then he would not weep over their deaths.

All that he cared about now was finding Sophie and Helga. They were all he had left. Drawing in a deep breath, he took the reins of the horse the strangers had brought into his stable and tried to lead it outside. It was a lovely white stallion.

But when Chris tugged the reins, it let out a fearful cry and reared up, and it was all Chris could do to calm it down. Eventually he got it outside, but it seemed terrified, looking about and snorting nervously, seeming terrified but obeying him like it had no choice.

Then Chris spotted a much more familiar beast.

Watcher. The dog suddenly paced out from behind the house in the distance, staring at Chris. He, like the horse, seemed afraid.

"Watcher!" Chris called, feeling as if he had rediscovered the only other remnant of his family.

Watcher paused and looked at him for a moment...

And then turned and ran. He didn't stop, disappearing into the fields.

Chris stared, feeling yet another surge of pain deep inside. Watcher was part of the family. Why would he run when Chris called? He had *always* loved Chris. Watcher was *his* dog. Chris was his best friend, and he knew it. Didn't he? He'd raised Watcher since he was a puppy...

Why would Watcher run?

Trying desperately to swallow the thick lump in his throat and fight back even more tears from his burning eyes, Chris mounted the white stallion. Turning away from his home, with no idea where he was going or what he was going to do, he set the horse off at a trot.

He didn't look back.

Potential Energy
Lord Plutarch's Tale
by Justin R. R. Stebbins

Part 1: Brotherly Love

As it was at the time of creation, the earth was split into light and shadow. With blasts of terrifying power, the light would try to fill the void. But the black abyss paid no heed, and each flash was soon lost in darkness. The light shone with fierce fire, in a last dazzling display of energy, as the shadow relentlessly closed in around it.

This was how the two armies appeared that day on the field of battle. The mage-lords stood behind their horde of horrifying creations and unwilling slaves, watching as the legion of black-armored knights cut through them like grass, moving ever forward. The magi were at the peak of their power, hurtling spells of unimaginable fury into the heart of the enemy soldiers – spells that could break mountains asunder... but they were forced to watch their magic dissipate, like a meaningless light show to amuse peasants, as the enemy marched on unheeding.

The land beneath the feet of the ebony knights was blasted, twisted, torn asunder, cursed to be forever barren, like the earth of the Great Wastes to the South laid bare by the Mage Wars of Sinkarya. Forever after, the battlefield would be known as the Scar, a place no man would dare to tread. Yet the knights trod it that day, plodding and climbing over the cursed ground without pause.

The magi who had instilled unthinkable horror into the lives of so many – shattering the minds of innocent Achaean men and women with otherworldly things never meant to be glimpsed by mortals – now found themselves cowering before the strength of the Void Iron Knights.

Sir Durand led them, slicing a bloody swath through the magi and their minions, his eyes ever locked upon his goal: the tall golden war-chariot of Ildrius, Mage-Emperor of Achaea. He slew the twisted, unnatural beasts that pulled it, not pausing to watch their hideous forms crumble to dust under his feet as they returned to the dark realms from which they had been summoned. He looked ever upward, to the top of the throne-chariot's golden stairs. To Ildrius, the knight's obsidian form looked far more terrifying than the beasts he had just slain.

The Emperor's gaunt and bent figure rose from the chair at the top, wracked with terror and anguish, but also with rage. To his credit, the usurper of the Imperial throne refused to cower, to beg, or to flee. He fought to the last, in his own cowardly way, opening a gate to the nether realms from which spewed a flock of hellish bats, crows, and harpies. Through them all, Sir Durand cut like a scythe, until he slammed the fingers of his black gauntlet atop the head of the golden lion that adorned the arm of the usurper's throne. Then he pulled himself up.

They say his black blade sliced through so many layers of arcane shielding before it pierced the Mage-Emperor's chest, that the blast of power from the broken spells melted the gold of the great chariot, leaving a mound of riches in the center of the Scar. They also say that when Durand drew his long sword from Ildrius's chest, the Mage-Emperor's heart came out with it, and it was blacker than even the Void Iron of the blade.

But the stern Sir Durand would not have wanted such fanciful tales told of his deed that day in the shadow of the Iron Pikes...

Here, the young man closed the book with a sigh.

"He's a fine one to talk about 'fanciful tales'," said Septimus Plutarch.

Behind him, his sister giggled. "Now Septimus, you know better than to criticize our most beloved ancestor."

"Yes, especially not in front of our Lord Father, who would have me follow in his footsteps."

"You would make a grand historical chronicler, Septimus."

"A grand chronicler of the greatness of others..."

Septimus rose from his chair and placed the heavy tome back on the bookshelf. His family had a massive collection of books.

It was not quite the great Library of Xandropolis, but most of the important works were here. Septimus had spent the majority of his years studying them, since his skills with the sword were no match for his arrogant warrior brothers.

Growing up as the youngest of seven sons had been difficult. All things considered, he preferred the company of his only younger sibling: his sister Octavia. He found her music a soothing background while reading, though he seldom complimented her on it. She was strumming on her lyre even now. Septimus usually pretended to find it irritating.

She looked up at him then, her dark blue – almost violet – eyes smiling. He knew she was well aware of his true feelings, though he always tried to hide them behind his own eyes, which were similar in color but not so vibrant. They both had very dark hair, as did most of their pure-blooded Achaean family, the Plutarchs. Named for their vast wealth, the House of Plutarchus was one of the oldest houses in all of Achaea. Their ancestors had stood beside Exar I of Coria himself when he had forged the First Empire.

As a reward, they had been given the great castle of Pluton Hold, just north of Coria – now called Coronaria, capital of the Empire – in the shadow of the great volcano named Vulcan's Forge. Though the mountain had never erupted in all of recorded history, it was also never truly dormant. It just loomed there, nestled among the unimaginably tall peaks of the Jagged Edge, spewing a never-ending cloud of smoke. Septimus could see it even now, outside the window of his room, which was built high in the black volcanic-stone towers of the Hold.

"Your skill with the lyre has improved," Septimus deigned to say.

Octavia giggled again. "My friend has been teaching me. Truly I prefer the lute, but others seem to find it somehow...

common. Not distinguished and ancient enough for my distinguished and ancient blood. In the south, around Justantion, they use a bowed lyre, which I also prefer..."

Septimus ignored all this dull talk of musical instruments and gave a dirty smile. "This friend you're referring to wouldn't happen to be Cordia? The blonde with the green eyes? Mmm... Is she back in town? I thought she'd run off to Templaria."

Octavia pursed her lips and made a scolding motion with her fingers. "Yes, she's in town, but she told me not to tell you. Must you try to get all my friends into your bed? It's disgusting."

Septimus chuckled, rubbing his smooth-shaven chin. He'd been told his deep chuckle was charming. In fact, it was one of Octavia's musical friends who had told him that. Septimus took great pride in his personal charisma. While his brothers had busied themselves trying to make conquests on the battlefield, he'd made far more conquests of a different type, more suited to his own skills...

Suddenly, the door to Septimus's room burst open, interrupting his pleasant reverie. In stepped Paulus, the loyal family servant. The grey-haired, sour-faced old gentleman had served the Plutarchs all his life. Septimus's father Lord Titus, head of the House of Plutarchus and master of Pluton Hold, had grown up with Paulus, as they were nearly the same age. They hardly seemed to say two words to each other now, but there was a silent mutual respect there that allowed Paulus to lord over Titus's children, despite being low-born and uneducated himself. Septimus utterly despised the man.

"Master Septimus," Paulus said, without even looking at whom he addressed, "you are summoned to the great hall. Lord Titus and your brothers are waiting for you."

Pointedly reclining in his chair, Septimus said, "And what of Octavia? She is Father's daughter – is she not summoned as well?"

Octavia made a face at him, angrily imploring him to leave her out of it. He paid her no heed.

Paulus glanced between them, stumbling to form an appropriate response. "She is not... That is, your father did not specify, but he indicated... He said to fetch his *sons*."

Though she truly did not like Paulus either, Octavia forced a smile. "It's quite alright."

Septimus snorted. "It's not alright at all. Octavia, if by some good fortune my brothers and I all kill each other, and you come to inherit, I hope you'll fire this lout."

Paulus stiffened even more than normal, if such a thing were possible. "I shall tell Lord Titus of your disrespect toward me."

"You may also tell him I said you were an idiot and recommended he replace you with a trained monkey from the Sunset Islands. But enough; I tire of talking about you. I'll head to the main hall now. You can run along."

Paulus bowed and left, and after replacing his book, Septimus followed. Octavia waved goodbye and continued practicing her music. Plutarch felt his bare feet sink into the luxurious carpet of the castle hallway. He tightened the belt on his night-robe but did not bother putting on any more formal clothes. It was a nice enough robe: a deep royal purple lined with silver, even if he did occasionally sleep in it.

Septimus headed downstairs. Just outside the doors to the main hall, he ran into one of his brothers. It was Varius, his father's fourth son – one of the lighter-haired ones. Septimus suppressed a sneer. He had to suppress a sneer around all of his brothers, but it was perhaps worst around Varius.

Thoroughly outshone in martial prowess by their father's eldest two sons, Varius was forever trying to prove himself in the only thing he was good at: swordfighting. 'Varius the Blade,' he liked to instruct others to call him. He could barely sit a horse and was no good at commanding troops, but he was a master with a sharpened length of metal. Their father had assigned him to coach Plutarch in the art of the sword, and instead, Varius had simply done his best to humiliate him. Plutarch was better with a pen than any kind of blade, and Varius loved to rub this in his face.

"Septimus," remarked Varius, grinning and swaggering like a swashbuckler – the idiot could never stand still.

Septimus looked down his tall aquiline nose at his shorter brother. "Varius."

Varius hooked his thumbs on the belt that held up his leather trousers. "Been exercising your sword-arm any since we last met? Perhaps we should spar again later, though I see you're not carrying a sword on your... robe."

"Are swords all you ever talk about, Varius? I always have to resist thinking of innuendo when speaking with you."

Varius snickered. "Still sharpening your wit instead of your blade then, I guess. I could lend you my sword, and I'll fight with just my dagger. We could do it now!"

Septimus rolled his eyes. "A sword for me and a dagger for you? That does sound physiologically accurate, but Father is waiting for us, so please, just... keep it in your pants."

Varius laughed, bobbing excitedly on his heels. Then he moved past Septimus and opened the great oaken doors to the main hall. Septimus followed him. The rest of the family was already there, seated around the tremendously long table amidst the tall statues and long banners of the House of Plutarchus. Their ghastly family emblem, a helmeted black skull on a field of purple, stared from the flags with hollow eyes.

As he took his seat, Septimus scanned over those present. At the head of the table sat Lord Titus Plutarch himself, a gaunt but straight-backed old man with hardly a hair on his head, and with eyes so cold it was hard to believe a soul resided behind them. Septimus had his doubts that one did. As usual, he was clad entirely in black. They were fine clothes, of course, but where other nobles valued color as a sign of status, Lord Titus spurned it.

On either side of him sat his two eldest sons, Adamas and Albus. Adamas was dark-haired, as stern and emotionless as his father, and a master of all the arts of war. Albus, the younger of the two, was the first of the three lighter-complexioned, sandy brown-haired Plutarchs. He was supposedly a tactical genius on the battlefield, beloved by his troops for his confident yet affable attitude.

The next two Plutarchs were the other light-haired ones. First was Claudius, the least ambitious of all the Plutarchs and a major disappointment to his father. For this reason if no other, he was the only brother that Septimus could tolerate, even if he had no respect for him. Claudius simply lived a life of luxury on the family wealth, and Lord Titus tried to ignore him so long as he caused no scandals. Seated opposite him was Varius.

After Varius, their Lord Father had apparently lost interest in thinking up individual names, for the rest of his children were simply numeric. Quintus – number five – had taken up religion and become a priest in the temple of Zeus, much to his father's annoyance. He took his job seriously, however, and was always irritating the rest of the family with reminders to respect the gods. Perhaps it helped him feel superior to his brothers.

Then came Sextus, the most forgettable brother. Well aware that his position lay far down the ladder, he did everything he could to ingratiate himself with the eldest son, Adamas. He served as his squire, eagerly following him around everywhere he went and overzealously enforcing his orders. The little toady made Septimus sick.

Of course, Septimus had plenty of cause to jealously resent all his brothers, for he was the youngest. Except, of course, for Octavia, but Lord Titus hardly seemed to acknowledge her existence. Once his wife had borne him a daughter, he had reportedly lost all interest in her. She'd passed away when Septimus was still a child; he had barely known her.

Septimus scooted his seat around to the end of the table – the squeaking of the chair legs echoing in the great chamber – so that instead of sitting opposite empty air, he now faced his father across the long field of polished wood. Lord Titus looked at him and frowned deeply, but made no comment, neither about Septimus's attire nor his reclined posture. Instead, the old man cleared his throat for silence and then addressed the whole room.

"My sons, I called you here for an important occasion," he said, his voice coarse but strong. "Adamas and Albus have been assigned to lead two Imperial Legions to the Black Lands to suppress a rebellion. Word is that the rebel houses may even have the support of a barbarian tribe who sailed their longships into the Empire through Rognosst Swamp. This is an opportunity for the eldest sons of our house to show their greatness. Varius and Sextus will accompany them, as their lieutenants."

Sextus grinned sycophantically at this. Septimus tried hard not to gag.

"And Septimus," said the Lord of House Plutarch, startling his youngest son, "you will accompany them as chronicler of the campaign."

Septimus coughed. "What? Father, I was about to head to Coronaria to serve as a Quaestor..."

"An ancient position," Lord Titus said dismissively, "largely worthless now, and it was my impression that you had no desire to serve in it anyway."

"I do not, of course. In truth, I had... other plans."

Titus gave an amused smile, and said condescendingly, "And pray tell, what plans did you have in mind?"

Septimus's lips tightened. He knew he shouldn't say anything, but it was difficult to resist. He'd been keeping his scheme a secret for so long, and now the judging eyes of all his older brothers and his father were laughing at him – even Sextus, the stupid little toady.

Septimus straightened in his chair, leaned over the table, and placed his hands out flat upon it, looking across into his father's eyes. "Consider this: The Empire is full of ancient, blue-blooded patrician families with virtually no land holdings. Compared to the young and upcoming new bloodlines, earning their money through conquest and trade, these venerable old houses are practically poor. Over the centuries, they've lost everything save the value of their names. They're desperate for financial help, but they have nowhere to turn. The only bank with enough money to loan them is the Iron Gauntlet, and what Achaean noble wants to deal with the *Dvergar*?

"So here is my plan, Lord Father: I will go to Coronaria, serve my years as a Quaestor and then an Aedile, and use the knowledge I gain of economics, the families in the capital, and their finances, as well as their respect... to open a bank here in Pluton Hold. Whatever meagre pittance I inherit of our great wealth should still be enough to start the venture. Men will flock from across Achaea for an alternative to banking with the Dwarves. Our wealth and influence will increase a hundredfold. So... what do you think?"

Silence fell over the room. Every small squeak of leather echoed off the ceiling. Septimus looked at his brothers. Adamas was stone-faced as usual, impossible to read – as was Lord Titus. Albus was frowning thoughtfully. Claudius actually had the guts to raise his cup to him, with a nod. The rest looked like they had hardly even understood his proposal.

Then Lord Titus simply shook his head. "That's the most ridiculous thing I've heard in my life, boy. You think I'd let a son of mine stain the family name by becoming a damned professional moneylender? We *have* money, son. We needn't *make* it like some upstart young merchant family – we need only manage it."

To the surprise of all his brothers, Septimus appeared unfazed by this rebuke. He crossed his arms and leaned back in his chair. "If you're offering to put me in charge of the family's finances..."

Titus waved his hand. "I'm offering no such thing. What I am offering you is a chance to follow in the footsteps of one of our family's most esteemed names and become a great historian."

Septimus's lip twitched with a barely-concealed sneer. "Yes, a chronicler of the exploits of greater men – my esteemed brothers."

"A chronicler," said Quintus, the priest brother, "of the will of the gods! A holy calling." But no one paid him any heed.

Albus, the light-haired second son, licked his lips and forced a smile. "Now brother, there's no need for this attitude. If you feel that way, we will give you a command position! Won't we, Adamas?" Adamas's stone face carved itself into a frown, but Albus went on: "Why, if we conquer some new land for the Empire, you might even have a governorship–"

"You think I want to govern some backwater frontier swamp or barbarian dung-village," Septimus snapped, "while one of you two inherits the wealthiest hold in the heart of the Empire?

Don't throw me a bone, Albus – I don't want your table scraps. I can make my own way in the world."

Lord Titus rose from his chair then, and placed two fingers upon the table, leaning forward with an air of finality. "Enough of this! Septimus, you will accompany your brothers as their chronicler, and if either Albus or Adamas sees fit to offer you a greater position than that, you will thank them kindly and accept it. You are *not* going to make your own way in the world – you're going to help make the way of the House of Plutarch. Now, I would have a word with you alone. The rest of you wait here."

Septimus refused to look cowed. He kept his head held high as he leapt to his bare feet and padded around the table to join his father, the eyes of his brothers following him as he moved. He gave Albus a nod, hoping his elder brother would not take his earlier outburst personally. He had no real problem with Albus – only with his father. And perhaps Varius. And Sextus. And possibly Adamas. Well, he certainly had no *love* for any of them.

Lord Titus moved with measured step, never looking back as he led his youngest son toward a door on the side of the great hall and into a small study room. He closed the door behind him and motioned for Septimus to take a seat on one of the deep purple cushioned chairs. Septimus did as instructed, picking up a glass from the table and sipping it, without knowing what it was. It turned out to be green wine, a very rare and valuable elven drink. Septimus decided he would finish the glass.

His father sat down opposite him and locked his fingers together beneath his chin. "Septimus, I wanted to have a word with you in private."

The younger man swirled his wine and huffed. "Well yes, that's why we're here."

"I want you to know I understand how you feel. You are a man of great potential, who feels he is being held back. I want you

Part 2: A Change in Plans

Septimus Plutarch did not look back. It was one of his policies in life, established at a young age. He made his decisions and stuck to them, and then dealt with the consequences. Looking back tempted one to turn around and *go* back, and Septimus preferred to move forward.

So now, as he rode from Pluton Hold on the road to Coronaria, alone except for the horse pulling his cart, he kept his eyes trained on the path ahead. Though eventually he got bored of this and began taking in the familiar scenery once again. Far away to the west, he could just make out the shadow of the Iron Pikes, rising up from nothing. Nestled in those lonely mountains were the fortresses and mines of the Iron Gauntlet, the guild of dwarves who controlled the trade of their special metals and crafts, and had the wealthiest bank in Achaea – the bank with which he hoped to compete someday.

And just north of those peaks lay the Scar, the blasted landscape where Sir Durand du Vide, the First Inquisitor, had defeated the Mage-Emperor Ildrius so long ago. Plutarch had ridden by it once or twice, but there wasn't much to see, for the Empire had erected a low but solid stone wall around the blackened land, warded by runes carved by the Inquisition. Many an adventurous young Achaean dreamed of scaling that wall and venturing into the Scar to find the mound of Ildrius's treasure that supposedly rested at its heart. A few had attempted it, but they either came back with naught but wounds and strange tales, or never came back at all.

Plutarch looked at all these things that lay off to his side, but still he did not look back... until he heard the sound of another horse approaching. Then he turned his head and cursed.

The family servant, Paulus, rode his steed up beside Plutarch's cart and matched its pace, then said loudly, once again without looking at him, "Septimus, your lord father does not want you leaving. You are to meet up with your brothers Albus and Adamas at our manor the edge of the Shadow Sea."

Returning the favor, Septimus didn't look at him either. "*Our* manor, Paulus? Really? You must be going senile, with all the times you forget you're not a Plutarch. Unless one of my relatives has been foolish enough to adopt you... or marry you, perish the thought."

"Where are you going, Septimus? Coronaria? Stop your cart, turn it around, and ask me not to report your transgression to your Lord Father. Hurry up now. Perhaps if you ask nicely, I'll consider it."

"Honestly, Paulus, if you speak to my brothers like that, I'm surprised none of them has killed you in a fit of rage by now." Septimus could feel his own ire rising, but as always, he refused to show it. "You're lucky I'm so tolerant."

Paulus drew his horse closer to Septimus's cart and finally deigned to turn his wrinkled old head and look at him. "I wiped your bottom when you were an infant, boy! Perhaps your brothers simply respect me the way you should."

Septimus snorted. "I *highly* doubt that."

"Damn it, Septimus – stop your horse and look at me!" Paulus reached out and grabbed Septimus tightly by the arm, as if threatening to pull him from his cart.

Then something happened. First, Septimus felt a surge of fury go through him like a wave of heat, and then Jupiter himself looked down from Olympos and threw a divine thunderbolt, which burst from the heavens and, with a mighty flash of light and crash of thunder, struck Paulus dead.

At least, that's what Septimus assumed happened when he saw the unfortunate old man blasted suddenly backward, away from Plutarch, flying off his horse to land sizzling in the ditch beside the road, with smoke rising from his tangled form.

Paulus's horse bolted in fear. Septimus stopped his cart. As his brain worked to comprehend what had just occurred, he climbed down and approached the old man's corpse. It was a twisted, blackened mass; it barely even looked human. The flesh had been warped into strange shapes and patterns of massed scar tissue. One thing was patently obvious:

He had been killed by magic.

A chill ran down Septimus's spine. He looked at his hands. They looked perfectly normal, but he knew he'd felt a surge of power go through him before Paulus died.

The voice of his father echoed in his mind: *"I too was seventh in line..."*

Suddenly, Septimus remembered an old superstition, and he didn't know whether to laugh or cry.

"Seventh son of a seventh son..."

He said this aloud as he stared at his hands, turning them over as if looking for a magic rune to appear. Stories claimed that magi were born with bizarre birthmarks, or other distinguishing characteristics such as colorless hair, or heterochromia – eyes of two different colors. Septimus could recall seeing no such markings on his own body. But tales also said that magi were usually born under unique circumstances, such as during a solar eclipse, or at a place of magical power like an ancient crossroads... or when a seventh son bore a seventh son.

Terror gripped him in its icy embrace, and he found himself looking away toward the Iron Pikes again, imagining the final battle between Sir Durand and Emperor Ildrius. Since childhood, he'd often envisioned himself on the winning side, striding into battle in that black armor, dauntless against the godlike power of the mage-lords.

Now he stood on the opposite side, and imagined that unstoppable legion of Inquisitors hunting him down like an animal. He could feel all of his well-laid plans – and even those of his father – crumbling down around him.

And then the mood passed.

Plutarch looked at his hands again, and the feelings of fear and doubt faded as quickly as a cloud of sea-spray in the wind. *Never look back.* Fear was a waste of time. He glanced over the colossal ruins of all his best-laid schemes – a mental sight that would have broken a lesser man – and, without a thought, swept them aside to begin building new ones. All his life, he had sought to gain power with his intellect, through political or economic means. But fate had granted him a far greater power, one even his great warrior brothers could never hope to achieve. And he would use it.

The words of his father continued to echo in his thoughts: *You are a man of great potential... We must use what we are given...*

It was time to go to work. First, he needed to dispose of Paulus's body, for if it were discovered, the Inquisition would soon hear of it and begin a search. Perhaps he could drag it to the bog he'd seen nearby and sink it into the mud. It would have to do. Luckily, there were no other people on the road at the moment, and he was quite far from any settlements, so hopefully there were no witnesses. He reached down and gingerly touched the corpse's dry skin. Despite the manner of death, it was not hot to the touch. He tried to lift it, but it proved surprisingly heavy. He had no idea dead men weighed so much.

A thought struck him: This was the first man he'd ever killed. Shouldn't he feel something? Remorse? Pity, at least? He felt nothing. Only annoyance, as if he'd stepped on a bug and now had to clean it off the floor. Did this make him an evil man, he wondered? Then again, it was only Paulus. He doubted if anyone who knew the bitter old prune would truly feel remorse for putting him out of everyone else's misery.

"If only I knew a spell," Plutarch muttered as he struggled to drag the cadaver, "to raise you from the dead, just so you could walk your own sorry corpse to the bog."

When he finally made it to the little patch of wetlands, he had some difficulty pushing Paulus's stiff body to a spot deep enough for it to sink. Once Paulus had disappeared out of sight into the mud, Septimus did his best to bend some of the grass back into shape to cover his trail as he made his way back to his cart.

He climbed back up into the seat and picked up the horse's reins. He considered his next move. He needed to arm himself… but not with weapons.

"*Scientia potentia est,*" Septimus said to himself, and he smiled.

First, Septimus returned briefly to Pluton Hold – carefully avoiding notice – and visited the library, taking all the most obscure books and scrolls on magic, along with some other subjects to camouflage his intentions. He loaded these into his cart and then headed for Coronaria. He took a slightly different road this time, to avoid the marsh where he'd hidden Paulus's body. Fortunately, all of the roads between Pluton Hold and the capital were safe to ride – probably the safest in all the Empire. Which would make Paulus's death all the more suspicious, but Septimus had no time to worry about that.

So, I'm a wizard now, he thought as he rode. *I should grow some sort of beard. A forked one, perhaps. And buy a cape with a tall collar. No pointed hat though.*

He tried to laugh at these thoughts. Not so long ago, he'd dreamed of wearing void-iron armor…

Soon enough, the walls of Coronaria, Capital of the Empire, loomed over Septimus's head. Extending from the top of the wall to the hills beyond the city stretched a long ramp. A gatehouse stood at the point where the ramp touched down. It was toward this that Septimus headed, merely nodding at the gate guard, who took one look at his face and the family crest embroidered on his surcoat, and then waved him on his way.

These were the gates to the city's Sky Bridges, which extended from the elevated central districts, over the outer poor districts, and then over the outermost wall. The bridges allowed the wealthy and noble, the important and powerful, to pass over the crime-infested, poverty-ridden "Iron Ring" without ever having to set foot in it. They were a marvel of engineering, dwarfing even the great aqueducts that fed the city water, especially in width. They were wide enough for four carts to ride abreast.

As Septimus rode, he looked down over the edge at the slums below. They looked so dismal, like an entirely different world, which he was happy to have never experienced. He wondered if he might end up hiding in such a place eventually, on the run from the Inquisition. As he looked, he saw what appeared to be a child clad in black crouched atop one of the tallest rooftops. She looked up at him, her eyes so big he swore he could almost make out their color – they looked green. But when he blinked, he found she had disappeared.

Septimus turned his gaze ahead to the elevated inner districts: the Bronze, Silver, and Gold Rings surrounding the tall central citadel. In the Bronze Ring lived the merchants and the younger noble families, still separated from the oldest Patrician houses in the Silver and the government buildings of the Imperium in the Gold. Here in the Silver, Septimus found the city's library. Though nowhere near the size of the great library at Xandropolis in Kemhet, it was newer – relatively speaking – and boasted quite a selection of rare works.

Septimus Plutarch headed straight in, collecting a pile of books and scrolls under one arm as he walked between the towering shelves. He headed to the stairs, down to the lower floor where the rarer works were kept. He had perused these shelves many times, and knew where to find what he was wanted. The selection of works on magic wasn't enormous, but it was a place to start.

He sat down at a secluded alcove and spread his books and scrolls upon the table. Without further consideration, he dove in.

And found nothing.

For hours, he pored over tomes and lengths of papyrus and parchment, and yet he came up dry. He found only simplistic information, magic history, the basics of magic explained at great length, and references to other arcane works that were nowhere to be found in the library. There was no concrete information. Never before had he fully considered how easy it was to say so much in writing, without actually saying anything at all. He learned nothing.

The most interesting passage he stumbled across was a single paragraph referencing an actual spell:

Many a wanderer in arcane ruins or the Blasted Wastes has attempted to reveal the hidden treasures of the magi through spellcasting, to no avail. For no matter how many times a mundane man mutters the phrase "vide arcanum," no secrets will be revealed to him unless he bears the Gift. All words have power, some say, but only a born mage can cast a spell.

Septimus shrugged and murmured, "Vide Arcanum."

What happened next surprised him so much that he sat bolt upright, nearly falling out of his chair. A message appeared out of nowhere, fading into view on the blank lower half of the very same page, written in a halting script with bright red ink:

Magus, heed these words: Your brethren await you, down the stairs in the ruins at the corner of Silver Way and Old North Street. And remember, seek not the Schola. They will make you a prisoner.

Septimus had never heard of this 'Schola.' He wondered if it might be some archaic word for the Inquisition. Of course, the entire message might be a trap laid by that very group. He would have to be careful. But he could not simply ignore this – it might be his only path to true arcane knowledge, the kind he was having no luck finding in this library or the tomes he'd taken from Pluton Hold.

Septimus hurriedly slammed his books shut and rolled up his scrolls, and then went about replacing them on the shelves. Since they'd been covered in dust when he found them, he tried to gather some dust from nearby and scatter it back on top, eager to cover his tracks. It looked far from perfect, but it would have to do. Then he walked briskly back outside.

The sun was setting as he made his way down the well-paved Imperial highway – down Silver Way, the oldest road of the Silver Ring. Old North Street was also ancient, and at their corner stood an archaic ruined temple overgrown with grass and vines. Stories said it was actually a temple to one of the titans – Ouranos perhaps – whose worship had fallen out of favor long ago. The locals now used it as a park. Some of the fallen stones there were so well-worn from the rear ends of sitting visitors that it was hard to imagine they'd ever been anything other than benches.

But Plutarch hesitated to approach. "This was far too easy..." he muttered to himself.

What if there was a secret Inquisitor outpost beneath the ruins, with sentries waiting day and night on the slim chance a mage would happen across their bait – their hidden message? And yet, what other choice did he have? How would he ever learn the secrets of magic without help? It was not as if the hidden magi rumored to live among men in the Empire would simply reveal themselves to him. Would they?

Septimus sat down on one of those well-worn benches to think. He drummed his fingers on the smooth stone, watching the men and women who walked by – especially the women. The Imperial capital was truly a place of beauty, he mused as his eyes roved up and down the legs of one young maid, watching the way her dress flowed over her hips.

Then, something in the air seemed to change. He felt a tingling in his skin, very subtle – an extremely mild version of a sensation he had only experienced once before: when he had unconsciously blasted his father's obnoxious manservant straight to Hades.

Septimus had the presence of mind not to look around wildly. Instead, he leaned back on his seat, stretching, and glanced to his right – the place from which, somehow, he felt the sensation must be emanating.

And saw a woman staring straight at him.

She was very striking – not only because she was beautiful, with a pale, blue-eyed face framed by long crimson hair – but also because she was tall, probably taller than Septimus. Her shoulders looked broad too, though her dress was perfectly tailored to draw attention away from this, accentuating the feminine curves of her body rather than her rather masculine stature.

The pale woman stared at Septimus, and then reached up with one finger and traced an invisible line under one eye, in the shape of a hook.

In a chillingly serious tone, her sultry voice alluring with a slight lisp, she said: "I see you."

With a graceful wave, she beckoned Septimus to follow her. He knew how dangerous it was – that it could still easily be an Inquistor trap – but what choice did he have? If it were a trap, then he was already as good as caught. They could not have found a better way to lure him in: an invitation from a beautiful woman. The prospect of learning to tap into his magical potential wasn't bad either.

He stood up and followed the woman. She led him into the heart of the overgrown ruins, down a flight of stone stairs, to a dark room, half caved-in, that youngsters of Coronaria often used as a secret meeting place. The half-collapsed "room" was really little more than a shaded area full of rubble, but the woman led him inside anyway. Then she approached the ancient stone wall and held her finger out toward it. Without touching the stone, she traced in the air the same symbol she had drawn under her eye earlier.

Soundlessly, the stonework of the wall slid backward. The pale woman squeezed into the opening that appeared, and Septimus reluctantly followed.

It took his eyes a few minutes to adjust to the dim lighting he found inside. The only illumination came from candles on tables, and each table was littered with books and scrolls, or potion bottles and ingredients. It was all very arcane, exactly like one would expect to find when walking into a secret mage lair.

But the people were not what he expected at all. There were only six occupants, counting the pale woman, and most looked like they had walked right in off the street. They came from all walks of life: two poor and wearing rags, two middle-class merchants, and two wealthy nobles dressed in all their finery. Four were old, two were young, and half were men, the other half women. It was strange to see such a diverse group united for what he assumed was a single cause.

A few, however, definitely stood out. Four of them had skin so pallid it seemed almost translucent, with visible dark veins and a red tint to their bloodshot eyes. Three of these actually had the hook symbol tattooed under their eye, like a black talon, marking them as an obvious member of the cult. Were these some sort of branded slaves, bound by magic, Plutarch wondered? Such a thing had been commonplace under the rule of Mage-Emperor Ildrius, according to the histories...

The pale woman waved to the room in general and said, "Friends, this son of Plutarch is to be welcomed into our midst. Perform the first of the mysteries while I prepare myself."

One of Septimus's eyebrows went up at these last words, and he watched with some anticipation as the pale woman stepped behind a curtain at the back of the room, concealing herself from sight. He wondered what exactly the mysteries of this cult involved.

The other five cultists quickly gathered in a circle before Plutarch and began to chant. Septimus tried to make out the words, but they were from no language he'd ever heard. The tone of the chant was undeniably ominous, deep and thrumming. Septimus stepped closer, peering into the center of their ring, watching. He fully expected some great flash of light, or an oddly-colored flame to sprout from the floor, or a demon to be summoned into their midst.

Instead, they simply stopped chanting and stepped away from each other, and then went back to whatever they were doing before. The two oldest started carrying on a hushed conversation, while two others resumed studying books and potions. Septimus turned to the last one – a relatively young man, but with pale skin and the mark under his eye – and tapped him on the shoulder.

"And what in Hades," he asked coolly, "was all that about?"

The man blinked at him with eyes that were colorless save for the bloodshot red around the edges. "That was the First Chant."

"Does it... do anything? Cast a ward of protection over this hideout, or...?"

The pale, hairless little man stared at him. "None know for certain, but it is ancient and important – a tradition passed down by magi since the days of Ildrius, the Mage-Emperor. Why he and his magi performed it, well, that has been lost to time."

Plutarch had to resist rolling his eyes – he had little respect for meaningless traditions, no matter the group that performed them. "Right. Very impressive. Who are you, exactly? Closing act at the local carnival?"

The candlelight glinted in the shorter man's beady orbs, which did not change as his mouth spread in an unsettling smile. "Not exactly. I am called Cold-Eyes, at least here in this place. We are the Hidden. For so we have remained since the fall of the Mage-Emperor, walking among normal, mundane Achaeans, right under their noses, gathering in secret and collecting what magical knowledge we can, to save it from the void-iron claws of the Inquisition. And meanwhile, we infiltrate the highest ranks of the Imperium, to one day take back what is rightfully ours."

As Cold-Eyes continued intoning his rhetoric, Plutarch scanned the books stacked on the tables, which bore strange titles like *Arcanum: On Runeworkes and Magick Obscura* and *Transmutation: The Most Difficult Magic*.

"So, there is actual useful information here?" he asked. "More useful than your rituals, I hope. I could find no helpful knowledge in the libraries."

Cold-Eyes breathed rapidly in something approaching laughter. "Of course you couldn't! The libraries have been... *cleansed*, by *them*. By the Inquisition. Just like they wish to cleanse the world. They suppress even the *existence* of magic, so that many in the Empire believe it's nothing more than a fairy tale, denying what they see with their own eyes. You know why? To keep people *calm*.

So they think of mages only as a distant fear, a threat from which their precious Empire protects—"

"That's enough, Cold-Eyes," interrupted the voice of the pale woman, who now reappeared, stepping out from behind the curtain.

Only she did not look like the same woman at all. Not in the slightest bit.

She hardly even looked like a woman now. She was clad in armor – dark-tinted metal over robes of black and deep violet, standing straight and broad-shouldered and at least an inch taller than Septimus. Her hair was much shorter now, a mess of deep red tangles interrupted by scar tissue weaving its way up her scalp, causing nearly half of her head to be bald. The network of scars covered half her face too, coming down over her mouth – hence the lisp. The transformation was such a contrast from her previous beauty that Septimus felt genuine fear at the mere sight of her.

Her eyes were sunken and dark, but gleamed in their shadowy sockets with a fierce blue fire – strangely beautiful still. Beneath her right eye – the one on the good side – was tattooed the black claw mark of the Hidden. But her skin, however pale, lacked the dark veins and unnatural wrinkles he saw on the others, including Cold-Eyes. It was still smooth in the places where it remained unburnt.

"Welcome to the Hidden, son of Plutarch," she said, waving her clawed gauntlet toward him.

Septimus gave his most charming half-bow. "My Lady. You may call me Septimus."

"And you," she snapped, her armor clanking as she stepped forward to tower over him, "may *not* call me Lady. Do not flatter me with gracious niceties. I get plenty of those when I walk the streets, disguised by magic to appear how I *once* did. Here, there is no such pretension. I know the way I truly look to your noble eyes. And I do not care."

Septimus felt the slightest twinge of fear, and he licked his lips and tried to look as respectful as possible, never breaking eye contact. "My apologies..."

"Septimus Plutarch," said Cold-Eyes, bowing his head, "you stand before Vae Victis, Dark Spellsword of the Hidden Council."

"*Vae Victis*," Plutarch said, translating the High Imperial phrase: "*Woe to the conquered*, yes? Strange thing to use for a name. But it suits you."

"Suits a scarred and hideous dark magus, you mean?" she rasped out something like a laugh.

"Scars? I hadn't noticed them. Your beauty blinded me to such minor imperfections. But now that you mention it, who dared to do this to you? The Imperial Inquisition, I assume?"

"You are bold of tongue," she said, the lisp from her burned lip now more pronounced. "Bold, or proud and foolish. We will see which. No, this was not the work of the Black Order. These scars came from the hands of 'simple' peasant folk. Despite being fair of face, I never fit in as a girl – too tall, you see, and too able to defend myself, and with hair an unnatural shade of red.

"That's why the gang of boys were stalking me that day, and saw me practicing the magic I had only recently discovered within me. That's why they seized me – not without some difficulty – and dragged me back to the village leaders, who were all too willing to accept their sons' accounts of what they had witnessed the freak-girl doing in secret.

"At first, they tried to cut out my tongue. I wouldn't let them – I was too strong – so they decided it would be easier just to burn me. So, they gathered a pile of wood and tied me to a stake in the center. But they made the mistake of leaving me conscious, so I could feel the pain of the flames. That was the last mistake they ever made. I didn't yet know how to control my magic, but the agony of the fire awoke it. When the Inquisitors arrived days later, they found a crater surrounded by blackened bodies."

Septimus cleared his throat, at something of a loss for words. At length, he said, "Impressive. I only managed to kill the family butler."

"Your noble status is an asset," said Vae Victis. "We are always looking for new members in high places. One day, when the time is ripe, they will be the key to seizing power in the Empire once again, and bringing about the rule of the next Mage-Emperor."

"Or!" Cold-Eyes interjected, with a mad look in his namesake orbs. "Or the return of the original!"

Septimus blinked, looking back at the dismal little room and all the robed men and women in it, all staring at Vae Victis where she towered above them. "You can't possibly mean Ildrius is still somehow alive?"

Cold-Eyes rubbed a slender finger over his hairless chin. "There are those who say he is. Could someone so wise and powerful truly allow himself to die? Would he not have had some backup plan? Tales speak of spells that can anchor one's soul to an artifact, allowing life after death..."

Septimus sneered. "What does it matter if he is? What fool would want to bring back Ildrius? He was a madman."

As Septimus had expected, a murmur spread through the room. Cold-Eyes even audibly gasped, quite theatrically. Again, Plutarch almost rolled his eyes. But Vae Victis only let out a cold laugh.

"You truly *are* brave, Septimus Plutarchus," she said. "I'm starting to like you. 'Tis not your fault you have been deceived by the lies put forth under the orders of the Imperium – even those penned by your own historian ancestor. Ildrius performed certain... experiments on the weak, true, but only so that humanity as a whole might grow stronger. Had Ildrius ruled for longer, he would have led us down the path to immortality. Instead of being the puppets and playthings of the gods, the giants, the titans... we would have been their equals. We would have been gods ourselves."

Septimus snorted. "Lofty goals, certainly, but if Ildrius were truly worthy to lead us down that path, then he would be the one telling me this now, not you. As it is, he failed. He and all his mightiest peers and apprentices, servants and slaves, cut down in the height of their power."

Finally, Vae Victis merely shrugged. "It's a moot point. Unless he is found, he cannot return to power. Perhaps someone else could rule better – there are those who think so."

Septimus nodded slowly, wondering if everyone in this hideout was completely mad. "If my station is such an asset, I should warn you: my family is expecting me at our manor near the border to the Black Lands. I should have been there already; my visit to the library was a... detour. I'm supposed to document the glorious conquests of my two oldest brothers as they slaughter some pitchfork-wielding bandits and call it 'squashing a rebellion.' So, if you want me to remain incognito, just lend me a few of your *'Magic for Beginners'* and *'Baby's First Spell'* books, and I'll be on my merry–"

"No," Vae Victis cut in, raising a gauntleted hand. "We have a hidden lair in the Black Lands, a storehouse of forbidden knowledge. Cold-Eyes will travel there ahead of you. He will then meet you outside your estate and lead you there. We can't risk our precious knowledge falling into the wrong hands and exposing you. Besides, you need more than books to learn magic. You need hands-on training. Your Gift must not be squandered. Some in this room are not so blessed by fate."

Septimus glanced back at the others in the dark little room. They looked away as soon as he did so, as if in shame. Plutarch's eyes went wide, and he turned back to Vae Victis.

"Let me see if I understand this..." he said slowly, trying to keep his voice low enough so only she would hear. *"You and I are the only real mages in this room?"*

"If you only consider those born with the Gift to be 'real mages,' then yes. The others – those who look pale and sickly, like Cold-Eyes – are just warlocks: men and women who sought to be more than what they were, by selling their soul to a demon in exchange for power. With each use of this power, they lose more and more of their humanity. They can fight it by fueling their spells with soulstones and other tricks, but the demon is always waiting, for as long as it takes... to inevitably claim what is theirs.

"A deadly high price, but who can blame these ambitious souls? Do you have any idea the rarity of your Gift, son of Plutarch? There are perhaps a million people in this, the capital and largest city of the Empire. Among them, I doubt there are even ten magi. We may be the only ones. In all the vast lands the Empire holds, there are perhaps a few hundred... and many of them now live in chains in Karak du Vide, prisoners of the Inquisition. The key to making sure you do not join them... is to remain Hidden."

"We happy few..." Septimus muttered sarcastically.

Vae Victis did not seem to hear him. "You should go now," she said, with a commanding tone. "You've tarried in here long enough. Your family must not suspect."

Septimus snorted. "They'll probably be more suspicious when they see me riding up to the manor like a good little boy. But you're right. So long then, I suppose. I'll... be in touch?"

"We'll make sure of it," Vae Victis said ominously as he rose to leave.

He tried not to think too hard about that. He had only just discovered his power, and already one group was trying to control him. Previously, he had wished for more power over his life, over his own destiny, and he had hoped this "Gift" would give him that. But now, between the threat of the Inquisition and this Hidden cult, he felt more under the control of others than ever before. But that would change, he told himself. That would change.

Just as he reached the door, Vae Victis called out to him one last time: "And Plutarch! One thing to remember: always remain calm. If you let your emotions get out of control..."

"Yes," Septimus said, "then I might accidentally blast my pompous brothers into ash. Wouldn't that be a shame."

He traced the sign over the stone door, and again it slid right open... just like magic.

Part 3: Before the Storm

Septimus Plutarch arrived at his family's manor on the edge of the Black Lands two days later, still traveling alone. He took his time, resting often and poring over the tome he'd stolen from the Hidden lair in Coronaria. He knew they would realize it was missing, but would they do anything to him, as valuable as he was? He doubted it.

And I'd be even more valuable if I knew how in Hades to do some real magic, he thought as his cart rattled over another hill. The manor came into view then, resting in a lush valley below him, between a shining blue lake and the dark forests of the Black Lands. The mansion itself rose like a fortress tower, tall and grey, surrounded by a stone fence topped by black iron spikes. It contrasted sharply with the placid surroundings. The Plutarchs were known for their somber architecture and decoration.

A servant greeted him at the gate as he swung it open. "Hail, Master Septimus! Your brothers sent word that they would be late, though we were expecting you a good deal earlier as well."

Septimus frowned thoughtfully as he loaded his books into a satchel, then took it with him as he dismounted. "I see. So, none of my brothers are here? When should they arrive?"

"I don't know, m'Lord – within a day or two, I think."

"Take care of my horse and carriage. I'll be in the study. If anyone else arrives, let me know. Just knock and shout it through the door; it will be locked."

The servant nodded, though Septimus did not see it, for he had already moved past him into the manor. There were some more servants inside cleaning, who bowed when Septimus entered. He nodded to them as he strode past, heading straight up the stairs to the study.

It was a spacious room on the second floor of the manor, with a shining wood floor, plenty of comfortable chairs – one behind a large desk – and glass doors opening to a balcony overlooking the lake. Septimus tossed his bag into the nearest chair and withdrew the stolen Hidden book, which bore the title *A Translation of Nirav Sadar's Study on Elemental Lightning*, by an anonymous translator. Septimus recalled that Nirav Sadar was an ancient mage-king of Sinkarya, whose empire had been destroyed in the mage wars that created the Endless Waste far south of the Empire. The title had caught Septimus's eye because his own unexpected magical murder of Paulus had looked like lightning.

But he'd already read enough of the book along the way, so he just deposited it on the desk and picked up a silver candlestick. He had failed time and time again to cast any of the spells mentioned in the book, but he was determined to keep trying. Striding out onto the balcony, he looked down. There was only a short gap between the side of the building and the defensive wall below, with nothing but grass and the lake beyond. No servants would see, hopefully, if he succeeded in blasting the candlestick. So, he set it carefully upon the balcony railing and then stepped back to the doors.

He casually stretched out his hand and said, *"Voco Fulmen."*

Words, the tome had said, helped to concentrate the mind. The shorter and more specific the words, the more concentrated on a single idea the mind could be. This meant, supposedly, that although specific spell incantations had been found to have certain effects, *any* words could be used to cast most basic spells, no matter what the language. High Imperial was favored due to its terse and accurate nature.

But this sage advice had been no use for Septimus so far, because once again nothing happened.

He concentrated now, furrowing his brow and pointing one finger directly at the candlestick. He was a surprisingly good aim with a crossbow – one of the only martial contests in which he was a match for some of his brothers – so how different could it be to aim a spell? He tried to think of lightning, images of Zeus tossing thunderbolts, even the Nordic god Thor with his thunderous hammer.

"Voco Fulmen!"

Nothing. Why in Hades wasn't it working?! He stamped out onto the balcony and grabbed the silver candlestick in his fist, preparing to hurl it into the lake if he could manage to throw that far. But as soon as his fingers closed around it, something happened:

The candle on top exploded.

Septimus looked at the candlestick. There was smoke rising from where the candle had been resting, and blackened bits of wax dotted the balcony. He wondered why the candlestick itself had not been harmed.

He walked over to the desk, setting the candlestick down and picking up a new one. He stared intently at the candle, trying to rekindle his earlier feeling of rage and concentrate it on the new target. He stirred up his emotions, bringing them to a boil.

"*Voco Fulmen!*" he snarled.

Nothing. He swore and slammed the candlestick down upon the table. Was it a bad spell?

But his thoughts were interrupted by a sound coming from behind him: "*HAHAHAHA!*"

Septimus wheeled. It was Varius, his cocky swashbuckler brother, swaggering into the room and clapping as he laughed. His leather vest was hanging open, his brown hair was a mess, his face unshaven, and he smelled of alcohol. Septimus felt the chill touch of terror run over his skin. *He'd been discovered.* Just a few days since his first act of magic, and already his secret was out.

But the situation could still be salvaged...

"What are you laughing at?" Septimus said, eyes narrowed as his fingers inched toward the sword sheathed on his belt.

"My brother, the world's worst swordsman," replied Varius with a lopsided smile, "is now the world's worst wizard as well! He can only cast spells by accident! Oh, things could not have worked out better. Go ahead, draw your sword, brother! I'd welcome a final duel!"

Varius's blue eyes flashed, and his sword appeared in his hand as suddenly, Septimus thought, as a bolt of lightning. Its tip was pointed toward Septimus's throat, and though he still stood some distance away, he knew Varius could close the gap just as quickly as he'd drawn his blade.

Septimus took a step back. "What are you talking about? You're going to kill me? Why? What could you possibly gain?"

"Well, for one thing, by a stroke of luck, the Inquisition is already on its way here! They're traveling with our esteemed eldest brothers, heading into the Black Lands to search for some secret mage stronghold. They might be working with the rebels. It's all so perfect! Now to finish it!"

Septimus unsheathed his sword just in time. As he'd predicted, his brother closed the gap in two graceful steps, striking at Septimus as fast and hard as he could. It was all the younger brother could do to deflect it. As he blocked the jab and stepped back, Septimus picked up one of the silver candlesticks from the desk behind him.

He pointed it as his brother, but Varius just laughed and mocked him: "*Voco Flumen!* Hahaha!"

"*Flumen* means *river*, you complete *idiot*," Septimus snapped between gritted teeth. He despised the thought of being killed by a moron.

Varius rolled his eyes. "Oh, whatever."

The dance resumed, steel ringing against steel. Septimus put all his effort into remembering his swordfighting lessons, parrying Varius's attacks and trying to keep his brother at bay. But no matter how hard he tried, he found himself being pushed back. Soon he realized, much to his shock, that he was standing out on the balcony now. The wind whipped over him, catching his short cape like a flag. He had nowhere to run.

"Why?!" Septimus shouted. "What do you gain from killing me? The satisfaction?! We could be allies! Your blade and my magic!"

Varius laughed again, almost madly. "Oh yes, your magic is so impressive! Just as impressive as my swordsmanship, certainly! That must be why father made you his heir!"

Septimus's eyes went wide, and somehow he deflected Varius's next attack almost by reflex, as if his desire to live had just increased. "What – are you saying – how could you –"

"I picked the lock to his room one night just like I picked the lock to this study! He'd been writing his will, naming you above even Adam and Albus! Above me! Above *six brothers!* I refuse to see that happen, and now that I know your secret, I know it never will!"

With newfound determination, Septimus threw himself into the fight. Blade clanged against blade. But Varius had new energy as well. With rage that matched Septimus's determination, he forced his younger brother back more and more, until Septimus knew the balcony railing must be right behind him. He glanced back to look, just for a fraction of a second, and that was all it took.

Varius knocked Septimus's sword away, sending it spinning out of his grip, through the air and over the edge of the balcony. Then he stabbed Septimus. The younger brother felt the cold steel sink into his side. He screamed.

And then he looked up, right into Varius's eyes. His brother stared back at him, surprised at his courage. Septimus reached up...

and grabbed the blade of Varius's sword. He felt hot blood trickle down his wrist where the edge started to sink into his fingers. He let the pain combine with his outrage and fear, channeling his emotions.

"Voco Fulmen," he said.

Varius went rigid for a fraction of a second, then shook violently as a flash lit the air, even brighter than the light of the sun. Arcs of lightning crawled along Varius's blade and into his arm, snapping and cracking, leaving burns on his clothing and flesh as they traveled over him.

Then it was over. Blackened and stiff, Varius toppled backwards, letting go of his sword's hilt as he fell. Removing his hand from the blade and gripping the hilt instead, Septimus pulled the blade from his side, groaning as he did. With a great effort, he stood, wiped off the blade, and slid it into his own sheath. He didn't even look down at Varius as he shuffled past his charred corpse.

"Live by the sword..." he muttered.

Then he saw movement. The door to the study was still open, and a servant was standing there.

"Voco Fulmen!"

He did it reflexively, pointing and saying the words. This time, the lightning came when called. It split through the room with a sharp crack... but his aim was off. It only left a charred hole in the door next to the servant. He got a good look at her then, as she stared at him with her eyes wide. She was young, he thought, very young. He moved his finger to the right, toward the girl's face... but he hesitated.

Then she was gone, running back through the hall and down the stairs. The last living witness to his magic had escaped. He'd held his lifelong dreams in the palm of his hand, and in a moment of weakness, he had let them all fall away. Cursing himself, he took off after the girl. Maybe he could still catch her before she told someone. Maybe he could convince her not to speak of it.

Or maybe he'd have to kill every servant in the manor.

He sprinted down the stairs, taking two steps at a time, but on the way, he tripped and nearly fell. This caused pain to shoot through his wounded side. Swearing again, he steadied himself and resumed his pursuit.

He heard voices in the distance, shouting: "Magic! Septimus killed Varius with magic!"

He swore under his breath. By the time he reached the bottom, he knew he was too late. He caught a glimpse of two servants fleeing out the main door. All the doors in the hall were open. They all knew, and they were all gone.

He couldn't believe his misfortune. If what Varius had said was true, then he had been set to inherit his father's lands and titles – everything he'd ever wanted. And he'd beaten Varius. For once, he'd felt completely confident and in control of his life, on the road to being Lord Plutarch, the secret mage prince of Pluton Hold. But now that brief, tiny moment had passed. It had lived for but a fraction of a second. Once again, he felt it all crumbling down around him. All his plans, everything he had tried to build.

He looked at the great hall of the Plutarchus manor, with the portraits and tapestries of his father and forefathers hanging on the walls. Suddenly, he hated all of it. He wished *it* would crumble down around him. He walked out onto the wide purple carpet that spanned the hall, standing in the center of a great star of Astra depicted thereon. Then, without even thinking about it, his emotions swirling like a tempest within him, fueled by the pain of his wound, he raised his arms...

Without calling for it, he felt the Power surge through him. He felt it tingle over his skin, like a thousand tiny ants. It felt like the first time he'd felt the touch of a woman, combined with the first time he'd first been burned by fire.

Lightning poured from his fingertips. arcing up along the floor and the walls. A bolt snapped across the room and straight into the face of a painting of his eldest brother Adamas. It fell to the floor, burning. Fire began to trail along the blackened walls. One, two, three thunderclaps split the air, and he felt the floor of the building tremble. A chandelier hanging overhead fell and crashed at his feet, sending shards of broken glass onto him.

He didn't care. He could feel the energies of the universe flowing through him, and suddenly he felt more like himself than he ever had before. Why should he be concerned about the trappings of man, when he held in his hands the power of the *gods?* This was who he truly was, what he was meant to be – his destiny since the beginning, finally discovered. He had found his true potential. He felt free, without a care in the world as he watched his old life burn. The agony of his stab wound was entirely forgotten. He laughed aloud with joy.

Then a section of the roof fell down, blazing with flame, crashing to the floor just to his left. It woke him from his ecstasy. He turned and ran from the building, out into the courtyard. He glanced back to see Plutarch manor burning behind him, and he tried to cast one last parting bolt in its direction... but nothing came. Perhaps he'd drained himself, or perhaps he still didn't quite have the knack of it.

He ran to the stables, but there were no horses there. Perhaps the servants had taken them all. Still on a high from unleashing his magic, he couldn't bring himself to care. He simply strode out the front gates, turned toward the forest, and ran.

What could possibly stop him?

"Help! Help us! He's got magic!"

The caravan slowed as the hysterical woman approached them on horseback. She approached the leaders of the group: Adamas and Albus Plutarch, the former dark-eyed and grim-faced as always, and the latter friendly and reassuring as usual, telling her everything would be okay.

"Calm down, lass," Albus said, trotting his horse up near hers and putting a hand on her arm. "Take a deep breath and tell us what happened."

The girl breathed deeply, trying to fix her hair and clothing – and then she saw the rest of the riders in the caravan, and her eyes went wide again. "Are those... are those Inquisitors?"

Albus glanced back at their companions. The ebon-armored Inquisitors had been headed toward the Black Lands to stomp out an outpost of the Hidden there, when they'd joined forces with the Plutarchs so they might travel together. The Plutarchs and Inquisitors had talked much along the way, and Adamas had come to admire their selfless dedication to such a necessary cause. Albus just found them a bit creepy.

"Oh, thank the gods!" the servant went on. "They must've sent them! Praise Olympos! You must stop the mage!"

"Who?" Albus asked. "Who is this mage?"

"Lord Septimus!" the girl blurted. "It's Septimus Plutarch!"

Albus went pale as a sheet. Adamas set his jaw. The Inquisitors exchanged glances. One of them pointed to a rider and sent him ahead to scout.

"You must be joking, woman," Albus said, gripping the girl's arm again. "Make sense!"

"I saw it, milord!" the girl gasped. "Lord Varius burst into Septimus's room, and they fought, and Varius stabbed him, and then *Septimus killed him!* With a blast o' magic! He tried to blast me too! Then he started blowing up the manor! It's on fire!"

Adamas, eldest son of Plutarch, sat up taller in his saddle and finally spoke, drawing all eyes to him. "Let's move!" he commanded. "To the manor!"

By the time the caravan arrived, the lakeside mansion had been burning for hours, and it still blazed now – a towering inferno bearing the symbols of their family. Albus felt righteous indignation. Adamas simply felt the cold desire for justice.

The two brothers looked back at their comrades from the Imperial Inquisition. There were only three of them: an Inquisitor-General, his lieutenant, and a channeler. The Inquisitor-General's name was Burkhard. He was old, with silver hair, and he wore his void-iron mail like a second skin. Clean-shaven and straight-backed, his black tabard bearing the white Inquisition emblem was immaculately straight and clean.

His lieutenant – named Karl Metus – wore heavier armor and never fully revealed his face, leaving his helmet on at all times with only the ventail open to reveal his chin, which seemed curled into an eternal scowl. Why he kept his eyes hidden, the brothers could only guess.

From atop his mount, Inquisitor-General Burkhard looked down at Adamas where he stood outside the gates of his family's manor. "Master Plutarch, we will do our best to bring your brother back alive for trial, if possible. We were supposed to wait here for a contingent of Ebonguards to help us clear out the Hidden stronghold, but we should be able to handle Septimus on our own. From what the servants said, it sounds like he's inexperienced, as well as wounded."

Adamas nodded his head low, his dark brows casting shadows over his eyes. "He'll be brought to justice, I swear it."

Albus, running a hand through his light brown hair, gave his brother a worried look. "Adamas... go easy on Septimus. I doubt the boy even knows what he did. The servant said Varius had *stabbed* him. You know Varius..."

"*Knew* Varius," Adamas corrected. "Unless our witness is a liar, Septimus killed him – killed his own brother."

"Possibly by accident," said another voice, with a thick Southron accent.

It was the channeler, whose comrades called him Basileus. The Plutarch brothers had never seen a man with darker skin. It was almost as dark as the black tattoos that covered it, including a tattoo of the Inquisition's emblem over one of his eyes. He had long, black hair as well, thick and curly, and wore little more than a ragged black robe over his tattooed muscles.

Channelers underwent special rituals so that they could absorb magic through their runic tattoos and "channel" it back at their enemies. The Plutarchs had asked Basileus whether his skin tone was a result of the rituals, but he said it was natural, as he was from the land of Axa, far to the South. He was well-educated in the arts of magic, even moreso than Burkhard.

Basileus went on: "Magi can lose control of their powers during times of stress, emotion, pain... I have witnessed it personally many times. It is why they can only be allowed to live in secluded, controlled communities like on Karak du Vide. Septimus will go there, if we can take him alive. Hopefully, he will see reason."

Inquisitor-General Burkhard's lieutenant, Karl Metus, added grimly: "But if not, we will do what's necessary."

"I understand completely," said Adamas. "I can come with you..."

"No," said Burkhard, "I will not be the man to get either of the eldest sons of Lord Plutarch killed. No offense meant, my Lords, but without void-iron armor or the tattoos of a channeler, you are as helpless against your brother's power as if you were fighting naked. Now, the three of us should be off before Septimus gets too far ahead. Metus! Release the dogs!"

Other than their three horses, the Inquisitors had two more animals with them: a pair of dogs – sturdy bloodhounds with thick muscles visible beneath their short black and grey coats. Their short, pointed ears twitched to and fro as they sniffed the ground around a pair of footprints left by Septimus. Metus let go of their leashes, and off they dashed toward the forest. In a rumble of hooves, the Inquisitors followed.

The sky grew overcast, the world dim and grey, as Septimus followed the northern road into the Black Lands. He carefully kept his distance from the road itself, traveling through the forest to its right. He hoped it would not rain. He had no idea where he might find shelter in these bleak woodlands. He had no precise idea where he was going, just a vague understanding of the local geography and locations of towns where he could stop and rest. He had enough coins in his pouch to last a while.

Luckily, his injury was not slowing him down much. The magic he'd cast on the metal had heated it, causing the wound to cauterize – and it wasn't as deep a cut as he'd feared. Nonetheless, he used his dagger to cut strips from the purple cape of his House and wrap them around his waist as bandages. Then he put his shirt back on, fastened up his surcoat, and kept walking.

The worst thing was the headache. The pain came in waves, making him feel dizzy and sick, so that he had to stop and rest at intervals. Had all the magic he'd unleashed caused it? The thought was slightly mortifying. Gods should not get headaches.

Suddenly, he spotted a lone traveler on the road. Clad in a grey cloak and robes, the man was easy enough to recognize by his hairless head and pale, very nearly translucent skin and eyes.

Septimus shouted a greeting to him and emerged from the brush onto the well-paved Imperial road.

"Cold-Eyes!" he exclaimed with confidence. "Fancy meeting you here."

"Master Plutarch," the warlock said in his raspy voice, giving a very small bow. "I am pleased you have found me! Is that blood on your clothes?"

Septimus shrugged. "Only a flesh wound."

Cold-Eyes nodded eagerly. "Our stronghold is not far, in the forest due east of here. It rests on a place of magical power, so even though I cannot sense it, you should be able to find your way there. The stronghold is located beneath another ruin, and–"

Septimus held up a hand to stop him. "Cold-Eyes, I would ask a question of you. This is important, but merely hypothetical. If I were to suddenly, say, be discovered and lose my influential position in my family and the Imperium... would your organization still have a use for me?"

The little necromancer squinted his pallid eyes at him, as if he had trouble seeing clearly. "I... hope it will not soon come to that, Master Plutarch. But you are a born mage! Lady Victis emphasized how rare and valuable you are, no matter your position among the nobility."

"How comforting," Septimus said sarcastically, and then he sighed. "I just wish I could have seen my brothers one last time, to tell them that father was going to name me his heir. To rub it in their faces, and then tell them I don't even care anymore..."

Cold-Eyes blinked with incomprehension. "Wait... you don't mean...?"

Septimus paused at the sound of distant barking. It was not an uncommon sound in and of itself, but he was on the alert. He recalled something he'd read in a book, about the Inquisition using a special type of bloodhound, kin to an ancient breed developed by the Venatori for hunting monsters...

"They're coming," he said.

Cold-Eyes blinked. "What? Who?"

"A parade of frolicking nymphs, of course," Septimus said dryly. "Who do you think?"

He was about to clarify with the truth when the truth itself rode up before them. First came the two dogs, and behind them three Inquisitors on horseback. The one in the rear whistled, recalling the hounds, who immediately ceased their snarling and snapping and ran back to their master.

Then all three Inquisitors dismounted. Two were clad in that daunting black armor, one in plate and the other only in mail. The third was nearly naked, but his skin was almost dark enough to be void-iron itself. The white of his eyes shone like beacons of light against it.

Septimus glanced at Cold-Eyes. He had not thought it possible, but somehow the pallid little hedge-wizard had gone even paler. He was terrified.

In a fit of panic, without even thinking, Septimus stretched out his arm toward the first Inquisitor. "*Voco Fulmen!*" To his relief, it worked: with a crack like thunder, the magic energy split the air and burned the man's tabard in half, so it fell to the ground in blazing pieces. But the Inquisitor himself didn't even pause in his stride. His black armor was not even smoking.

"You're wounded, Master Plutarch!" said the Inquisitor, his voice echoing behind the void-iron mask that peered out beneath his black hood. "Surrender, and we will see to your wounds. Fight, and we will be forced to put you down!"

Septimus tried to think of a plan, but his headache flared up again, clouding his thoughts. In the meantime, Cold-Eyes attacked. With a hissing snarl, he mouthed an incantation, and Plutarch turned to see an astonishing sight: a column flames emerged from the ground at the little man's feet and then twisted themselves into a ball of heat between his hands. The fire was horrifyingly unnatural: the tongues of flame were solid red, illuminating the grey road with their hellish crimson light.

Letting out a strange, otherworldly hiss, Cold-Eyes sent the sphere of red flame hurtling toward the group of Inquisitors. But without hesitation, the channeler simply stepped in front of it, letting the blast of crimson fire disappear right into his body. The network of tattoos on his ebon skin began to glow white, as did his eyes...

Septimus turned and cast his one and only spell again – "Voco Fulmen!" – but he only got the words halfway out before a pain shot through his head, interrupting him. He then felt the pain shoot through his arm as well, and he nearly dropped to his knees. No bolt of lightning came, only pain.

Forcing himself to move, hoping to escape while Cold-Eyes was still distracting the Inquisitors, Septimus Plutarch ran. He fled straight into the woods and did not look back.

"I'll go after him!" shouted Inquisitor-General Burkhard, tearing off the last remnants of his burning tabard. "You two finish this one!"

As their leader dashed into the forest after Plutarch, Basileus and Karl Metus advanced on Cold-Eyes. Basileus channeled the energy he'd absorbed and sent it flying back at his attacker in the form of a beam of raw arcane power. At the last second, Cold-Eyes shouted a few words and conjured a magic shield that deflected the blast. The magic was sent flying outward in all directions, striking the nearby ground and tree branches, twisting them into unnatural shapes. A loud wind rushed through the forest, as if nature herself were protesting this attack upon her laws.

Basileus just kept walking, with Metus on his heels. The latter Inquisitor then dashed forward, striking Cold-Eyes's magic shield with his sword. The void-iron blade cut right through, slicing into the warlock's arm. Cold-Eyes stumbled back with a cry and sent out a gust of red flame from his hand. Basileus simply reached out and caught it, and then channeled it right back into the necromancer's face.

Cold-Eyes screamed as his flesh was burned and scarred and twisted.

"Violent and wielding demonic magic," said Karl Metus, his voice echoing within his helmet. "Let's put him out of his misery."

Basileus nodded. He drew his dagger and knelt down beside the suffering servant of the Hidden. "This won't hurt long," he said. It was the last thing Cold-Eyes ever heard.

Septimus ran faster than he'd ever run in his life. He was no expert, however, at making quick time through the forest. He kept tripping over vines and getting hung on briars, and all the while he could hear the indomitable Inquisitor-General smashing through the underbrush behind him like a void-iron boulder. Along the way, Septimus kept trying to conjure some kind of magic, but nothing came. It only seemed to make his headache worse.

He passed a particularly large dead tree. Summoning all the energy he could muster, he stretched out his fingers toward the base of the grey old pine – and this time, perhaps fueled by his fear and desperation, it worked. The log exploded into splinters and flame. The fire spread rapidly, and then the towering inferno crashed to the ground, blocking the path behind Septimus.

He had long since resumed running, not looking back. He hoped the blockade would slow the Inquisitor down for a while, because he had no more strength left in him for spellcasting. It was all he could do to concentrate on the vague feeling of magical energies in the area, trying to follow them to their source – to the Hidden refuge.

Soon, he saw some ruins of an old fort up ahead, covered in vines. It was an unimpressive place, just a small crumbling tower with a tiny ring of stone walls at its base. The gates had long ago been smashed, and the intact iron portcullis was wide open, so Septimus dashed inside. He looked around desperately for some sign of the Hidden, and his eyes soon landed on a note nailed to a wooden post. The note bore the Hidden symbol – the black hook under a narrow eye – and below it was written:

If one of our brethren reads this, know that we have abandoned this location until the Inquisition are done sweeping the area. All Hidden should leave the Black Lands immediately.

If one of our enemies reads this, know that GODS NEVER DIE. EMPEROR ILDRIUS WILL RISE AGAIN!

Septimus balled up the bit of papyrus in his fist and tossed it to the ground. It was clear the fortress had been inhabited recently, for there were tracks of men and animals all over the hard-packed earth. But everything of use had been taken when the Hidden fled, apparently. The only thing left was a massive amount of hay and animal feed in a loft above the stable.

Suddenly, Septimus had a truly wild idea. It was desperate and would likely never work, but he had little choice except to try, or die trying.

He would not be taken, he told himself. He would not be caged. He would achieve his destiny.

The old Inquisitor-General took caution when he reached the ruined fortress. He was out of breath from running so far in full armor, especially after dodging the burning blockade Septimus had put in his path. He paused a while, leaning against the stone wall until his strength returned. His breath echoed within the confines of his black metal mask, which was impeding his breathing, but which he dared not remove yet.

He looked into the ruined courtyard, the gates of which lay wide open. Inside the low stone walls was a wooden stable, with its loft smashed open and crumbling. Hay was scattered everywhere, so thick on the ground that it rose up nearly to Burkhard's black-armored knees as he waded into it. The stuff was everywhere. He moved toward a wooden post, to which was nailed a crumpled paper bearing the unmistakable mark of the Hidden.

The moment he reached the note and began to read, he heard a loud metallic clangor and then a crash behind him. He wheeled to watch helplessly as the iron portcullis dropped down over the entrance. His eyes moved upward to the gatehouse above it, where a man in dirty but well-made noble finery – including the now-tattered purple cape of the Plutarchs – stood confidently with his arms crossed, gazing down.

"Septimus," said Burkhard, sheathing his black longsword, "come down here, and let us speak. I do not wish to harm you..."

Septimus Plutarch threw back his black-haired head and laughed. "Oh, you can skip all that, Inquisitor. I once dreamed of being one of you, so I know very well your order does not suffer a mage to live a free life. I have no time to talk."

Burkhard threw out his hands. "So, what will you do then? Run? They all run, Septimus. No one can run forever."

"I don't intend to," said the mage, and then he cast his spell.

By the grace of the gods, or some other power, it worked. The lightning set the scattered hay ablaze immediately. The flames spread with startling speed, and Burkhard was forced backward. But he was trapped in the small, cramped courtyard, and soon the flames had engulfed all of it. He had nowhere to run. And while the lightning that sparked the fire was magical, the fire itself was not. And void-iron did not block natural flame.

Burkhard was roasting in his armor, coughing from the smoke, unable to breathe behind his void-iron mask. He tore the mask from his face and tossed it away, gasping for air. The metal faceplate bounced between the bars of the portcullis to land in the grass outside the gate.

Burkhard stumbled after it, hoping to get some fresh air near the gate, but the hay was spread slightly beyond the portcullis, all of it blazing. He walked to the iron bars and peered out through the smoke... and saw Septimus Plutarch standing there. The wizard looked down at the void-iron mask, picked it up, and turned it over in his hands, gazing at the triple bar design that hung down over its narrow visor.

Gazing at Burkhard, he slid the mask into his satchel. "I've heard that if an Inquisitor loses any piece of void-iron gear," Septimus said, "they are obligated to search for it relentlessly until it's found. Well, they'll be searching for me anyway..."

Burkhard said nothing. He stood there, leaning against a wall, choking silently as he was baked alive in a void-iron oven. The stare he leveled at Septimus was as cold as the flames were hot. He refused to bargain or beg for mercy.

"You'll burn for this, freak..." hacked the old Inquisitor between ragged breaths, "just as surely as I'm burning now... A stake and a bonfire... await you. They will cure you... of your curse... once and for all."

A million speeches rushed through Septimus's mind at once. He thought of all the things he wanted to say to Burkhard: to justify himself, explain his actions and his plans, to taunt the Inquisition... but what would be the point? He hadn't the time to waste breath on a dying man. So, Septimus said nothing, nor did he stay to watch the mage-hunter breathe his last. He knew the other Inquisitors would be on their way, and in truth, he didn't care if they managed to save Burkhard. They would scour the world for him regardless. All he could do was keep moving.

As he walked away from the burning tower, he considered the events of the last few days. It felt as if he'd gained and lost everything at least three times since that meeting with his family in Pluton Hold. He thought of his sister Octavia, whom he might never see again. He wished he'd gotten a chance to tell her how much he actually enjoyed her music.

And to think, for a few brief seconds, he'd held in his hands everything he'd ever wanted. He'd been heir to the title and lands and gold of Lord Plutarch. And a secret wizard.

But even as he had lost these trappings of power, his own power – his *true* power – had only increased. Wealth and property and prestige could be snatched away, just like love and family. But the churning storm inside of him, the power that arced from his fingertips? No one could take that away. And it would only grow stronger. He would see to that.

Albus and Adamas Plutarch had followed the Inquisitors, against their wishes. But by the time they caught up with them, Karl Metus and Basileus were just preparing to head into the woods after their commander and his quarry. They were in too much of a hurry to protest the Plutarchs following them, so all four plunged in together. Metus led the way, with his two bloodhounds on their leashes sniffing out the path.

As it turned out, they were not needed. Burkhard had left an obvious trail as he smashed his way through the underbrush, and the smoke from Septimus's fires marked their destination. They passed his burning tree and forged on, heading toward a larger pillar of smoke that rose ominously in the distance.

When they arrived at the abandoned fort, the inferno inside was still blazing. But all that was left of Inquisitor-General Burkhard was a heap of void-iron armor against the wall, with a dancing flame where a face should have been. Karl Metus fell to his knees at the sight, and Basileus closed his eyes and bowed his head. If they said any prayers for their fallen comrade, they did it silently.

After a moment, Albus Plutarch spoke: "I am sorry. As Adamas said, we will do everything in our power to bring our brother to justice for his crimes. His guilt is now clear."

With grave seriousness in his gravelly voice, the dark-haired Adamas fell to one knee. "I will do more than that. I offer my service to the Inquisition, in payment of the debt of this man's life. I will help you catch my brother myself, and continue to serve after that, for as long as I am needed."

Albus shot his older brother a concerned look, but he knew better than to try to dissuade Adamas once he had set his mind on a course of action. He only said, "Adam... you know that Father won't like this. You're his eldest – his heir – and Inquisitors have to give up land and titles when they join the Order. Not to mention, when Sextus hears... You know he follows you everywhere."

"It doesn't matter what they think," said the stern Adamas. "It only matters what must be done. Tell young Sextus he may follow me, or follow *you* with my blessing. But this is my duty."

Albus just blew out a long sigh, shaking his head.

Meanwhile, Adamas looked up at the two mage-hunters and said, "Inquisitors... will you have my sword?"

Metus and Basileus exchanged glances. The former nodded his helmed head. Basileus smiled and turned back to Adamas.

"We will give you a new one," he said.

The elderly woman strolled leisurely through the marketplace, smiling at each stall she passed. Her silvery white hair tied up in a bun, a shawl over her head, standing hunched in homemade clothes, carrying a basket of herbs from her garden... she was the very picture of a kindly old grandmother. No one who saw her would have thought her capable of harming a fly.

But once out of sight of prying eyes, she slipped deftly into the shadows of an alleyway. She removed her shawl and stood up straighter, striding into the darkness with confidence. Ahead of her loomed another shadow, in the shape of a man in a cape and hood. He stepped out into the dim light to meet her, but his face remained in the shade of his crimson cowl.

The old woman said, "Hello, young man. You're the one who wishes to join the Schola Arcana?"

The hooded man raised a hand, on which he wore a fingerless black glove. A faint blue light appeared in his palm, barely illuminating the alley before it disappeared again when he closed his fist.

"Of course I am."

She smiled. "So confident! I heard about your experience with the Hidden. You say you joined their organization, but sensed its foulness and managed to escape? That speaks well of you. Many are too late perceiving the evil of that group. You were lucky!"

"They were mad, hoping to resurrect and restore an insane Emperor who was already defeated once. I have better things to do."

"Well, of course you do. But if you can lead us to any of their strongholds, we would most appreciate it. We would love to liberate any magical knowledge they may be hoarding. We have great libraries of our own, and you'll have unrestricted access! They're located far, far away from this mundane world. One can study there in peace."

The shadowy figure bowed slightly. "I thank you. It is an honor."

"Oh, so formal! Your parents raised you well."

"I wouldn't give my father too much credit. You should meet him first. You might change your mind."

"Ah well... In any event, all well-meaning magi are welcome within our halls. It's been ever so long since we found any." The old woman gave a little laugh. "But listen to me! I must be losing my wits. I haven't even introduced myself! I am usually called Susana, sometimes Susana the Silent, for I prefer to listen rather than speak. One learns more that way. And what, pray tell, is your name?"

The man threw back his hood. He had blue-blooded Achaean features, with high cheekbones and an Imperial nose. His hair was black, his eyes sapphire... and he had a small forked beard on his chin.

"I am called Plutarch," he said politely, as a smile spread over his lips. "*Lord* Plutarch."

Hunted
Caiden's Tale
by Maegan A. Stebbins

Rain. A slow, steady drizzle and a fine mist clouded their path. The road to Pikeston was a long one, a wide but winding dirt trail passing in and out of hamlets full of quaint homes. Each one, Gwen imagined she could live there, quaint as they were with their thatched roofs and buckets under the windows that ordinarily held colorful flowers.

But in the growing cold, everything looked grey and lifeless. Winter steadily crept over the landscape, though it hadn't yet turned the rain to snow. Still, a chill in the air and her own self-consciousness had Gwen pull the neck of her blue cloak higher, taking a deep breath of the moist dirt and fresh rain. A less pleasant scent than the petrichor of *warm* rain, like the smell that always seemed to cling to her partner.

Said partner who rode alongside her on his large brown horse gave her a quick look. She, orphan Gwenevere Vergil, had never imagined becoming a Venator: a member of the Empire's dedicated monster hunting order – and never had she imagined having a partner like the man whose one blue eye regarded her now, his other eye covered by a black patch.

Caiden Voros looked every bit a soldier – or maybe one who had borderline given up. His dark hair was a mess of short spikes that stuck out this way and that, and a stubble darkened his chiseled, handsome face. Whereas Gwen stood a bit shorter than average, Caiden towered over nearly everyone they met, but perhaps still more impressive was his heavy build of pure muscle, with arms thick as tree trunks.

Gwen felt she hardly matched up. Green eyes peered from the shadow of her hood, and she fidgeted briefly with her short brown ponytail she currently had draped over one shoulder. Her lithe, athletic form and her sharp features were actually very attractive, as well, though she hardly thought of herself that way.

The rain lightened just enough for Gwen to see a cluster of cottages in the distance: they were nearing the edge of Pikeston, their destination, a town in the Black Lands of the Achaean Empire. She didn't know much about it, but she had always heard it was generally a quiet, unsuspecting place, if full of superstition.

Now she finally returned one of the glances Caiden had been sparing her for most of the journey and said, "How're you holding up?"

"I'm fine," Caiden replied, like he always did. Gwen almost wanted to reach over and smack him on one of his big arms, but she resisted. How many times had she heard that exact phrase, and how often did she actually believe it?

Despite his words, she watched as he reached up to readjust the strip of black cloth tied around his throat. Underneath it, he wore a choker made of cold iron: a strange and darkly magical metal used to ward off the powers of the Fey... powers Caiden carried, himself. Neither he nor Gwen truly understood his abilities, but they'd learned a lot in the years they had been partners. It was a mystery Gwen remained confident they could eventually solve – and get Caiden the help he really needed. Help to... well, not go insane.

Gwen shivered at some unbidden memories.

That choker, despite its original purpose as a collar for prisoners, helped Caiden keep his own mind. She knew how much he hated it, but especially as they neared a thicker patch of civilization, he would certainly need it.

Right now, however, they were 'just' monster hunters. They had a job to do.

"So," Gwen said as she threw off her deep blue hood and shook free her brown ponytail, "any theories?"

Caiden huffed. "About what?"

"The monster."

"What do we even know right now?"

"Not much, but I enjoy wild speculation," Gwen replied with a smile as their horses strode into town. "Anything you've always *wanted* to find?"

He grunted. After all this time, Gwen could almost understand Caiden's nonverbal language of actions, grunts, huffs, and other largely guttural noises. This one she guessed to mean a disdainful, *"Not really."*

"Kind of hard to beat what we've already faced, isn't it?" she thought aloud, but Caiden had no answer for that except a quietly amused huff.

They reached the town limits – and it felt haunted.

Although Gwen hadn't expected much activity in the rain, this felt wrong. Instead of an outdoor market or the remains of one, watchmen on patrol, or even a few wandering civilians, they found only stillness and empty streets. Gwen frowned as the one person she finally caught sight of was already running – actually *running*, like doom was at his heels – into the nearest building and slamming the door shut behind him.

"Whatever it is," Gwen said quietly, almost afraid to raise her voice to even a normal speaking level, "it's really got everyone spooked."

Caiden rumbled in pensive agreement.

They passed by an equally as silent inn with a few candles visible through the windows, as well as several stores and homes, on their way to the largest building: a tall, two-story structure almost certainly belonging to the local ruler. Its windows all stood dark, the very air around it still. Gwen didn't need Caiden's strange abilities to feel the palpable fear blanketing the entire town.

They stopped and dismounted, hitching their horses to a post just outside before Caiden stepped up to knock on the door. At first, no one answered. Gwen exchanged yet another look with Caiden's one eye, shadowed grimly under his sharp, heavy brow that seemed eternally furrowed.

"When was the last time *anything* had a whole town this spooked?" Gwen asked.

"When the streets were filling with undead," Caiden answered darkly. "Otherwise, never seen anything like it."

"Well, that was... an exceptional situation," Gwen murmured. She didn't like to remember her visit to Caiden's home city.

Finally, heavy footsteps approached from the other side of the door, which cracked open with an ominous groan. A pair of dark eyes peered at them from the shadows of the building, staring as if they were mad to simply be standing in the streets – at least until the stranger noticed their deep blue cloaks and silver brooches shaped like arrowheads: the symbols of the Venatori. Then he pulled the door open wider, revealing a tall, barrel-chested man wearing a simple hauberk of quilted armor, a long dagger sheathed on his belt. Whoever he was, he didn't exactly dress like a count.

"Only someone claiming to be monster hunters would dare be outside at sundown at a time like this," the man said, stepping aside and motioning them into the dark home. "If there *is* such a thing as a 'monster hunter...'"

"That's why your Count summoned us," Gwen replied as they entered. Caiden had to both turn his shoulders slightly sideways and duck to fit through the doorway. The man eyed Caiden for a long moment before shutting the door behind them, latching it with a heavy makeshift wooden bar. Gwen blinked.

The man noticed the expression she wore. "Can't be too careful," he said, ushering them down a dark wooden hall decorated with a few hunting trophies, the floor covered by a finely-patterned rug of deep green. "You two know what's going on?"

"No," said Caiden. "We were told there've been monster attacks. People were killed. Not much else."

The man scoffed. He led them into a larger, open space, where another fellow in the finery of a noble sat beside a fireplace. A third man, dressed in armor and wearing weapons similar to the one who had answered the door, stood looking around the room as if something could spring out and attack at any moment.

The older man in finery stood, his beard and wiry mustache looking unkempt for someone of his station. "Venatori," he said, "I am Count Goran Vulpowicz. I summoned for you days ago, and the Venatori send me only two hunters here almost at *dusk?*"

Gwen sighed. They had dealt with more than one ungrateful ruler who assumed the Venatori were still numerous and well-equipped, an order at every Imperial noble's beck and call. They were mistaken. For ages, the Venatori had all but fallen apart, turning small and weak and underfunded. While most people called them useless now that monsters had all but passed into legend in the Empire, the moment they were *needed*, they were suddenly supposed to be powerful and obedient.

Caiden briefly held up a hand to stop the Count from babbling. "We came as soon as we could. Now tell us what's going on."

That placated Count Vulpowicz, at least mildly. He started to pace as he continued, "Very well, though I don't understand what exactly is wrong with your order, unless all that poisoning muddies your minds. The creature only strikes at night. It... leaves no trace, except perhaps some blood and viscera. But it seems to occasionally eat its victims whole, maybe it even holds them with some kind of dark magic—"

"Stop speculating," Caiden said. "Give us facts."

"Leave the speculation to us," Gwen added with a small smile, trying to soften the blow.

Vulpowicz paused and furrowed his brow, but he said, "Fine. That makes sense, I suppose. Anyway, we often find no trace, is my point. It's almost like someone cleans the damn place up after it. Three or four times we have found blood and lots of it, but every other time, we discover almost nothing. People simply disappear.

"At first it was on the outskirts of town, around the forest, especially toward the north. Now, the monster has grown bolder and attacks the town itself. Someone was killed on a street-corner two nights ago, and last night, someone's home was broken into and they were gone. Her bedroom was full of blood, but there wasn't even a trail. In fact, we have found *no* trails at all, nothing leading to or away from the sites of the killings or anything unusual in the forests surrounding the town."

The Count continued pacing, staring hard at the floor. Already, Gwen mentally ran through the possibilities. If it always struck at night, it could be an undead – but why? Undead didn't simply *happen*, they had to be the result of some curse or someone using dark magic to raise them. And undead generally weren't as clean and impossible to track as Vulpowicz implied with this creature.

Visions of red eyes, pale skin, and fangs crossed her mind, and Gwen shivered. *Vampires.* No, it couldn't have been. A vampire wouldn't have eaten its victims or left blood everywhere – right? She had to assume that. Thank the gods it wasn't a vampire…

But there remained another possibility: the worst one. She hoped, even more than she hoped against vampires, that it wasn't *that*. Maybe it was just a beastman, one who wandered out of Rognosst Swamp. The swamps weren't very far off. And a beastman would have been intelligent enough to not leave a mess every time or to leave tracks, if it was careful enough…

There were other creatures, too, but she doubted it could be any of those this close to civilization.

While she lost herself in thought, Caiden nodded and said, "Alright. We'll handle it from here."

"What?" Vulpowicz demanded, rounding on them. "You will 'handle' it? Absolutely not – you're not going to wander off into the woods and come back with some ridiculous tale of how you gloriously slew a monster. Hesker," he gestured to the man who had answered the door, "Dalibor," he motioned to the other one who still stood guard, "you will go with them."

Instantly, Gwen tensed. Barely a second later, she and her partner locked gazes. Caiden's nostrils flared and his brow furrowed still worse. They knew how something like this ended.

"No," he told Vulpowicz. "I don't know what you think this is, Count, but we're not bringing anyone else along."

Vulpowicz scoffed loudly, motioning his two men out of the building. Quietly, they followed his orders, though the one he had called Dalibor looked apprehensive. Gwen felt sorry for him, but they still loyally left out the front door.

"You *will* take them," Vulpowicz insisted, "because I said so. And if you don't, your order will be hearing from me, and so will the Emperor. I'll have you both punished for disobeying an Imperial noble. You may have grown into some kind of wild rangers, but you're still under the Empire's command." He resumed pacing. "You will take my two men along. Only *then* will I donate coin and spare silver to your order for your supplies and those strange weapons you craft."

That made Caiden hesitate. The order could certainly use the donations. He opened his mouth, then closed it again in silence. Despite no other outward appearance of breaking discipline, his hands curled into fists the size of stone bricks by his sides.

So Gwen spoke instead, saying, "We'll take them if you insist, and we'll do everything we can to protect them, but just know... you're adding another level of danger to this – for everyone. There are a lot of reasons we only hunt with other members of our order. We're trained in this, and we go through a lot to be able to use our potions to give us an edge." She paused. "Your people might not come back."

"It's damn likely they won't," Caiden added flatly. "You'll be sending loyal men to their deaths. You really wanna do that?"

Count Vulpowicz sniffed. "Go, Venatori, and take them with you. Bring me this beast's head as proof."

Neither of them said another word; they simply turned and left, joining the two men – Hesker and Dalibor – who waited outside. From the corner of her eye, Gwen saw Caiden size them both up in one glance each, but it took Gwen a bit longer.

Hesker, the first man they'd met, looked like a capable warrior, and his short, ashen hair told of possibly a military background. Dalibor looked nervous and lanky, despite wearing similar armor and weapons. Not incapable, but certainly not standing with the calm confidence of Hesker, whose back remained straight as an arrow and whose face betrayed only a hint of apprehension. Dalibor fidgeted and ran a hand through his dark hair, scratching his head.

Appearances, of course, meant nothing. For all his muscles, Gwen knew perfectly well Hesker would be just as useless in a fight with any kind of monster as a toothpick would against a knight on horseback. Which was exactly why the Venatori existed: to do what others, even the greatest soldiers, could not... to hunt monsters, creatures beyond most people's comprehension, things they only ever met in their nightmares and rarely even thought of as real.

"If there's anything you have to do to get ready," Caiden said to the two quiet men, "do it now. We're hunting tonight."

Dalibor's eyes went wide, and Hesker almost choked on nothing. "*Tonight?*" Dalibor sputtered. "That's when the thing comes out!"

"Yeah. If you don't want to come, don't let the Count throw your lives away for you. You should stay here. Whatever it is, it's not gonna go down easy."

"We're coming," Hesker said. Beside him, Dalibor opened and shut his mouth a few times before saying nothing.

Caiden huffed. "Fine."

"If... you have any loved ones," Gwen said cautiously, "you should tell them what you're doing. Just in case."

Hesker nodded, walking off. Dalibor, however, only stood there fidgeting. And he kept standing there, even as Caiden told Gwen he was going to double-check his gear. Gwen knelt to do the same, removing her belt of potions and quiver of arrows and laying them out on some cobblestones under the eaves of the Count's home, where things were still relatively dry.

From her pack, she slid out her bow and proceeded to string it. Nearby, she heard Caiden checking his crossbow, but it was Dalibor who wandered into her view. She glanced up at him and forced a quick smile.

"My name's Dalibor," he said reluctantly, crouching down nearby. "I know the Count mentioned that, but I figured I'd properly introduce myself."

"I appreciate that," Gwen replied. "I'm Gwen Vergil, and my partner is Caiden Voros."

He nodded. "So... you're Venatori. 'The hunt never ends.' Is that right?"

"That's right," said Gwen; what he'd spoken was the motto of their order.

"Seems pretty dark..." Dalibor mused aloud.

Leaving her face, Dalibor's eyes locked onto the small array of potions instead, eying each one. A few were in clear bottles but others were in simple vessels of clay, their contents a mystery. Potions weren't something ordinary people generally used – or *could* use. Most were made from materials and toxins that would kill someone who hadn't inured themselves to the assorted ingredients, some of which came directly from parts of monsters. Venatori were poisoners, however: anyone could use potions if they built up to them over time, but few would ever do such a thing outside their order. So when Dalibor kept staring at them, Gwen knew what was coming. She'd heard it many times before.

"Are those potions?" he asked.

"Yes," Gwen replied as casually as she could manage. And she was about to drink one, which she knew would raise more questions, but it needed time for the effects to settle in before they went hunting. Taking one of the smaller bottles, she uncorked it and swallowed its contents down while Dalibor watched in something between fascination and horror.

"What was that one?"

She corked it again and put the empty bottle away. "It heightens our senses – all of them, including pain. That's the bad part, but at least we'll be able to see and hear and even smell more than we normally could. It helps us hunt and track, especially at night, and quickens our reflexes to fight something like a monster." She gave him another quick look. "Another side-effect is it makes our eyes glow. Just a little. But don't be surprised when you see it."

He blinked, his face growing pale. "And this one?" he pointed to another on her belt.

"That's a regeneration potion, as we call them. They can heal wounds relatively quickly and heal even very bad wounds, but it's... not a fun process. This one," she pointed at another, "is so we can breathe underwater." She wasn't going to explain how *that* one worked; it really would scare Dalibor to death. "We don't always carry one of those. And this last one is the most important – but I've never had to use it. Most of us never do, but we always try to carry one, if we have enough supplies to make them... it isn't easy to brew these."

That captured Dalibor's imagination. "What is it?"

Gwen hesitated. How could she even begin to explain this?

"It's a potion for lycanthropy – the curse of the werewolf. It's probably the most valuable one here, and the most difficult to make, too. Werewolves spread their curse through bite, or so they say. The Venatori code states that once someone becomes a monster, especially a werewolf, they lose their soul. They are no longer human and won't ever be themselves again. But even after the bite, if you take this potion before the next full moon, you won't turn if you can survive the potion's effects. Most don't, not even some Venatori, but… it's not impossible, and it's the only chance someone has."

With all color now well and truly drained from his face, to the point that Gwen wondered if he would simply fall out on the spot, Dalibor kept staring.

Gwen finished, "Like I said, they're hard to make, but we try to keep one around. You don't exactly hunt werewolves very often, but… you know, just in case."

"Have *you* ever met one?"

"No. I hope I never do." Self-consciously, she picked up the bandoleer of potions and slid it back over her chest, buckling it in a hurry. "Anyway, we don't always carry the same potions, but some are kind of… standard, like the one I just took. We try to prepare for hunts specifically so we don't get weighed down carrying too many bottles."

Dalibor's interest in the potions themselves was long spent, however. "And – it isn't a werewolf behind these attacks. Right?" he blurted.

"I hope not," Gwen said, "but we can't ever know what we're hunting."

With that, Gwen rose to her feet again, strung bow in hand. Snatching up her quiver, she threw that over her back once more, quickly running her fingers through her differently-colored fletchings to count her arrows. Dalibor stood with her, breathing rapidly enough to be running for his life.

"What's that on your neck?" Dalibor suddenly asked, and Gwen put a hand over the mark she knew he meant: a pair of perfect scars, puncture marks—

A vampire bite. Something she never wanted to think about, never wanted to *remember*, ever again.

"It's none of your business," said Caiden as he rejoined her, towering at her back. Gwen felt a wave of relief and released a small sigh, hand still covering her neck.

"Venatori have a lot of scars," she added, her voice low.

Dalibor eyed Caiden up and down, probably counting every visible scar on what little skin Caiden left revealed, like the large set of scars from human teeth that marred a lower side of his neck – and the set of deep scratches on one forearm. Those were just a few. Then, of course, there was the eye patch...

"Yeah," said Dalibor. "I get it... I'm sorry for asking."

"It's fine," Caiden said, his voice finally coming out in slightly less of a growl. "Now, we need to move."

Every scar is a reminder of a mistake, Gwen thought to herself. Caiden's words, not hers. She knew perfectly well how he thought of his scars, and even that much had taken her years to wring out of him. From the way Dalibor looked cowed and nodded, she had half a mind to explain to him that Caiden didn't mean any harm. In fact, he undoubtedly cared more about Dalibor's life than their own Count Vulpowicz did – but there wasn't any time for discussing how Caiden's years as a centurion hardened him and his methods of communication.

Hesker returned as well, sauntering up and saying, "I heard you talking. I want one of those potions for lycanthropy, in case this *is* a werewolf."

Gwen hesitated. "Chances are it *isn't*; werewolves are very rare. We've met a dragon, and we've still never met a werewolf." *And a werewolf is far more likely to kill you than leave you bitten*, Gwen thought, but she didn't say that out loud. Instead, she continued, "But if you do end up needing one, which I hope none of us will, I'll give it to you. It's just as likely to kill you as help you, though."

Hesker crossed his arms. "I'm here to do Count Vulpowicz's bidding, and I need the supplies to carry it out properly. Give me the potion, or I'll go ahead and report back to him right now."

Over her head, Caiden rumbled in frustration and reached for the potion on *his* belt instead— but Gwen quickly rested a hand on his arm. Caiden gave her a sharp look, though her touch did make him freeze. Ignoring his glare, Gwen took her own potion in question off her belt and offered it to Hesker, who snatched it and tucked it into a pouch he wore over his chest.

Caiden huffed.

With that, however, Caiden led the way down the deserted and steadily darkening streets. Gwen hurried to stay beside him, while Hesker and Dalibor stayed a few feet behind, already starting to whisper harsh and grating questions to each other. Not wanting to overhear anything they said, Gwen focused on Caiden instead, even while he kept looking around as if the monster was already out in the streets, maybe even lurking around the next corner.

"You shouldn't have given him your potion," Caiden said, the angry edge in his voice unmistakable.

"It'll be fine," Gwen assured him. "What're the chances we'll actually run into a werewolf, anyway?"

"I don't like bringing them. Every time we've involved someone who isn't a Venator, we've regretted it. More for their sakes than ours. We're not here to get people killed."

"I know, I... thought about that," Gwen replied. "It's a weird hunt already, even without them." She managed a tiny laugh. "We didn't even get to scarf down some food yet. I guess that's what we get for reaching town so late."

Caiden said nothing, but Gwen knew him well enough to pick up on the hint of disappointment over not getting to eat. Maybe that was what had him in such a foul mood.

"And usually we have *something* to go on..." Gwen said. "He didn't give us anything. I guess there *isn't* anything. Are we just going to try to track it?"

"Right now, yeah," Caiden said. "I'm going to check the perimeter of the forest for any tracks. Then we can go deeper in, look around. Maybe it has a lair nearby." He glanced at her, his expression softening for the first time since they had reached Pikeston. "Wouldn't be the first time."

Gwen nodded. Letting feelings get the better of her, she allowed herself to lock gazes with him a moment longer, and... he did the same, for some reason. Surely not the same reason, though – right?

Then he suddenly blinked and looked away again. Gwen self-consciously followed suit.

Sunset had since turned to dusk, and darkness descended upon the silent streets. They neared the edge of town where the stillness only grew heavier, thicker, burdened by unknown and possibly imminent peril. Gwen knew her biases played into the tension that seemed palpable in the very air, yet she couldn't shake the feeling that even she could almost feel the town's collective and growing terror as night fell... and they dreaded the arrival of the monster.

Behind them, Hesker and Dalibor picked up the pace, staying closer. Rain came down harder, as if strengthened by the coming night. Caiden and Gwen pulled up their blue hoods as they entered the forest, the shadows of their cowls emphasizing the soft glow of their eyes from the potion. Caiden drew the large *bauernwehr* hunting knife from its sheath on his back and made a mark on the first tree they passed.

Mist obscured much of their view, turning the trees into tall, imposing spires that rose suddenly from the darkness around them. Everything appeared in a deep bluish hue thanks to her enhanced senses – despite having used the potion to enhance her senses a few times now, she had still never gotten used to it. And even so, the trees still looked like great black figures, but at least she could confidently see anything if it came at them in the dark.

Their two companions, however, didn't share that ability. Hesker and Dalibor remained remarkably silent during the trek around the perimeter of the forest as she and Caiden searched for any sign of the monster's passage. Dalibor started to sputter more than once, but Hesker always quieted him with a hand on his shoulder or a quick gesture.

There should be *something*, somewhere: a scratch on a tree, sets of prints leading to or from the town, some leftover blood, or maybe some fur caught on a branch it passed – if it *had* fur. Whatever it was, she or Caiden would find it. Every sight, every smell felt ten times stronger. If even a hint of blood had touched any surface, they would find that, too. They were essentially hounds on the trail.

The night pressed on. Minutes became hours, time dragged, their two new companions grew ever more restless... and still nothing – nothing at all.

Then, finally, they stopped once more beside a tree marked by Caiden's knife. Caiden swore under his breath, kneeling and examining the ground.

"Anything would leave tracks in mud like this," he muttered, "but I haven't seen a damn thing in the forest *or* outside it."

"There oughta be *something*," said Dalibor. "The thing's come out of the woods every single night."

"Maybe we're looking in the wrong spot," Gwen said. "Should we go deeper in?"

Standing again, Caiden double-checked his great, bayonet-bearing crossbow. "Yeah," he agreed. "Stay behind me."

"Then I can't see anything," Gwen quipped with a tiny smile, trying at all to lighten the mood. Caiden snorted.

As they continued, an ever-heavier shadow grew over her mind of just what they were hunting. If it had come out of the forest like they all suspected, every monster she could think of would leave some kind of tracks... except one.

"Hang on one minute," Gwen said, halting Caiden in his tracks. Carefully, she drew two arrows with blue and white fletching from her quiver. She held one toward Dalibor and the other toward Hesker. "These arrows have heads of solid silver. Whatever we're fighting, it might be vulnerable to it, like beastfolk and... werewolves and vampires..."

"Wait," Dalibor blurted, "so that's *true?* I thought that silver business was fairytales. It sounds preposterous."

"It isn't. *Don't* waste them. These are some of the only things that can even slow down monsters like that – they can save your life."

Hesker silently took his offered arrow while Dalibor did the same, though the latter's hands shook so violently Gwen almost wondered if he could even aim. Why Count Vulpowicz insisted on sending them along, she had no idea. Maybe he didn't like these two men very much, except the problem was that they could very likely get her and Caiden killed, too.

Still, she tried to remain optimistic. Even if, beside her, she could practically sense Caiden's malcontent with her giving away two of her precious silver arrows. Not because he was concerned for their value, though... she knew that well by now. But she was just trying to keep their two new companions from getting killed – hopefully.

That done, they resumed their already long and arduous hunt. Gwen allowed herself to slip into thought, wondering, fearing...

Reality pulled her from her musings as they entered some forested foothills. The corners of the Jagged Edge Mountains, which ran almost the length of the world, reached even this far west.

And Caiden stopped. Gwen halted behind him, tensing. He held up a fist, giving her a look over his shoulder with his one blue eye, and silently motioned to his left – his blind side – at a shape in the dark mist and pouring rain.

There, she saw the yawning maw of a cavern opening into one of the larger hills. Gwen held her ground as Caiden gestured with one palm down for her to stay put. Biting her lip, she nodded in return. Hesker and Dalibor seemed to pick up on the signs well enough and held their ground, too, despite shifting on their feet and clutching their weapons with white knuckles. Maybe the two locals weren't so bad of hunters as she and Caiden had first feared.

She watched as he stepped into the darkness so deep even her enhanced eyes couldn't penetrate it, not from here. Focusing, she listened instead, barely realizing as her grip on her bow tightened until she looked even more frightened than the two town watchmen at her back.

Movement. A few deep breaths. Then...

"*Shit—!*" Caiden almost yelled.

Heart in her throat, Gwen raised her bow – only to see Caiden come practically flying out of the cave, thrown by something within. Claw marks on his chest trailed hot, reeking blood. Nothing should have been able to pierce the deepsilver chain shirt he wore under his leather. He landed flat on his back with a loud grunt, scrambling to righten his hold on his crossbow and take aim at whatever now emerged from the cavern—

The moment Gwen saw it, she froze.

Towering from the shadows, rising higher and higher still as it straightened its back, was nightmare incarnate: the most feared devourer of flesh, dealer of death and of curses. Its dark silhouetted showed arms heavy with muscle, and it stood taller than any man could ever dream. Dark brown fur coated much of its form that she could make out, the lengthy fingers of its great hands ending in long, dark claws dripping blood. Caiden's blood.

The creature was far from man or beast. Despite its hands, its legs were like an animal's, its feet massive paws and its spine ending in a ragged wolf's tail. Where a man's head should have been on its wide shoulders was a bestial, maned neck... and the head of a wolf.

"*Werewolf,*" Gwen breathed.

Everything happened at once.

Shouting to the gods, Dalibor could only uselessly scramble back in horror – Hesker loosed his arrow, the shot going wide.

The werewolf moved faster than any of them expected. Baring its massive white fangs, blood-red eyes seeming to glow through the sheets of rain, the monster charged forward and scattered its attackers. They tripped over themselves trying to escape. Hesker and Dalibor fell back onto each other in a flailing pile. Caiden managed to get to his feet despite the blood running down his front, aiming his crossbow, while Gwen regained her footing and took aim as well.

Caiden's bolt sailed by the werewolf as it cleanly dodged – but Gwen's arrow struck true.

With a disturbingly human scream, the werewolf recoiled at the silver arrow that lodged itself in one massive shoulder. It whirled to face them and snarled – a blood-curdling, unearthly sound like the growl of a human distorted and mingled into the overwhelming voice of a beast.

It charged— away from them. Off into the night.

Loping on all fours at a pace that would shame even the best horses, the werewolf disappeared, leaving no sign of its passage.

No paw print, no hand print, nothing. *That* was why they couldn't track it. Werewolves, so they said, were the ultimate hunters: untraceable. No one knew how they did it. Gwen hadn't ever been sure she believed it until now – but the dark magic was real.

Rushing over to her partner, Gwen took a closer look at the wounds in his chest – but Caiden waved her off, the scowl on his face speaking a thousand words of his agony. He coughed, just once, as he pressed a hand on his bleeding chest. In spite of the pain, only made worse by the potion they had taken, he still straightened up.

So Gwen steadied herself again, nocked her last silver arrow, and called out, "After it!"

Hesker and Dalibor had since regained their footing, Hesker wielding only an ordinary arrow after losing his silver one. The two locals rejoined them. Gwen took the lead this time, plunging off into the darkness in the direction of the werewolf's escape. No one spoke, breathless, faces pale and covered by sheens of sweat.

Onward they went. Dalibor took a breath to say something, but Gwen quickly shot him a glare to silence him. No doubt the werewolf already knew where they were, but they needn't draw even more attention to themselves.

Despite the look, Dalibor hissed, "We'll die out here!" His next few words came out far too loud – he raised his voice and practically cried, "Why are we *still hunting it?* We should come back in daylight – won't it be a man then!?"

"This isn't *our* hunt anymore," Caiden answered sharply, grim but factual. "But if we fight back, maybe we can survive."

His words silenced Dalibor and Hesker both, though they exchanged a horrified stare. For her part, Gwen kept moving, not wanting to spend too long in one place. Now they maintained a tighter formation. With Hesker and Dalibor at the back and Caiden close by her side, they had eyes in every direction, but she feared it wouldn't be enough.

They pressed on. But they saw nothing, not even any sign of blood. Maybe the werewolf had moved too fast to leave any behind. For what felt too long, they slowly trudged onward, staying alert despite the endless mist and pouring rain leaving them blind and dumb, making continuous noise in every direction and dampening their vision – literally. Then, ahead, Gwen finally spotted something.

On the ground rested her silver arrow, snapped in half. Gwen snatched up the half with the silver head, tucking it into her pack in spite of the blood. They couldn't afford to leave behind any silver, no matter the circumstance.

But doing so meant she paused, even for just a moment. Behind her, Hesker took a few too many steps, ones that led him only a short way into the unforgiving darkness. From that darkness, Death struck.

Hesker's scream pierced the night, turning Gwen's blood to ice. Through the steady downpour of rain, she heard a meaty crunch and a final, jagged breath. Everyone whirled to face where Hesker had disappeared, and Gwen led the charge – only to almost trip over a freshly mangled corpse.

His neck was snapped, his throat torn open – his head almost ripped off his spine. The monster had left Hesker there in a bloody mess, twisted and lifeless in the dirt, his body trampled and broken. Kneeling and setting aside emotion in the face of the mission, Gwen quickly pulled the pack Hesker had worn free of the pile of gore. Rifling through it, she found its contents smashed.

The potion she had given him was destroyed. But she didn't even have time to stand, much less to tell anyone what had happened.

Fast, heavy footfalls came rapidly from behind her. Terror raced up her spine as she scrambled back to her feet to wheel and face Death once more – but it didn't aim for her. It went for Caiden.

The werewolf emerged from the darkness on all fours, lunging with such speed no one could react before it had one of Caiden's legs in its jaws. It pulled him off his feet, dragged him through the mud, then flung him away like a plaything – this man made of pure muscle. To the werewolf, he was still nothing.

Up it rose, standing on its hind legs like a man once more, great clawed hands bared. Caiden flew right past her and slammed hard into Dalibor, sending them to the ground in a heap while Dalibor cried to the gods for mercy. Gwen moved before she thought, acting on instinct alone. She dropped her bow and arrow and drew her silver dagger, a measly and pathetic thing under these circumstances – and she put herself between the werewolf and its victims, who struggled to untangle themselves and stand.

The werewolf struck again. With one quick backhand, it effortlessly disarmed her, knocking the dagger from her grip.

Teeth flashed in the darkness. They went straight for her throat.

Gwen lifted her free arm, catching the werewolf's jaws. It bit down hard – and harder still. Pain exploded through her wrist, her hand, her entire arm— bones snapped, crushed in its grip. She screamed.

Then the *werewolf* cried out.

Its blood-dripping jaws released her as it leapt back a pace, stumbling on one leg and letting out another nightmarish, distorted scream. Gwen's knees buckled under the pain from her arm, but she managed to stay standing – and gathered her wits enough to see one of Caiden's silver bolts jutting from the werewolf's leg.

Behind her, Caiden had collapsed again flat on his back, blood everywhere – but he still held his crossbow.

The monster paused. The very air trembled under the power of the werewolf's bestial growls as it watched them, blood red wolf eyes flaring with rage, darting between her and Caiden...

Until Dalibor moved.

Sobbing and still begging the gods for mercy, Dalibor ran, his bow and single silver arrow long forgotten. Gwen had never seen a man move so fast, especially half tripping over himself and the underbrush. In seconds, he faded away into the mist—

And the werewolf roared. The sound made Gwen's life flash before her eyes.

It came straight for her. She flung herself to the ground trying to avoid it. The impact sent pain rocketing once more through her bitten and broken arm, and she cried out again. The werewolf barreled over her and Caiden both, trampling them. Claws scraped her shoulder and crushed the breath from her lungs. Caiden somehow muted a yell as it all but mauled him effortlessly in passing.

The werewolf didn't stop. It ignored them, sights set on easier prey. Its growls silent now, it ran so gracefully it didn't even seem injured as it bounded after Dalibor. Moments later, she knew, it would catch him.

Just like that, their would-be quarry disappeared into the night. In its wake, it left only death – and a failed hunt. An *incredibly* failed hunt. The werewolf would easily survive its wounds, Dalibor would become its next meal, and the most they could hope was that it would move on... but it would only terrorize a different town.

For what felt like a long while, Gwen couldn't bring herself to move. The pain was too great. Hopefully, the werewolf wouldn't come back and simply finish them off.

Some dark part of her wondered if, at this point, that would be a mercy. She almost wondered why it had even let them live at all. Maybe it... knew.

Finally, she gathered her strength and moved. Her arm protested, practically screaming at her, but she ignored it.

She hauled herself over to where Caiden remained spread on his back, blood seeping from the open gashes on his chest and stomach. Still more covered his arms and shoulders, and from the way he breathed, she guessed the monster may have broken a rib or few. And his leg... the werewolf had maimed his leg when it had bitten him. The potions he wore hanging from the belt on his waist had been broken.

Miraculously, though, two other potion bottles remained unscathed on his harness. The wave of relief that washed over her then almost made her fall back onto her side, but she fought the urge. Caiden still had his potion: the one that, tonight, mattered more than life itself... the one that could reverse the curse of the werewolf's bite. Hopefully.

With those other potions they had taken enhancing pain reception, Gwen marveled at how either of them remained conscious, but especially Caiden. He struggled to breathe, his one eye trying to fall shut on him as it fluttered, blinking and attempting to focus on her face.

"Gwen," he grunted, his gaze set firmly on her mangled arm.

She steeled herself, straightening up against all odds to answer firmly, "You're worse off."

Carefully, she peeled some of the destroyed mail and leather armor away from his wounds. Her touch, no matter how careful, dragged a deep and agonized groan from the back of Caiden's throat. He went rigid, and she winced, quietly moving her good hand up to rest on one of his massive shoulders. His brow knit still harder, and he rumbled something under his breath. Gwen couldn't quite make it out, but she had a guess.

No warrior wanted to die on his back, bleeding out from his wounds, having failed to do his duty. Especially not Caiden Voros. She wouldn't let that happen, not to him.

"You'll make it," she said quietly, giving his shoulder as much of a squeeze as she could with such little strength left.

First, she carefully took hold of his harness with her good hand and tugged him over toward a tree. Silent and with his jaw set, he tried to help, dragging himself on one elbow as much as he could manage. He coughed, gagging on some blood that came up in his throat, but she somehow got him propped mostly upright against the tree trunk. The way he grunted in pain before he finally went still rent at her heart.

Taking one of the few remaining potions, this one for helping his wounds heal, she uncorked it and pressed it to his lips. Even Caiden hesitated at the smell, but he drank it down.

Neither of them spoke, and Caiden fought to remain quiet in the face of such pain. Gwen managed to remove some of his shredded armor to start cleaning his wounds, fishing into her satchel and using all supplies available to tend and bandage his many injuries.

Stitching one-handed wasn't easy, but she still stitched the worst of the claw-marks over his torso, and she wrapped his bitten leg while he did his best not to uncharacteristically squirm and moan. Even with her own broken and bleeding arm, she could only imagine the pain he was in from all the maulings.

Now for the hard part.

Carefully, treating it with more care than she would treat even a priceless artifact, Gwen removed the last intact potion from the harness around Caiden's shoulders: the 'cure' for lycanthropy...

as long as the imbiber could survive – and as long as it was taken before the next full moon.

A full moon that would rise all too soon.

The moment she uncorked it, Caiden's energy returned. His one eye opened and locked onto her. And he scowled, the faint blue glow that still lingered in his eye now highlighted by the dark slant of his sharp, low-set brow.

"No," he said firmly, trying to move but going rigid and falling still again. "Gwen, that's *yours*."

"Mine's on Hesker's body," Gwen replied, trying to sound calm. "Now hold still and drink this."

He growled. "I'm... not gonna make it, Gwen—"

"Yes you are," she almost snapped before even realizing. Pausing, she swallowed. "Yes, you are. We've been through worse."

They *hadn't* been through worse.

With that, though, she moved closer again and all but forced the liquid down his throat. She tilted his head back, bottle against his lips, and he finally relented, swallowing before it could run out and down his face. Only when he drank every drop did she finally toss the empty bottle aside.

Caiden swallowed one more time for good measure, his head resting against the tree as he went limp again. Despite his eye that barely remained open, he halfway murmured, "Think it'll come back for us?"

"It's had its meal," Gwen replied darkly, "and it fended us off. Once it... feasts on Dalibor, it'll move on for tonight, I think. Sunrise isn't *too* far off now, so I don't think it'll risk coming back."

"Shouldn't have brought those two," he said, his words slurring into a deep growl as he grated words out between waves of pain. "They... got us killed."

Gwen shook her head. "We didn't have a choice. It was one mistake after the other. Colder hunters would've just abandoned them, so at least we *tried* to do the right thing."

"Gwen... go drink—your potion."

He faded fast. The weight of his wounds and the strength of the potions hit him at once. Steadily, his ragged and pained breathing slowed and evened out.

He sagged against the tree, and Gwen sidled closer, gently taking hold of his harness again to tug him over to her instead. Unsurprisingly, he weighed a solid ton, but she leaned against the tree for support and held Caiden against her. Draping her good arm over his chest let her feel it rise and fall.

Caiden would be okay. Gwen would make sure of it.

How long she stayed there, she didn't know. Carefully, she bandaged her own bleeding arm, just enough to not pass out. The steady rain finally slowed to a drizzle and then to a gentle stop, and Gwen threw back her hood, shaking her ponytail free again. Clouds gradually floated away to reveal the stars... and the pallid visage of the gibbous moon.

The sight of it gave her a chill. How could something so beautiful be so haunting? How could the moon awaken such a curse? That moon had made a man turn into a monster. A man whose soul was long since gone, taken by the beast he had become.

More time passed. Gwen didn't know how much. Finally, Caiden stirred—only to go stock still when he saw her arm over his chest.

His ragged breathing stuttered, and he looked back at her.

His eye found hers again. The one eye he had left carried more weight than most men ever saw in their lifetimes. His stare was one of trauma, of darkness: a stare so heavy it had taken Gwen years to remain still and not balk under his gaze, and in the time she'd known him, it had only grown worse still.

But as his eye met hers, she felt the full force of that weight land heavily on her shoulders. She had lied to him, to Caiden. To her partner. To her best friend—

Most importantly, she had lied to the man she loved.

No, she never told him. Did he feel the same way? She didn't know. Now she would never know.

His face changed. His scowl lightened, disappeared – and turned to fear. Horror. Outrage. Then, eventually, to sadness. All the while, Gwen could only sit very still and try to bear it, watching him process so much emotion.

"Y-you... you *didn't*," he breathed in a tone she had never heard from him before.

In spite of everything, she forced a very small, deeply unfelt smile and answered in a small voice, "I'm sorry, Caid. I lied. I gave you the only cure we had."

Gwen had never experienced heartbreak, but the pain that crossed Caiden's face shattered something in her. His hand shot up, grabbed her unwounded arm. She slipped her arm from her grip to slide her fingers between his.

Again, his breathing stuttered.

"It's fine," she said in hardly a whisper. "I made my choice."

"You can't do this," he said. The command in his voice stumbled, wavered. "There's another way— there's still time. We can make it back to Greywatch..."

"There's not *enough* time," Gwen answered, quiet but resolved. "We can't make it back and get another potion before the next full moon."

He struggled, but he could barely move. "I don't care," he suddenly snapped, his fingers tightening around hers. "I don't *care*, Gwen— don't do this. I won't *let* you do this."

She only squeezed his fingers back. "It's our code."

The pain on Caiden's face was like nothing she had ever seen. "To hell with the code—"

"Caid…"

"*No.* You're… I…" He paused, took a breath. "Don't do this."

Gwen hesitated. They both knew what being bitten by a werewolf meant.

"When someone turns," she said slowly, "the person is already dead, Caid. Their soul is gone." She paused and took another breath. "I've made peace with this. It's our code. And… I want to die with my soul."

"There's another way," he protested, almost in tears. Almost. Gwen realized suddenly she had never seen him cry. "There *has* to be. And dammit, I'll *find* it – I swear I will."

She looked down at his armor instead, unable to look at his face. Now she stared at the silver arrowhead brooch on his cloak. His was personalized with the head of a wolf. Ironic, in a very dark way.

And she replied quietly, "There isn't." She swallowed. "I can't risk it, Caid. I don't want to be a monster, and I don't want to risk… hurting you, or – worse. I can't do that. Please don't ask me to."

He pulled in another shuddering breath, steeling his voice this time. "I'm not asking you to, Gwen. I'm *telling* you: don't do this. You've asked me before if I trust you— I do. If you trust *me*, if you've *ever* trusted me, then… trust me now. Trust that I can find another way." He looked her in the eye yet again, but she still couldn't look back. "Trust that I can save you."

He tried to move, maybe even to stand – but he couldn't. Gwen kept her arm around his shoulder in an attempt to steady him, but there wasn't much she could do. Still, despite his shivering and cringing, he faced her. Gwen let her arm slide away from him as he sat before her now, all his grave wounds suddenly ignored. They no longer mattered.

All that mattered to him, it would seem, was her.

One of his hands slowly lifted toward her face, gently cupping her cheek. His fingers brushed under her ear. Without even meaning to, she leaned into his touch as tears suddenly welled into her eyes. Not wanting to meet his gaze and know he watched her cry, she pinched her eyes shut.

She felt his breath on her face, warm and – against all odds – full of life. Maybe even full of hope.

His lips touched hers. His hand on her face cradled her head as Caiden kissed her.

The kiss lasted both forever and nowhere long enough. He fell away, his hand sliding from her face, and he roughly collapsed back against the tree, awkwardly pressed on his side. When she opened her eyes again, Gwen saw him passing back into unconsciousness.

She couldn't speak, her voice lost the moment his lips had touched hers like he'd stolen it. The tears running down her face said more than words ever could.

"Stay alive," he practically whispered, his voice fading as he slipped away, going limp against the tree.

Unconscious, Caiden looked almost dead. Skin pale and coated in sweat, covered in blood and bandages, if anyone saw him, they could have mistaken him for a corpse. But the steady rise and fall of his chest, labored though his breathing was, assured her he was still alive. He would get through this.

And, briefly, Gwen didn't know what to do.

For so long, she could only sit there, heart racing, drowning in a thousand feelings she at once knew yet didn't understand. Everything overwhelmed her like a cresting tidal wave. All this time, her feelings, his feelings— *their* feelings...

But it didn't matter now. It couldn't matter. Or was that all that *did* matter?

She couldn't hurt him. She would never. And if she became like the thing that had bitten her, she *would* – she could maul him, do this to him all over again or worse, and she would never even know. She would never even remember. And she could pass that curse on to him, too. That was how it continued, or so they said.

One morning, she could wake up, and he would be dead by her hand. By her... claws. Claws and fangs. She would be nothing more than a mad beast, out for flesh and blood.

No. That would never happen.

Silver didn't burn to the touch yet. It wouldn't hurt, not for long. This was what she had to do, and she wasn't afraid. Her only regret now was knowing... was thinking... all the things that could have been, the feelings she should've acted on, things she should've said, should've *done*—

She couldn't go back.

Reaching over, she drew the silver dagger from the sheath on Caiden's chest. Her own remained somewhere in the dirt, cast aside by the werewolf. There was no time to go and find it. All she had to do was use this and not miss her heart.

Hour after hour, or however long it was, she stayed there. She never left his side, waiting until the sun rose, making absolutely sure nothing found and attacked him in the night. The moon sailed across the ever-clearer sky, and were it not for the constant prickle of fear on the back of her neck, she could have sat and named all the stars and constellations through the black-fingered branches of the forest.

Sunlight slowly returned to the dark woods, banishing the mist from the night before. Caiden started to look better, too. Color returned to his skin, and he was no longer sweating, his breathing almost normal.

Every other hunt, they returned... mostly successful. If nothing else, they always at least managed to return alive.

Sometimes that was all they could ever ask for, often bearing wounds that left too many scars. Every other hunt, around this time, they would be heading back to some little inn to share a meal and to crash, get some much-needed rest.

All those wounds and potions had taken so much out of Caiden, Gwen wasn't sure when he would wake up. But maybe that was a good thing. He wouldn't have to be awake when it happened.

Still gripping that silver dagger, Gwen finally, slowly, got to her feet. She wanted to say something more to him, to apologize, but she knew it was no use. Her arm hurt, ached incredibly, but she ignored the throbbing of the barely wrapped wounds and broken bones, shutting it out from will alone.

Off she went. Many paces she walked, trying to get some distance. Either way, he would find her – but she wouldn't be the first thing he saw when he woke up. Preventing that was the last thing she could do for him.

Finally, she stopped and knelt, setting the silver dagger aside long enough to undo the clasps of her armor and open it over the simple shirt she wore underneath, pushing the protection away from her chest. Then she took up the dagger again, closing her eyes.

Was there, she wondered, any crueler thing than Fate?

Gwen took a deep breath and said, "Wise Grey-Eyed Athena, I beg your mercy: please, welcome me into your arms. But more than that... please look after Caid – my partner, Caiden Voros. And please let him forgive me for what I have to do."

Better to die with her soul, to die knowing she had saved him, than to live as a curse not only upon herself but even more a curse upon him. She couldn't do that to him. She *wouldn't*.

She had to be strong for both their sakes.

Caiden awoke with a start.

Pain erupted through his chest then through his whole body when he sucked in a breath. Pounding filled his skull and blurred his vision, and he shook all over. Blinking, he tried to focus.

Gwen.

At first, he thought he still felt her lying against him – but she wasn't there. And neither was his dagger. His *silver* dagger. His stomach lurched.

"No..."

A surge of desperate strength let him stand, every ounce of pain that had once left him weak and useless all but forgotten. Even his bitten leg miraculously held him up as he turned in circles, looking everywhere, trying to find her, his head throbbing so hard he thought he might actually pass out again. But he couldn't – not now.

Footprints. Faint ones. He saw them there in the wet underbrush and the dead leaves, and he'd know those footprints anywhere. He followed them without hesitation.

Even as he limped through the forest, he quickly unbuckled the choker around his neck and pulled it off, trying to sense her, trying to find her— and the foreign emotions rushed into him like they were desperate for a home, so powerful he stumbled and had to catch himself.

He felt a faint trail, something left over from maybe hours, maybe minutes ago. The emotions were so strong that time didn't matter. They would linger in these woods for years.

Sadness. Regret. Determination...

Love.

"*Gwen!*" he cried, his voice ringing through the empty and silent forest.

With mad energy, he crashed through the woods, shouldering branches out of his path and ignoring how they scraped and prodded into his bandages, how they cut at his arms.

Morning fog still covered the ground in a fine haze. In that haze, he found her.

Gwen rested on her back. She looked almost peaceful, except her unbroken hand still clutched the silver dagger plunged deep into her own heart. Blood stained the ground around her and the long, deep blue cloak on her back.

Her eyes were shut, her expression utterly placid – but a faint trail of tears stained her perfect face, porcelain in death.

Caiden stopped in his tracks, his heart in his throat. This couldn't be real. It wasn't happening.

Time stretched. Nothing changed.

He fell to his knees, vision hazy with a rapid flood of tears that escaped his one eye. On the ground before him lay everything he cared about most, everything he had *left*, with a dagger in her heart.

In utter silence, he bent low over her, choking on his own breath. Again he felt for her, for her soul, but he'd never had to do that before. She had always been there. He'd *always* felt her, even when he wore the choker, even when his abilities had been so dampened he could barely feel anything himself.

Now he couldn't feel her soul, her spirit, her emotions – her joy and her love of life, her endless questions, the amusement as she ribbed him, the hints of anxiety...

She was gone. Or... was she? He didn't feel her anymore, but he felt – *something*. Like a faint spark, a soul not yet passed away. It felt not quite there, but not quite gone. It didn't feel right.

That wasn't possible. He was lying to himself. Then again, maybe that was what it felt like to be there at the passing of someone he loved. For all he knew, those were his own feelings still clinging onto that thing that betrayed him yet again: hope.

Slowly, he removed Gwen's hand from the dagger. He pinched his eye shut and took the blade, himself, drawing it from her heart – and then casting it aside in hatred. All his training told him to keep it, to save it: it was solid silver, it was valuable. He didn't care. He would never touch that dagger again, and neither would anyone else. It would be buried and forgotten by time.

Crossing her arms over her bloodied chest, he paused long enough to look at her face one last time. To think about the way she smiled – and the way those deep green eyes would regard him no more. He set his jaw, swallowed, and took a difficult breath.

I'm sorry, Gwen. He wanted to tell her, he wanted to talk to her, to speak, to have her answer – but it was a childish notion. He knew that.

In silence, he wrapped her in her cloak and took off his own, using both to cover her entire body. Ever slow and gentle, he took her lifeless form in his arms. Her limp head fell against one of his shoulders. Of all the things he had ever faced in life, it was that which almost broke him.

For a moment, he stood still, lowering his head to touch hers. Until the lingering and insistent pain of his wounds became too much for even broken love to ignore. Bleeding out from a shattered dream wouldn't make meaning of her sacrifice.

He started walking, limping back toward the town, eye set dead ahead. Autumn had since crept into winter, leaving the woods as chill and as dead as Caiden's heart. The loss that wrapped his soul and crept ever deeper into him was like nothing he had ever felt.

He liked to tell himself that he'd never actually been in love. He did this when he had almost acted on something he felt was foolish, on what she never would've felt back and returned. Love was something from a fairytale. Certainly not meant for someone like him.

It was only now, too late, that he knew love was real. He had known it since the moment he'd met her.

Carrying the one thing he held dear, Caiden strode in silence and sorrow toward the rising sun.

When he reached the border of Pikeston, Caiden approached the first wagon he saw. The old man standing nearby didn't say a word as Caiden gently rested Gwen in that cart, then turned to him and gave him every coin on his person. Exuding feelings of remorse and sympathy – and memories, things Caiden never wanted to see, memories of death and of loss – the old man merely nodded in understanding and hitched his horse to the cart.

"I'll have someone send it back for you," Caiden said as he climbed into the cart and set the horse off at a walk into town. His voice came out low, grating, distant. Getting off his legs and giving his wounds some desperately needed rest should have been at least a small comfort, but it wasn't.

As the horse took him back into Pikeston, before anyone was around to see, Caiden silently fastened the choker around his neck once more and tied the black cloth over it. Curious onlookers slowly gathered as his cart rattled into town. More than once, Caiden threw a look over his shoulder at Gwen's body, wrapped in their cloaks, resting in her bed of hay.

When he stopped before Count Vulpowicz's home, Caiden clambered out of the cart. He landed on his good leg and still almost staggered from the impact lancing up into all his other wounds. He grunted, caught himself, and somehow straightened up.

He approached the door and didn't stop walking. Barely making effort to kick, he knocked the door in with his sheer size and weight.

"Gods!" shouted Count Vulpowicz, rushing down his stairs – and stopping the instant he saw Caiden. He blinked, staring. "Venator? Where are...?"

His words came out like stone. "They're dead," Caiden answered. "Killed by the werewolf. It escaped. It probably won't come back."

"Werewolf?" Vulpowicz echoed, his voice high and shaking. But it faded fast and he furrowed his brow, demanding, "A *werewolf*? They're – they're *real*?"

Caiden said nothing.

"So, you... you failed? Why did you even bother coming back here? I'm not going to donate food or weapons or men to your useless order if you can't even do your job – the Empire pays you rangers as it is. And you can't even protect my men! Where is Hesker? What about Dalibor? Did you get them killed too? I want that monster's head!"

Caiden took a step forward. That act alone silenced Vulpowicz in an instant. He went still as a mouse, shrinking, eyes wide while he craned his neck to stare up at Caiden's face.

It remained that way for a moment: Caiden standing over that shriveled Count. He stared deep into the Count's eyes... and, with every ounce of his willpower, managed to tame the storm of emotions tearing him apart.

He thought of Gwen. What would she think if he, for once in his life, acted on his temper like he used to so long ago? What would she think if he accidentally broke this man just because he was upset at having failed her?

So, he took a breath. A slow, deep breath. And he took a step back away from Count Vulpowicz, who remained too terrified to move.

"If the attacks resume," Caiden said, "the Venatori will send someone else."

Count Vulpowicz said nothing. Caiden didn't care. Without another word, he turned and left, going back to the cart. This time, when he turned the horse about, it was to go home.

Alone.

For more than two nights, he rode. He never spoke a word to anyone. Never really saw anyone, either. What few people he passed on the roads back to Castle Greywatch, home of the Order of the Venatori, he barely regarded. Talking was the last thing he wanted to do. Except maybe to his little sister or his mother, both far away and beyond unreachable.

Everything he cared about, what little remained, *was* unreachable and would be for a long time. Or forever.

Caiden had always prided himself on shutting out emotions. Turning memories into facts. He thought that often, reflected on it, accepted it was a necessary part of his job – his life. Somehow, he always managed. Even now, he managed to shut it all in. Contain his emotions, like he always did. Try not to feel the loss.

But it ate at him. The emptiness that had gnawed a greater and greater hole in his insides, ever growing, pitiless – it felt all the worse. The only thing that had ever quieted it, calmed it even for a moment, was gone.

When he arrived at the gates of Greywatch, he found greeting party as joyless as he felt. Someone must've seen him from afar and known what happened. One of the few Elves in the order, maybe. They had ways of seeing farther than Men; things Caiden didn't understand.

He wasn't sure if he was glad they knew. Maybe he could never be 'glad' about anything again. But he appreciated, at least, that his compatriots met him at the gates – and that they didn't say a word.

Those hunters he had worked alongside for years waited for him as he stopped the cart: Kiya, Henryk, Daisy, even Theron

Brennus, among others. No one spoke. No one had to. They knew what had happened: a Venator never hunted, or *returned*, alone.

In silence they waited as Caiden climbed from the cart, his wounds still weighing him down. When Kiya stepped forward to offer him help, though, he waved her off. She took a step back, clearly understanding. Caiden then went to the back of the cart, opened it, and— paused.

He swallowed. Took a deep breath, straightened his back still further, and carefully picked up Gwen's body once more.

When he walked past the other Venatori, they parted for him, bowing their heads. Caiden thought he saw a brief shine of tears in Kiya's eyes, and even in the eyes of some of the other hunters. Gwen had been well-loved by the order – an important part of the castle. The light, youth, and joy of Greywatch. She cared about everyone, and everyone cared about her... but not like he had.

Onward Caiden walked, the other Venatori in step behind him, as he led the way to the lonely little graveyard at the back of the castle grounds. Here, the Venatori buried those dead who had no families, no home to which they could return. And there, Kiya, Jed, and Forge – all seasoned hunters – came forward to begin silently digging a new grave. Several other hunters followed Theron Brennus's lead as he headed for a small workshop on the grounds. They went to make a coffin.

Caiden waited, staring straight ahead. He didn't move, didn't speak. There was nothing to say.

Soon enough, the coffin was made, the grave dug. Everything was arranged. Caiden stayed to see to it all. He saw to cleaning Gwen up, he saw to fixing her armor. He saw to taking care of her equipment. But he let her keep his cloak. As much as he wished he had something else, the cloak was really all he had to give.

What he took for himself, however, was her brooch: her silver Venator brooch. His was engraved with the head of a wolf, hers with an arrow. That, he tucked into a pouch on his belt. He had plans for it. He wouldn't see it go to waste.

Finally, the time came to bury her. But Kiya took him aside, back to the little workshop where some of the Venatori tinkered with wood during long and simple days at the castle, their brothers and sisters in arms their only company. Caiden had taken those days for granted.

She motioned to a simple wooden marker, offering him tools to carve on it. And she spoke the first words Caiden heard since he left Pikeston.

"Do you need help with this?" she asked, as gently as she could.

Caiden knew why. When he'd first came to Greywatch, he couldn't read. Never learned how. A lot of commoners didn't, especially when they were too busy fighting wars. Being a soldier. Caiden was one of those people. Gwen had tried to teach him, but they never got far. Maybe, though, they had gotten just far enough.

He had learned to spell at least *one* thing. Two things.

Caiden managed to answer, sounding as if he had forgotten how to use his voice: "Just make sure I get it right."

Into the wooden marker, Caiden carefully carved her name: *Gwenevere Vergil*. The moment he started, his lip twitched, and he sneered at himself, scowling at the wood and holding the tools so tightly one of the rusted old things cracked under his grip. His nostrils quivered and flared. A low sound briefly got caught in his throat. Rage, red-hot rage, filled his heart and overflowed, poured into his stomach, made him feel sick—

A hand rested on his shoulder: Kiya's. She was one of the few who had known his feelings for Gwen. Not because he told, but because she just... knew. If anyone who wasn't his sister was going to be with him right now, at least it was her.

But he got it done, like he always did. They all did. And the services were simple – quiet. The Venatori were hunters. But they were *monster* hunters. Like warriors, they rarely traded empty words about death in the field. Silence was the best means of understanding.

He didn't take another partner. Not yet. Caiden often wandered the halls like a lost specter, wondering what to do with himself. Drinking a lot. Even more than usual. He still hadn't taken off his choker, fearing what would happen, fearing he might go completely mad with no anchor to keep him sane. Hours on end he languished, feeling empty and directionless, more than ever. Felt like he was back on the outskirts of home, of Helos, the city he grew up in: the city whose young price had disgraced and cast him out, forced him to wander into the Venatori and take an unexpected partner... in more ways than one.

Now, here he was.

Two nights later, it happened.

Like he so often did, Caiden stared down from his window at Gwen's cold and humble grave. Evening steadily turned to night. But where darkness should have fallen, moonlight fell instead. Bright and full, the haunting silver moon shone from a cloudless sky...

And a howl pierced the night.

Instantly, Caiden went rigid. He had never heard a werewolf howl, not even after being hunted by one. The sound chilled him to the bone, made a shiver run up his spine and made him pinch his eye shut. A wolf howl, bestial, but... wrong. So full of rage, of hunger—

And of all its terrifying aspects, one thing frightened him most: he recognized that voice. It made no sense for him to recognize the howl of a werewolf, but he did. Somewhere in that bestial cry was the voice of a man he knew well, distorted and lost.

Caiden didn't know how long he stayed there, heart pumping ice, hands gripping the stone rimming the window of his room like he needed the hold on reality after hearing that howl – the howl of the same kind of monster that had taken Gwen. It filled *him* with rage, with sorrow – and then the door to his room flew open.

Theron Brennus, the most veteran hunter in the Venator order, regarded him with eyes wide and a terrified face paler than the moon.

Brennus spoke four simple words: "We need to go."

For a long drawn-out moment, Caiden stared at him. He and Theron Brennus had never gotten along.

But Brennus said, "We'll slay them, Voros. We'll kill them all."

And in that moment, Caiden knew – he understood. He felt what Brennus must have felt during his many years as a Venator. The same coldness that had so long ago penetrated Brennus's heart now lived in Caiden's, as well.

Though he didn't say it, Caiden knew Brennus needed a partner. This was him asking. With a quiet huff, Caiden turned to his gear and pulled on his harness, taking up his crossbow. From the small table near his bed, he picked up Gwen's silver brooch, turning it over in his fingers before he put it in his pouch again.

And he said, "The hunt never ends."

The story will continue in *The Prophecy of the Six, Book II – Bloodmoon...*

Wake Not the Sleeping Bull

Jörgen's Tale

by Justin R. R. Stebbins

What follows here is the tale, as best I can tell it, of Jörgen "Joe" the Lone Bull, Slayer of Giants, and founder of the Brotherhood of the Bifröst Banner. Most of it I was told by the man himself, and I have done my best to verify and gather more details from other eye-witnesses. Tales do tend to grow ever more exaggerated in the telling, however, especially ones as legendary as the saga of Jörgen, who rose from an outlaw to a great hero of the North. Yet, I would ask the reader not to think of this as a hero's legend, but instead as the tale of an orphan boy who dreamed of fighting for his homeland, but found that the wars of men were not as glorious as the tales told, and so forged a different path...

Part 1: Burning Bridges

Jörgen ran the whetstone down the length of his sword... once, twice, three times, over and over. The sword's blade was enormous, but so were Jörgen's arms, so he was able to keep his strokes long and even. After just a few, he set the stone aside, satisfied at the keenness of the edge. After all, *Skera* required little sharpening. Her weight combined with his strength was enough to cut any foe in twain, even when dull. That was why her name meant "Cutter."

Jörgen wiped the oil from Skera, taking special care to make sure her golden hilt shone brightly, the dragon heads on the crosspiece sparkling – and then he slid the great sword back into the sheath at his side. Jörgen was a giant of a man, a head taller than even most soldiers, and with shoulders that looked nearly half as wide. His entire body was covered in muscles like a statue of a god, and since he often went about bare-chested, few could miss this fact. His hair was a reddish brown, long and flowing, though he kept his beard trimmed relatively short. His eyes were a deep, bright blue.

"If you ever take a woman to wife, Joe," he heard a man's voice say behind him, "she'll have a hard time competing with that sword for your affections."

Jörgen laughed. "Yours would have an even worse time, Lindwurm! You've a sword *and* an axe!"

The man chuckled. "But I'd love any real woman more, so long as she didn't call me 'Lindwurm.'"

Jörgen made up nicknames for everyone, usually the names of beasts. In return – or perhaps in retaliation – his friends always called him "Joe." An Imperial soldier had once called him "Zho-er-gen" after reading his name on a wanted poster. Apparently, people in the northern parts of the Achaean Empire pronounced the letter 'J' strangely. His friends got a good laugh out of that, and would never let him hear the end of it. His real name was pronounced something closer to "Yorgen."

The man Jörgen called Lindwurm was actually named Ivarr. He stood nearly as tall as Joe, had bright orange-red hair, and liked to wear blue war paint in the traditional patterns of his clan: the Wurmtongues. The Wurmtongues were sea raiders, but Ivarr had never fit in with them. He hated ships, much preferring to fight on solid land. Hence his nickname: Lindwurm, meaning "Landwurm," a type of wingless, land-dwelling dragon-kin.

"No shame in being called Lindwurm," replied Joe. "They are fearsome beasts. Have you not heard of the great lindwurm Spangentail, who burrowed up from the very earth into the middle of an Imperial town? The Legionnaires' spears bounced harmlessly off his armored hide!"

Ivarr snorted. "Haven't you heard? They say Spangentail was slain not long ago... by a dwarf."

"Hmm..." growled Jörgen. "They say a lot of things. Come, let us practice the bow! You will throw the discus, and Jörgen will hit it with an arrow."

"The discus?" Ivarr scoffed. "*Pah!* An Imperial sport."

"All practice is good practice," said Jörgen. "Unless the Lindwurm thinks he cannot throw as well as an Imperial?"

"Oh, I can throw it. These discs are heavy though. Won't your arrow bounce right off?"

"Some arrows perhaps, but not Jörgen's. His bow is large as the horns of a great aurochs, and its arrows fly with the strength of one too!"

Ivarr smiled and shook his head. "Quit boasting and string this mighty bow of yours, Joe."

It was a beautiful day, practically perfect. The vast blue sky of Northrim seemed to stretch on forever – so huge that it was almost hard to believe it was made from the skull of a giant. Below, the great mountains and dark forests of Northrim covered the horizon in all directions. But where the two friends stood, there lay nothing but hills covered in green grass, which billowed in graceful, shimmering waves.

Jörgen tried to estimate the wind direction and speed as he strung his tremendous bow – actually an Imperial Longbow, which he had taken from a captured soldier of Illikon over a year ago. Joe's friend Stígander had taught him much about archery, but Joe had never been as good as him. Which was why he was keen to keep practicing.

"Throw!" Joe shouted as he nocked a long arrow shaft.

"I hope Ullr favors you!" Ivarr called from a nearby hill, where he stood with the pile of metal discs.

With all his strength, Ivarr launched the first discus through the air. And with all *his* strength, Joe drew back his bowstring, causing the boulder-sized muscles on his arms and back to pile even higher. He watched the flight of the discus for a fraction of a second, and then... let fly.

The power of the shot surprised even him. When the longbow shaft struck the discus, it didn't just knock it off course; it actually punched right through. The impaled discus spun once more – a wobbly spin with the arrow sticking out – and then careened into the grass. Joe and Ivarr both shouted excitedly and ran to inspect the 'kill.' Although they had grown up in different villages, they felt like boys playing together again.

Jörgen's family, a traveling clan from a far-away land, had died in the wilderness when he was very young, killed by monsters. Some warriors of the Björnings – the Tribe of the Bear – had found him, the lone survivor, and decided to take him back to their home, the Great Den called the Björnburg. He'd grown up with the other orphans there, mostly children whose parents had died in war, and whom no one else wanted. He had always been a bit different, sometimes bullied for his unusual size and funny accent and manner of speaking, but he'd never let this bother him too much. As a man with no homeland, he thought of all sons and daughters of the North as his brothers and sisters.

"Did you see that!?" Ivarr yelled as he found the fallen discus and picked it up. "Clean through! Was it a bodkin arrowhead?"

Joe laughed as he ran to catch up with him. "Of course! Jörgen did not wish to disappoint!"

"Joe, my friend, you are far too good at everything. If you wanted it, you could have women crawling all over you."

"One is usually enough for Jörgen," the big man replied.

Ivarr scoffed. "Not for me."

The conversation was interrupted by another voice, which said: "You boys should stop talking about women. Neither of you know a damn thing about 'em."

The two men laughed as they turned to see Hjordis walking down the hillside behind them. Hjordis was a shieldmaiden, a warrior-woman with stature and strength to rival most men, and a voice like grinding stones. She never even bothered to braid her long, strawberry blonde hair – instead simply tying some of it clumsily behind her head and then sticking a helmet on top. Hjordis was an old friend of theirs too, completing the trio of companions who had joined the Geatling army together after the dissolution of their little band of rebels called the Wolfpack.

"If you're done goofing around," Hjordis added, "the Jarl wants to see us. Apparently, he thinks you can lead us to victory, Joe, just like you led the Wolves."

Joe sighed. "Jörgen was never leader of the Wolfpack. He simply acted as its face and voice, when needed."

Hjordis blew out a sigh. "Joe, why in Midgard can't you just talk like a normal person? The 'Wildcat' thing's grown on me, but please stop speaking about yourself like you're someone else telling a damn story."

"Jörgen *is* telling a story!" Joe replied in his deep, booming voice. "The story of our band of brothers, who struggled valiantly to wrest our homeland's villages from the grasp of the Achaean Empire! 'Tis a tale worthy to be told!"

"Aye, and passed down through the ages!" added Ivarr.

It was true that Jörgen had never truly been in command of the gang of rebels called the Wolfpack, but many of its members had thought of him as the leader regardless. It was easy to see why. The phrase "larger than life" could very well have been invented to describe Jörgen of the Björnburg. His personality was as big as his muscular frame.

When Joe's laugh boomed through the air, it was hard to resist laughing with him, and when Joe was troubled about something, all his companions knew there was cause to worry. Everything else he did was big too: he talked big, ate big, walked tall, hit hard, and slept hard – and gods forbid he start snoring. He had earned the nickname 'Jörgen the Bull' as a young man by wrestling a bull to the ground with his bare hands. The 'Lone' part had come later, when he'd left his tribe to become an outlaw.

Hjordis gave a reluctant smile. "Well, that's exactly why Jarl Thorsten wants our counsel: because of the Wolfpack's reputation for fighting the Empire, against superior numbers. He's hoping we can help come up with ideas to split Imperial forces, set up ambushes, things like that."

"That was always Stígander's sort of thing," Ivarr said. "Wish we knew where he was right now..."

As they talked, they made their way back over the hills toward the army camp. As they crossed over the rise and Jörgen gazed out over the assembled Geatling army – over all of the motley tents and the horses and the training soldiers – his eyes lit upon the banners fluttering from the flagpole in the very center of the camp. At the top flew the silver ram upon a golden field that represented Horngöfgasta, the capital of the Geatling tribe. "Goatlings," the Imperials called them. Some embraced the name. Below it fluttered Jarl Thorsten's own emblem: Thor's holy hammer Mjölnir, flanked by a pair of ram horns, drawn in black on a field of yellow.

All Joe could think was: *Stigander never liked flags.*

Joe thought back to the last time they had fought together... the last time the old Wolfpack had truly been whole...

In the mountain forests on the eastern edge of the Imperial Territory in Northrim, a caravan of Imperial wagons made their way slowly over a rough trail. They were carrying supplies to a border fortress, escorted by twenty-two knights, with four legionnaires riding in each of the three wagons. Despite all the soldiers, the men of the Empire felt like unwelcome intruders in a strange land. They were from Achaea, where the roads were wide and paved with stone; where the forests were not so thick and dark and did not stretch as far as the eye could see; where the mountains of the Jagged Edge were not so close and so tall, their icy peaks reaching to the very heavens.

And the sunlight was starting to dim, as the dark trees of Northrim grew thicker around them.

Then one of those trees suddenly crashed down across the path ahead. The sound of its fall and of the birds it stirred from the trees nearby echoed off the distant mountains. A murmur spread through the ranks – talk of whether this was a bad omen.

But it was no omen at all.

A volley of arrows erupted from the trees, whizzing between the leaves and landing fletching-up in the ground ahead of them. There were more than two dozen projectiles – at least one arrow for each knight in the escort. The arrow shafts were long and fletched with red and green feathers. The knights and legionnaires drew their horses to a halt and reached for their swords, but did not yet draw.

A voice like thunder echoed from out of the trees ahead: "*HOLD, IMPERIALS!* Throw down your weapons and surrender, and you may live to be ransomed!"

Out of the forest stepped Jörgen the Lone Bull, bare-chested and fearless. The men of the Empire marveled at his size, wondering if he was half giant. He had muscles like mountains, and spread across his broad chest was the image of a long-horned bull aurochs, depicted in blue war-paint. Some of the soldiers had seen him before... not in person, but on a wanted poster.

"You're the one they call Zhoergen!" shouted a legionnaire from the front of a wagon. "The Lone Bull!"

"You indeed look upon *Jörgen!*" the barbarian replied, using the correct Nordling pronunciation. "And if you have heard tales of Jörgen the Bull and his companions in the Wolfpack, then you know to lay down your arms and surrender now!"

"I am Sir Edward Hartwin!" called the foremost knight, in a commanding tone, though it was no match for Joe's tremendous voice. "By my count of your arrows, you have no more men than we do. Perhaps fewer!"

"Ah, but our wolves are hidden with arrows at the ready, and you eagles are exposed!" replied the Bull. "Yet Jörgen does not wish to spill the blood of your warriors on his clean Northern soil. Take off your sword-belts and throw them in the dirt, then dismount and line up near the fallen tree! We will bind you and take your supplies, but not your lives."

A knight behind Sir Edward leaned over and hissed at his commander: "Surely we're not going to take this from–"

"Quiet!" Edward snapped at him.

But the knight sneered and slid his weapon out of its sheath with a shout: "The Imperium does not surr-!"

His words were cut off by the arrow that pierced his shoulder. The tip of his sword had only just left the scabbard when the missile struck. The knight released his weapon and clutched the imbedded arrow shaft, nearly falling from his saddle. The other knights stood still as statues, their hands on their sword-hilts but not moving.

"Next time, we aim for the throat!" Joe said. "Drop your swords!"

Sir Edward Hartwin sighed. At length, he took his hand off his weapon… and slid it over to his belt buckle. He unfastened his sword belt, let it fall, and then dismounted.

Jörgen smiled.

A few minutes later, all of the knights and soldiers were disarmed and kneeling in a line beside the great felled pine. The legionnaires seemed to have more fight in them than the knights. They glared openly at their noble-born comrades, as if this shame was their fault. Most of the knights had been born in the Northern Kingdom, after all. Some were part Nordling by blood.

The glares only intensified as the first members of Jörgen's rebel band started to appear. They came out of the forest in pairs and began tying up the Imperial soldiers, binding their hands and their feet. First came a pair of tall blonde Nordlings: Stígander and his sister Magnhild. Next were Ivarr and Hjordis. Last came an elf woman with orange hair and long, pointed ears – which raised quite a few Imperial eyebrows. Elves seldom mingled with mortal men. Only four more men came after that, all cloaked and masked beyond recognition.

"Is this all of you?" shouted an incredulous Sir Edward, as Magnhild bound his wrists. "Just nine!?"

"Perhaps there are more," replied the Northern woman with a smile. "You'll never know."

"They all have bows," a legionnaire observed. "They must have loosed at least three arrows each. A cowardly trick! And they say Nordlings are brave..."

Ivarr said, "We are! We're not the ones who surrendered!"

He let out a great guffaw, and the rest of the Nordlings joined in. The Imperials looked at each other with expressions of rage and shame, but they said nothing. There was nothing more to say.

An hour or so later, Jörgen stood surveying their haul: three wagons laden with Imperial supplies, and a group of captives, with only one injury among them. It had been one of the smoothest ambushes the Wolfpack had ever performed. He was proud of his little band.

Not that it was really 'his' band. Jörgen often served as the group's voice, as he had today, but only because he was so physically intimidating. Enemies were more likely to surrender when the huge Lone Bull stood towering over them. Officially, however, the group had no leader. Decisions had to meet with popular approval, and were often put to a vote.

From the campsite atop the hill behind him, he heard Ivarr shout: "Joe! Bring us that barrel of meat we found! This calls for a feast!"

Joe walked down the hill and inspected the barrels they had removed from one of the wagons. He detected the aroma of dried and spiced venison wafting out, from where they had cracked open the top. A rare find in an Imperial military caravan – practically a delicacy. It had probably been meant for nobles or officers at the fort. He lifted the heavy barrel easily and began carrying it back up the hill to where his comrades were camped.

"What a haul!" he exclaimed as he approached the others, who were circled around an unlit campfire. "The supplies from this caravan will help a lot of people, villagers and rebels alike."

Magnhild said, "The money from ransoming the Imperials will help too."

The next to speak was Fintan, a little old white-bearded hill-dwarf merchant. He had loosed a few of the arrows that the Imperials saw, but he wasn't technically a member of the Wolfpack, and preferred to remain out of sight. After all, if his face ended up on a wanted poster, it would be harder to keep trading in Imperial towns. And the others wanted him to keep doing so, because he often gathered valuable intelligence for the Wolfpack that way.

"Ransoming's too dangerous now," the dwarf said, as he lit a long smoking pipe. "Too much chance for treachery or ambush. Better to just let 'em go."

"I don't like it," grumbled Ivarr. "I don't like sending hardy soldiers back to the Empire…"

"We *have* to ransom them," retorted Magnhild. "We are *not* killing captives who surrendered."

"We could sell them as thralls to the Wurmtongues," suggested her brother Stígander, and Joe saw Ivarr nod in approval.

But Fintan nearly choked on his weed-smoke. "What?! Magnhild, what's gotten into yer brother? Doesn't seem like him to suggest such a thing!"

If the Wolfpack could have been said to have a leader, then Stígander must have been it. Although Joe was often the public face of the group, Stígander was usually the brains. He was an expert planner and a master of the art of the ambush, always using the terrain to maximum advantage.

Stígander was not his real name. It was a nickname, meaning "Wanderer." Everyone called him that… except for Joe, who called him Hawk. Joe remembered Magnhild using his real name once, a long time ago, but now he couldn't even remember it.

The Wanderer was a stoic man, keeping to himself most of the time. He and his sister both preferred the company of nature to that of people. His messy, dirty-blond hair was a shade or two darker than his sister's long golden braid.

Stígander stared into the distance, a grim expression on his sharp features, his heavy brow casting a shadow over his hawk-like eyes. "These skirmishes and raids against the Empire... Did a lot of good for Malir, didn't they?"

Fintan frowned behind his white beard. "That village was doomed from the start, lad, no matter what we did to try an' help."

"Exactly," said the Wanderer.

Joe dropped the barrel he was carrying and leaned upon it, thinking back to Malir. But he immediately stopped himself. He hated to even remember it. That battle and its aftermath had stunned the Wolfpack. For months, they did little but dwell on what had happened.

At last, Joe spoke up: "The Hawk has a point. Jörgen has been thinking of joining the army – taking the *real* fight to the Empire. Would any of you join me? You are all welcome. Even you, little badger!"

Fintan scoffed. "*Pff*. I've had my fill o' war, boy. Get that fool notion outta yer head."

"I can't, Joe," said Stígander. "I have something I need to do."

His sister Magnhild looked at him, her face full of concern. "You can't mean... Brother, I'm sorry, but you have to move on. No one can even remember her face, her name..."

"I know," said the Wanderer, his voice low. "It's some kind of curse... But there are a few places I haven't looked for her yet. I have to try one last time."

Joe knew of what he spoke, but only vaguely. Months ago, Stígander had come to them asking about a woman, whom he claimed was his wife. She had disappeared. He said that many in their group had met her, but no one could remember doing so. Even Stígander could barely remember her, and could not recall her name. A few in the Wolfpack thought he'd been stricken with madness, but the Wanderer was determined to continue his search, no matter how hopeless it might be.

Joe avoided mentioning that, instead merely saying, "But you'll come back, yes? This is not the end for our little band, surely! We don't have to join the army... Even these skirmishes and raids help, no matter what you think, Hawk."

Stígander gave a slight smile at last, though it was tinged with sadness. "Of course, Joe. You know I'd never abandon our little Wolfpack. I'll be back in a week or two..."

That had turned out to be the last great victory of the band of young rebels called the Wolfpack. Tragedy after tragedy had struck their little gang after that day. Betrayal, ambush, death, and the disappearance of the Stígander. Joe had not seen the Wanderer for many moons now. No one had.

Soon after the others had realized that Stígander was not coming back, Magnhild had left to search for her brother. Fintan had resumed his merchant life. And the rest had gone their separate ways, much to Joe's deep disappointment. In his youth, he'd expected his friends to stick together through thick and thin, forever. Or at least for as long as the fight against the Empire lasted. Yet all had ignored his invitation to join him in going to war. All except Ivarr, who was the only one to immediately accept his offer. Hjordis had sought them out later, after leaving her own tribe due to a dispute.

Together, they had decided to join the Geatlings. Joe would have simply joined the army of his own tribe, but the Björnings were still trying to maintain an uneasy peace with the Empire. As were the Wulfings and some of the other tribes. He respected them, but he did not agree. The Achaean Empire would never let them have peace nor freedom again, until they were driven out.

And yet, most of the warlike tribes were unsavory. The Frost Ravens were always at war, as were the Forsaken and the Chunni and other violent raider tribes, but Joe refused to fight for any of those. And he and Ivarr preferred the land to the sea, so they avoided joining the Wurmtongues. That only left the Geatlings, so the three of them had headed to the far northern town of Horngöfgasta to sign up to fight under the banner of the Goat.

Joe stood up, adjusting Skera where she hung sheathed at his hip, and began walking down the hill toward the war camp. "Well, let's go then! If Jarl Thorsten wants to see Jörgen, then Jörgen will not keep him waiting!"

Ivarr and Hjordis exchanged glances and shrugged, then set off behind Joe. He may not have been the leader of the Wolfpack, but he was certainly the leader of their trio. It was hard to say no to Joe the Lone Bull.

And he attracted plenty of attention. As they walked through the war camp, a couple of girls spotted them and began following, whispering and giggling to themselves. Hjordis audibly groaned. They were camp followers – civilians who attached themselves to military expeditions. Some provided valuable services, but others were like leeches. Hjordis figured these two were prostitutes.

"Jörgen! Is that really you?" one of them called out. "The Lone Bull? Jörgen!"

"You must excuse Jörgen, ladies," said Joe, glancing back at them with his broad, white smile, gleaming amidst his thick beard, "but he has places he must be."

One of them called out: "Is it true that the price on your head in the Empire is more than Guntram's and Bloodbeard's combined!?"

"No!" Joe laughed. "No, that is not true!"

"Is it true that you once arm-wrestled King Björnar and won?"

"Ladies, please!" Ivarr interrupted, walking backwards as he turned to flash them a winning smile. "Joe and I will both have time to talk after we've met with the Jarl."

The girls giggled again and exchanged glances. "Oooh, important business..."

Hjordis growled, and finally the two young ladies took the hint and disappeared.

The trio soon arrived at Jarl Thorsten's great war tent, which was adorned with trophies: the horns and skulls of beasts and the helmets and armor of Imperial soldiers. Thorsten was a charismatic leader. The Geatling tribe was famous for those, exemplified by their young King Wulfric. Thorsten – though still taller than average – was smaller and more athletically-built than the hulking Jörgen or Ivarr, but he still had a thick yellow beard, complete with a braided mustache.

"Jörgen, Ivarr... and of course Hjordis, as lovely as she is mighty," he said, with a deep, dramatic nod. "Welcome! Please, pour yourselves a drink."

Joe returned the Jarl's deep nod, for it was known that the Wolfpack seldom bowed to anyone. Then he helped himself to a cup of whatever Thorsten had in the keg standing in one corner of the tent. It turned out to be wine, much to Joe's surprise – Achaean, no doubt. The keg itself was probably another war trophy. Joe took a sip and then set it aside. He didn't care for wine.

"Jarl Thorsten," he said. "It is an honor. But if you are hoping for counsel on strategy, Jörgen knows little. He spoke for the Wolfpack, yes, but he did not lead it – not truly. Stígander did most of the planning."

"But I hear he left us in our time of need, sadly," replied Thorsten, taking a deep draught of wine and then shaking his head rapidly. "But, no matter! Your help in our last battle was considerable, Jörgen. I heard you unhorsed six knights single-handedly. Your legend continues to grow! I am happy to have you with us."

Ivarr snorted. "Six? I guess goats can't count! Joe unhorsed three, maybe, at most."

"This report didn't come from one of my 'goats'," said Thorsten, banging proudly on the ram's-head emblem on his large belt buckle. "It came from a Wurm like yourself – another mercenary."

"Ha! We Wurms can't count either," laughed Ivarr, before taking another long sip of wine and then giving an exaggerated scowl at the taste. "Except gold from our raids."

Hjordis cleared her throat and set her cup down on the table. "So, what are our attack plans for tomorrow, Jarl? We'll help however we can."

"Ah yes, back to business," said Thorsten. "Right you are, Hjordis. Women know how to keep men focused, don't they?"

Hjordis chuckled and let her eyes roam over the lean yet muscular young Jarl, up and down. "Hmm... we try."

"Today, we broke the local defenses of the village of Runwater," Thorsten said. "Tomorrow, we take the village. Runwater hasn't been there long. The Empire built it about a year ago, in an effort to move down the Rime and secure its mouth, since their great city of Rimegard sits further upriver. A force of Imperial knights have already arrived to protect the village, but if we attack early, while it's still dark, we should be able to seize the town before Legionary reinforcements arrive by foot."

"What's our role?" Joe asked.

"I want you leading the mercenaries and volunteers – the non-Geatlings. I'll be at the front, commanding my Geatling pikemen from my war chariot. You'll be right behind us, and rush to close any gaps that the Imperial cavalry might make in our lines when they charge."

"Shouldn't be a problem," said Ivarr, already grinning with anticipation. "I'll bring my longest axe."

"Go then, and get as much rest as you can," said Thorsten, standing and emptying his cup before tossing it away. "In four hours, we'll start assembling for the attack. Tonight, we beat back the Imperial march!"

Part 2: The Last War of Jörgen the Bull

As it turned out, Joe did not get much rest. For some reason or other, he was plagued by dark dreams and slept fitfully. So he decided to rise and visit the great runestone beside which they had made camp. Resting atop a hill, the stone stood nearly as big as a house, with one smooth side completely covered in carved drawings painted bright red. As he ascended the hill, the runes and etchings seemed almost to glow in the bright blue moonlight.

The hilltop was not unoccupied. In the trampled dirt around the stone sat several worshippers paying homage to the gods there. All wore cloaks of fur, and most had the animal's head still intact atop their own like a helmet. Otherwise, they were nearly naked, save for some warpaint. They looked terrifying in the moonlight, as if they were half man and half beast.

Most wore wolfskins, but others bore the hides of bears or rams with curled horns, and a few wore cloaks adorned with raven feathers. At first Joe thought they were shamans, who often wore ceremonial helms adorned with horns and wings and the like, but he quickly realized their true identity from their weapons and intricately-painted, naked skin...

Berserkers.

One of them heard him approaching and rose from his kneeling position. The man's entire body was painted blue-green, either by some temporary pigment, or possibly a permanent tattoo. His eyes gleamed out bright and fierce amidst the dark coloring, as did the false eyes in the wolfskin atop his head. He had a blond beard, but it looked dark in the dim moonlight, and the wolf atop his head looked solid black.

"Brother," said the man, walking over to Joe. "Come, sit with us."

"You are a berserker," Joe stated rather than asked.

"I am. I am a wolf-warrior, an *ulfhedinn*. My name is Nicklas of Clan Wolf. Or just 'Nick Wolf,' as most call me."

"Mine is Jörgen," Joe replied. "Both our names have Achaean roots, if I am not mistaken... Strange how much the Empire has influenced this land over the ages."

"Yes, I grew up in Empire-controlled territory. I've seen their 'influence' first-hand." Nick squinted then, looking into Joe's eyes. "You've never fought with a berserker before, have you."

This too was a statement rather than a question, and some strange wisdom seemed to gleam in the warrior's eyes, in which the moon was reflected as two bright white dots.

"I've seen them fight from afar," Joe replied. "Most men would have been frightened just to see it, but fortunately Jörgen does not get frightened!" He smiled and laughed, trying to lighten the mood.

But somehow the smile that broke out on Nicklas's darkly painted face only made him even more unsettling. "That's good! Neither do we. In battle, we do not feel pain, nor fear, nor weakness. We only feel rage. *Only* rage. Because, through the blessing of wise Odin, the spirits grant us strength – the spirits of the beasts on our backs. Many fear us, I know, and consider us monsters... but our powers are holy, granted to us by the Allfather himself."

Joe glanced at the other assembled berserkers, still seated in meditation... and then up at the runestone looming above them. "Is that him? Odin, on the stone?"

The Ulfhedinn turned to gaze up reverentially at the carved rock, his eyes wandering over the twisted, snake-like figures depicted thereon. "Yes, mounted atop his eight-legged steed Sleipnir, riding into battle against the Jötnar and their legions of monsters that will someday destroy all the world."

The wolf-warrior fell to his knees again as he looked at the carving, breathing deeply of the misty night air. In that moment, Jörgen felt as if he could sense the gaze of one-eyed Odin watching over them, and he too dropped to his knees. He had seldom given more than a few required thoughts to the gods, in truth. He'd attended sacrifices at some temple or other, now and then, as was expected, but he almost never took the time to truly sit and think about them...

When he felt it was right to speak again, Joe pointed at the red outlines of figures depicted on the stone, glittering in the moonlight. "What are those... twisted men, being trampled under Sleipnir's hooves? They are much smaller than the giants there. And uglier."

"Those are the Children of Chaos, bred by the Jötnar to fight the Noble Races, of whom they are deformed mockeries. They live the realm of the giants – in Jötunheim, which exists deep in the high mountains at the Jagged Edge of the world. The giants send them forth to attack our realm and raid and murder. It is our duty as servants of the noble gods to fight back these monsters, in order to keep the Ragnarök – the end of the world – at bay."

Joe nodded. "Do you think... Do you think they represent the Empire?"

Nick turned on him then, his half-man, half-wolf head whirling about, and somehow both pairs of eyes seemed to gleam more fiercely – the man's and the wolf's. "They 'represent' nothing! They are *exactly what you see.* The Chaos Races are *real,* Jörgen of the Björnings! Count yourself lucky that you and your band of outlaws never met any on your travels in the wilds. But perhaps you'd be wiser for it now... had you survived the encounter."

"I apologize, brother," said Joe, putting a hand to his heart. "Jörgen meant no offense. I'm just surprised that the North does not send more warriors to fight these monsters. They sound like an even greater threat than the Empire!"

"Aye," said the berserker, forcing himself back to a state of calm with surprising ease, "but they're a less immediate threat. Only the brave men and women who volunteer for that fight travel to the lonely border outposts like Endibraut Hall to keep watch over the Jagged Edge. Meanwhile, our kings and queens send us south to fight ignorant Imperials, disregarding the terrible doom living in the mountains, which waits, and watches..."

"Perhaps we should be there ourselves..." Joe said, speaking carefully and trying not to offend the ulfhedinn.

Nick nodded. "Perhaps... But this is a worthy cause too. My Queen sent me and my berserkers here, and she is wise beyond our ken. But you... You don't answer to a king or queen, do you, Lone Bull? Perhaps you could join us... We'll take men of any tribe, if they are willing and able to walk the path of the berserker. I see it in you, Jörgen. You even like to go bare-chested, as we do – that's what *berserk* means! Perhaps there is the spirit of a beast within you, hibernating... sleeping... and just waiting to be awoken."

Joe pondered these words, but did not reply. As he sat there amidst those painted and fur-clad warriors all meditating beneath the great shimmering runestone, he felt a combination of serenity and, strangely, anticipation... as if something terrible were looming nearby, or up ahead, and he could not quite see it. Then, far in the distance, he heard a wolf howl mournfully into the night, and all the wolfskin-clad berserkers around him immediately threw back their heads and joined in its song. Joe had seldom ever felt even a twinge of fear in his life... but just then, he felt a cold chill run down his spine.

"Joe!" he heard a voice hiss nearby, breaking the spell.

"Ivarr?" Joe replied, peering into the shadows at the edge of the hill.

"Yes, now come over here!"

With a parting nod to Nicklas, Joe rose and walked down from the top of the knoll to join his friend. He found Ivarr lurking in the shade of a tree, as if hiding from the moonlight... or, more likely, the berserkers. He was watching them with wariness in his eyes.

"What's wrong, friend?" Joe calmly asked, striding toward him.

"What are you doing, hanging out with their kind?" Ivarr said, still half-whispering in a frustrated hiss. "Come on, you know berserks can't be trusted, especially not on a night like this! They do strange rituals and cover themselves in animal skins so Odin will grant them the dark secret powers of beast-spirits... and sometimes it's too much for them to handle. Did you hear them howl? When their control starts to slip like that, especially in the heat of battle when they're giving into the rage, they can... *turn*. They become man-wolves, man-bears, and start attacking friend and foe alike! And once they've changed, they can never go back."

"Hmm..." was Joe's only reply – a deep rumble from down in his mighty chest. Then, after a moment's pause, it erupted out as booming laughter. "HAHAHA! Oh, Ivarr, you've got more in common with the berserkers than you think – you both like to tell tall tales of monsters and spirits!" He grabbed his friend by the arm and pulled him out from the shadows, throwing an arm around him and playfully punching his shoulder.

"Ow!" exclaimed Ivarr, rubbing his shoulder. "Easy, Joe! And they're not just stories! It's true, every word."

"You see? That's exactly what the berserker said!"

Ivarr sighed. "Let's just find Hjordis. The warriors are already assembling for the attack."

"Then let us join them! Jörgen would not miss this battle for all of the gold in Templaria!"

Together they searched for Hjordis at her usual tent, to no avail. She was not at their tent either. Joe stopped there to retrieve his armor: the simple sleeveless shirt of scale-mail he had deigned to bring along for the great battle. Ivarr laughed as Joe squeezed into the thing, which was a bit too small.

His helmet was more ornate. It bore a pair of long bull's horns, curving forward, so that they pointed straight toward the enemy. The size of the horns nearly rivaled those on the famed helmet of Guntram, chieftain of the Frost Ravens.

Joe and Ivarr, now fully armored, searched on. Hjordis was not at the feasting tent, nor with the other volunteers and mercenaries assembling in the field, strapping on their helmets and shields of many different styles and colors. So they started simply walking around the camp and calling her name at intervals. It was hardly a distraction or interruption to the rest of the camp, filled as it was with noise and bustle. Still Hjordis did not appear... until they passed Jarl Thorsten's great command tent.

They turned in surprise to see her toss aside the furs hanging over the entrance and strut out, still fastening her bodice over her mail hauberk. She blew out a sigh and smiled. "Yes? You called for me?"

"We..." Ivarr began, but he seemed to forget what he was was going to say.

"What were you doing in the Jarl's tent?" Jörgen asked quite innocently.

Then Jarl Thorsten himself appeared, stumbling out of the pavilion as finished strapping on his armor. He walked with a slight limp, and he winced when he stopped to stretch. Then he shook his head and slipped on his gold-adorned helmet.

Hjordis laughed heartily at him, then turned to her friends and said, "We were just... discussing strategy."

"Ah!" replied Joe, returning her smile. "Well, let us in on what you planned!"

Ivarr sidled closer to the bigger man and whispered: "Joe... They weren't actually discussing strategy."

"Oh?" Joe said, and then the confused look on his face slowly disappeared. "Ohhh..."

The Jarl cleared his throat loudly, throwing his fur cloak over his shoulders in order to appear larger as he strode up to them while trying not to limp. "I'm glad you're all here! Hjordis, you–"

She cut him off: "You should join your men at the front, my Jarl. I'll go with Joe and Ivarr to rally the mercenaries and volunteers."

Thorsten paused, staring at her for a second in thought before replying, "Yes. Thank you. Good luck to you all."

With a whirl of his cloak, the Jarl marched off toward the main body of the army, where the soldiers of his tribe were assembling. His limp seemed to be fading; he now only paused every other step. They watched him go, and then headed off to the non-Geatling section of the camp.

"I never let them give me orders after we've shared a bed," Hjordis clarified as they walked.

"You handled it well," Jörgen said honestly. "And congratulations, Wildcat, on getting the first conquest of the day!"

Ivarr snorted. "If only we could conquer the Empire by showing off our legs..."

"Ha!" Hjordis exclaimed, lifting her armored skirt a bit and tensing her thigh muscles. "These would snap any puny Imperial man like a twig!"

"I have no doubt," Joe said admiringly.

By the time they were done bantering, they had reached the assembled non-tribal forces. It was unfair to call them all mercenaries, for though some were fighting for gold, others had simply volunteered, like Joe, Ivarr, and Hjordis. They were only getting paid at all because King Wulfric of the Geatlings refused to let them fight for him and then go home empty-handed. There were men and women of all tribes present, from dark-haired Frost Ravens to pale Skridar hailing from the frozen far-northern reaches – all risking their lives to fight the Empire they saw as a threat to their homelands.

As they looked over the rows of fighting men and women, Ivarr elbowed Joe in the side. "They're all watching you, Joe. Maybe you should make a speech?"

"Jörgen is no good at speech-making!" Joe retorted, looking at his friend and then back at the crowd of warriors. Then, speaking loudly so all could hear, he added, "He is a man of action, not words! Perhaps his friend Ivarr would prefer to speak instead?"

Ivarr's cheeks went almost as red as his beard, but after a pause, he turned to sweep his hand in a grand gesture before the crowd. "Friends, brothers, sons of the North! You know of my friend Joe, but you do not know him as I do. He thinks he's not a leader – says he was the face of our Wolfpack, but not the brains. I say that makes him even more a leader! For who is the leader: a man who gives counsel behind a curtain, or the man who *acts* upon it? It is the one who acts - a man whom others look up to! A man they would follow through the gates of Hel and into the jaws of Fenrir himself! That man is Jörgen, the Lone Bull!"

A chorus of cheers erupted from the crowd – cheers and roars and howls and battle-cries. Weapons were shaken and shields were beaten. Joe even heard a few people chant his name, or at least his joking nickname: *"Joe! Joe! JOE!"*

Before the chanting could catch on, he interrupted: "Ivarr gives Jörgen too much credit! For too long did the Lone Bull and his Wolf friends hide in the shadows, striking only when the time was right. Only now does Jörgen see his error. The enemy must be faced head-on, if the North is to remain free. Jörgen does not ask to lead you; he asks for the honor to join you! Let us fight, together!"

The crowd cheered again, and finally Joe lowered his arms and looked back at his friends. Ivarr gave a slow clap and a nodded in approval, as if to say: You're better at this than you think. Hjordis was just laughing and shaking her head at the whole display.

"If you boys are done talking," she said, "let's get out there and fight."

Joe had not been in many *real* battles... In fact, not counting a few medium-sized skirmishes the Wolfpack had joined, this was probably only his second one. It was an odd and uncomfortable feeling, being just another soldier among thousands, fighting amidst so much death. It made the scuffles he had fought with the Wolfpack seem small and petty in comparison.

The sky was so grey that morning that it made all below look grey as well, even the billowing green grass of the open field where the armies stood ready to fight. The mercenaries and volunteers were positioned in the middle of the lines of Northmen, with a square of Geatling spearmen on either side of them, and a row of Geatling archers behind. This was to ensure none of them had second thoughts about fighting for the North.

Up ahead, the Imperial knights marched to meet them. They were all mounted – Jörgen had never seen so many horses in his life – and their armor seemed to gleam even in the dim grey light that filtered through the clouds above. Their lances were as long as the Geatlings' pikes, and a few bore long, flowing banners decorated with the eagle of Rimegard, the Imperial Crown, and a few other crests of lesser families.

Jörgen was not prepared for the sheer terror of an Imperial heavy cavalry charge. When those rows and rows of armored steeds started to build momentum, he felt the very earth beneath his feet begin to shake. The sound was like thunder unleashed by Thor himself from the heavens. The Nordling archers let a volley fly into the Imperial knights' ranks, but they barely seemed to notice. It did not slow them down; the charge only grew faster.

They plunged like an enormous speartip made of steel-clad men and horses... right into the center of the barbarian lines. Right into Joe and his compatriots.

Almost at the last moment, Joe remembered to draw Skera. He raised her gleaming blade high above his head and let out a bellowing war cry to inspire those around him. But it was cut short as, quicker than he ever could have imagined, the Imperial knights barreled through their ranks.

Joe saw men and women physically go flying, while others fell to be trampled under the avalanche of hooves. A few knights fell to the spears of the warriors in the first row, but not enough to slow the onslaught. Joe felt the urge to inspire his men to somehow push them back, but he knew that all he could do at this point was fight.

So, he gripped Skera tightly with one hand on the hilt and another on the foregrip, and then charged, leaping into the air to strike the first rider he saw on the chest. The blade cut through the knight's reins and struck him hard on the breastplate. He was knocked onto his back in the saddle, and Joe grabbed his arm just in time to pull him the rest of the way out. They both landed in the dirt, but the knight never had time to rise. The last thing he saw was Skera's pommel coming down toward his forehead.

At length, the knights' charge began to slow. First the berserkers entered the fray with terrifying beastly screams, filling the knights with fear. Then the great wedge of armored riders reached the line of Geatling pikemen at the back of the army, and their already reduced momentum was ground to a halt. Finally, the barbarians closed in around them, and all became chaos.

Joe had no idea how long the battle lasted, but by the time it was done, the grass beneath his feet was slick with blood. All of the Imperials were either dead, incapacitated, or had fled in a wild, unorganized retreat.

Jarl Thorsten, now standing in a heavily decorated war-chariot drawn by two horses, rode in front of the lines, shouting, "Take the village! You have one day to plunder! One day's plunder for every man! Take whatever you can carry!"

Joe saw the Jarl riding toward him. Without fear, he stepped out in front of the pair of horses. Thorsten spotted the great man immediately and drew his steeds to a halt. They whinnied and reared, but he managed to calm them, even as the sea of Northern warriors rushed past his chariot, headed toward the village.

"What is it, Jörgen?" Thorsten asked, trying to keep the anger from his voice.

"A day of plunder?" Joe said with outrage. "I thought we were freeing this village, not raiding it!"

"Have you never been on a raid, Joe!? Never been a-viking?" Thorsten replied, tugging at one of the braids in his yellow beard.

"This is no raid on foreign lands! This is our homeland!" Joe retorted.

"I have to let the men plunder! Many of them can't feed their families without the loot they take here today."

"And what about the families in the village?!"

The Jarl shook his helmeted head. "They're none of my concern! The damn overconfident Imperials should have evacuated!"

"The Imperials are gone; these are *villagers!*"

"They aren't Northmen, Jörgen!" Thorsten snapped, his anger no longer hidden. "This town was built by Imperials, settled by Imperials!"

"Imperials? These are not Achaeans from the south! Most are sons and daughters of the North, who just happened to be born on land the Imperials claimed! Many men in your army are the same – even the leader of the berserkers!"

"But *these* villagers followed the Imperial army, helped them conquer their own homeland, and built homes for the Empire! They've earned their fate! *Enough, Joe!* If you won't raid, then stay and watch. I'm heading to that hill to do the same. Join me or don't. *Ya!*"

With that, he whipped his horses back to a canter and sped off to the hill he had indicated, overlooking the village. Joe noticed Hjordis was already there, waiting for the Jarl. He was pleased to see her alive, and seemingly uninjured, though she was splattered with Imperial blood.

Jörgen heard a voice call out to him: "Joe!"

He turned to see Ivarr waving for him to follow. He seemed eager to head for the village and join in the looting. Joe gave him a noncommital wave and began walking ponderously in that direction, unsure of what to do as the chaos raged around him. Ivarr waited for a second or two, then nodded and ran off into town.

Joe had never been on a raid before – not a real one. He had grown up among the inland Björnings, not the seafaring Wurmtongues like his friend Ivarr, and he'd been an orphan and an outsider even there. He knew raids were a fact of life, but never had he seen one with his own eyes. Even now, he tried not to look, but the sounds kept drawing his eyes regardless.

As he strode into the village, gazing at the simple wooden houses, he heard women screaming, and turned to see families fleeing their homes. He heard animals crying out and saw warriors crudely butchering livestock, sometimes throwing a pig or sheep over their shoulders to carry back home. He saw men squabbling over loot and putting houses to the torch because they were decorated with Imperial banners or shields. Smoke filled the air.

He watched all of this and kept walking, in an almost numb state. Then one sight provoked a reaction: He saw a boy stumbling to climb atop his horse, but his legs were too short. The young lad kept slipping, startling the animal... as a pair of Northern warriors walked toward him, laughing. One of them raised a battleaxe and prepared to charge.

Joe stepped in front of him. The man stumbled and fell on his back, and his partner let out a curse. Without a word, Joe stared them down, until they turned and ran. Then he turned and pushed the boy up into his saddle with one hand, and slapped the horse on the rear with the other. The child never looked back. Joe could hardly blame him.

He walked on, the smoke thick in his nostrils, heading vaguely in the direction he'd seen Ivarr running. He'd lost sight of his friend, who had apparently been looking for an as-yet-unlooted house – for fresh pickings. Then Joe heard a terrified, tearful wail, and turned to see a woman running out of her home, carrying a baby tight in her arms.

Ivarr stepped out right behind her. He grabbed the woman by her clothes and pulled her back, gripping her arm and struggling. Joe took a step toward them, but not before Ivarr knocked the child out of the woman's hands. The infant landed on the ground with a sickening little thud, and made no sound after. Joe felt his heart crawl up into his throat. He tried to shout at his friend, but he couldn't seem to make a sound.

In three great strides, Jörgen made his way toward them. He saw Ivarr tearing at the woman's clothes, heedless of her cries. His vision red, Joe grabbed his friend by the shoulder and spun him around. Ivarr looked up at him, his blue eyes wild – they looked nothing like those of the friend Joe knew so well. This man who had feared the berserkers was now just as crazed as they ever were.

Joe punched him in the face.

Ivarr went down like a sack of rocks. The Imperial village girl screamed, picked up her baby, and ran. Joe never learned if the child was okay. He never looked back at the girl, and never saw her again. He just stared at his friend.

Because Ivarr was dead. Joe had hit him without thinking, filled with righteous indignation, too angry to hold back. By fate or misfortune, Joe's fist had struck in exactly the right way... or perhaps Ivarr had hit his head upon one of the stones beside the walkway when he fell... Either way, his eyes now stared blankly at the Northern sky. Joe crouched down, shook him, and listened for breathing... but there was nothing.

Joe stood up again. At first, he could not see or hear anything around him. The sounds of the looting were gone. All that existed for him was Ivarr's corpse... and his own bloody hands, at which he couldn't stop staring.

Then, slowly, the rest of the world faded back into reality. He heard the screaming, the crying, the burning, the shouting and breaking and laughing.

Joe tore off his helmet, letting his long hair fly free. Then he threw back his head and let out a terrible sound. It was half wail and half roar, like the sound of a bear that had just returned to the den and found its cubs lying there dead. By the time he looked around, Joe saw that every Northern warrior within earshot was standing still, gazing in his direction.

"Get out!" he bellowed. *"GET OUT!"*

A group of four warriors exchanged glances, apparently sure that Joe had gone mad, and decided to stop him. They dropped the loot they were carrying and approached him, their hands on the hilts of their weapons.

"Joe!" shouted the foremost warrior. "Jörgen! What's gotten into you?"

"I said *LEAVE THIS PLACE!*" Joe roared.

He reached down and lifted a great beam of lumber from the ground nearby. Then he heaved it sideways at the approaching foursome, knocking them all to the ground like bowling pins. Joe heard someone approaching behind him and turned to see two more warriors charging at his flank, one with a two-handed axe raised high above his head.

Joe waited for the axe to swing down, and he grabbed the haft, right between the warrior's hands. So great was Jörgen's rage-fueled strength that he halted its momentum instantly. Then he brought his other hand around, grabbed the stunned warrior's belt, and lifted the man high over his head. He tossed him bodily atop his companion, and down both went in a heap.

Those of his victims who could still easily move quickly scrambled to their feet and fled. Joe chased after them, roaring and swinging another plank of wood at anyone who came close. He charged a group of six looters, and they dropped their valuables and ran. More and more of the raiders joined the flight, assuming that Imperial reinforcements had arrived, some even running out of the Imperial houses and shouting for retreat.

From atop their hill, Jarl Thorsten and Hjordis watched in wonderment as somewhere between a quarter and half the army began pouring back out of the village, carrying very little plunder. Thorsten shouted down at them to halt and report what was happening, but he received mixed answers. Some said they'd heard that the Imperial Legions had arrived, while others spoke of a great monster or a demon-possessed madman defending the town.

Then they spotted Joe. By that point, he had long since ceased his rampage and gone back to retrieve the body of his former best friend. He carried Ivarr over one shoulder, walking at an even pace, heedless of the chaos around him, his eyes fixed on the horizon ahead. He strode right below the hill upon which the Jarl and his people had set up their command post. He didn't even glance at the gleaming chariot above him, or the king standing atop it. Thorsten shouted down at him, and Hjordis joined him.

"Joe!" she called out. "Joe, is that Ivarr? Is he okay? What happened? Dammit, Joe, answer me!"

As she ran down the hill toward him, he finally stopped and turned to regard her, and the look in his eyes made her freeze in her tracks. Joe glanced up at the Jarl, then back to her, his expression stony. She could tell that Ivarr was dead; he did not move at all.

At length, Joe said in a deep, monotone voice: "Jörgen is taking Ivarr back to his his people."

Still standing a good distance off, halfway up the hill, the Jarl responded in a carefully friendly yet commanding tone: "We'll take him there together, Jörgen, once we've seen this campaign to the end."

Joe did not look up at him; he didn't even respond. He just kept staring at Hjordis until she spoke. She looked back into his eyes – their blue appearing dark under the hanging grey clouds – and took a deep breath.

"The Jarl is right, Joe. We can still help here. Then I *swear* I will come with you to Wurmbreath Fjord, and we'll give Ivarr a hero's funeral."

"No," said Jörgen, his gaze still cold. "You can stay with the Goat-Lord, Wildcat. Help finish his 'campaign.' But Jörgen the Lone Bull is done with it. He will be taking a karvi, and enough thralls to man it. Perhaps he will send them back after reaching the Fjord, or perhaps not... but if Jarl Thorsten sends anyone to try to stop Jörgen... their blood will be on the Jarl's hands."

Jarl Thorsten stomped down the hill until he stood close enough behind Hjordis to hiss a whisper into her ear: "Is he serious? I can't tell when he's speaking like a fool."

Hjordis shot him a furious look. "Let's get back up the hill, Thorsten. I *suggest* you let Jörgen take the ship he wants, if you know what's good for you."

"Joe! If you think I–" the Jarl began, taking two steps toward Joe, but he soon stopped dead when the Lone Bull finally looked at him.

Joe's chest heaved, his breathing so hard that it stirred the hairs of his thick brown beard, and he bellowed in his tremendous voice: "Come one step closer, and tales will sing of how Jarl Thorsten took an Imperial village, only to die the same day from the bare hands of Jörgen the Outlaw, killer of men! Do you care how your saga ends, Goat-Lord? Because in this moment... 'Joe' does not."

Thorsten's nostrils flared, and he wanted deeply to draw his weapon and strike down this insolent rebel. The only thing that stopped him... was fear. When he looked up into the smoldering eyes of the much taller man towering above him, he found his hand began to shake, and he couldn't even bring it to grip his sword hilt.

After spending far too long a moment standing this way, frozen in terror, with his men watching... Jarl Thorsten did as he was told, turning about and stomping back up the way he'd come. Hjordis gave Joe one more long, meaningful look, but when he said nothing more, she turned and followed the Jarl. Joe carefully and reverently shifted Ivarr to his other enormous shoulder... and then marched on.

The karvi made good time from the mouth of the river and northward across the sea to Wurmbreath Fjord. The little longship was manned by a skeleton crew of thralls, wearing slave-collars bearing the mark of Jarl Thorsten. Jörgen had never approved of the practice of thralldom, especially when it involved making men wear collars, so he offered each of them the chance to go free if they desired it. Most did not, for they had families back in Horngöfgasta and the outlying villages, and they hoped to buy their freedom legally someday and become a real part of the Geatling tribe. To those, Joe offered a share of what little gold he and Ivarr had on their persons. The thralls were all happy to row for him then.

They made good time across the grey waves of the Boreal Sea, but even the fresh, crisp ocean air did nothing to lighten Jörgen's spirits. For most of the journey, he sat in the center of the ship, staring down at the coffin in which he'd placed the body of his friend. He wondered which crime was worse... Ivarr's attack on the woman and her child, or Joe's angry retaliation. Perhaps in some way it had been justice, but Joe had never meant to kill his friend.

Perhaps Nick Wolf had been right: there was a beast inside him, and Ivarr had woken it. It could have just as easily been Stígander he'd accidentally killed in his fury, he thought... but a voice in his head replied: *The Hawk would never have tried to rape a woman, or thrown her child to the ground in front of her. Perhaps that's why he chose not to join the war.*

War. For so long, Jörgen had wished to fight the war against the Empire in earnest, even if it killed him. And perhaps it had. After witnessing the horrors of war – the blood-soaked battlefields, the mass deaths of fellow men fighting to defend their homes, the slaughter of women and children – he felt like a different man. He could never go back to that.

Perhaps he would wander, like his lost old friend Stígander. He understood now why the Hawk had done it so often, and why he'd always wisely avoided true war. What Joe had to learn firsthand... perhaps the Wanderer had always known.

These thoughts and others filled his mind on the voyage to Wurmbreath Fjord. Fortunately for him, the journey was uneventful. Only when they finally reached the Fjord did Joe begin to seem truly alive again. He looked up at the great cliff walls of grey stone, whose sheer faces rose up out of the sea on either side of the inlet.

The dwellings of the Wurmtongues were quite a unique site. The cliffs were covered in ornate wooden walkways, with formed ladders and lifts and bridges to reach the caverns where many of the Wurmtongues dwelled. Great decorative carvings of sea beasts and battles and gods adorned the cliff faces, and everywhere were the colorful sails of longships. It was beautiful.

As their little boat slid into the shadow of the cliffs and headed for one of the docks jutting from their feet, Joe took a deep breath. With determination, he made good on all his promises to the thralls, setting some free with bags full of provisions and letting the others take the ship back, along with a little gold and silver for their time. Joe only asked one more thing of one of the freedmen: he asked him to help carry Ivarr's casket to his family.

Unfortunately, Ivarr's family proved difficult to find. Jörgen knew only that they lived on the southern cliffs. The main settlement of Wurmbreath Fjord lay at the inland end of the bay, at sea level, but Ivarr had lived in the high cave dwellings, from which the Wurmtongues looked down on every ship that entered their inlet.

Which was why they docked near the mouth of the fjord and made their way up to one of the cliffside dwellings via a rope-and-pulley lift. Joe asked every man he passed for directions to take him to the local Jarl. The chaotic dwelling places were awkwardly connected, when they connected at all. Some had rope-ladders and bridges, others stone-carved stairs with no railings between the walker and the sea far below. Joe tried not to look down, as the walkways swayed in the wind that blew through the fjord, howling like the souls of the damned as it blasted over the mouths of the many caves.

Eventually, they located the local Jarl's great cave near the very top of the cliff face, and they carried the casket inside. Lights streamed into the well-furnished and well-fortified dwelling from windows in the ceiling – windows of colored glass, which illuminated the carpets on the floor in a rainbow of hues. The workings of the cave were so finely-wrought that Joe wondered if the place had once belonged to seafaring dwarves. Now it belonged to a man... whom Joe quickly realized was not a Jarl at all, but the very King of all the Wurmtongues, Harald Bloodbeard himself.

He was seated on a throne carved from a single block of stone, but cushioned with thick pillows that looked like they had come from as far south as Parsanshar. The hue of Harald Bloodbeard's hair lived up to its name: his long, partially braided beard was a shade of red almost as deep as the stripes on his clan's dragon-adorned banners. He wore a hauberk of the finest scale mail, which looked like it may have been wrought from a dragon's own hide. The long, twisted horns on his gold-tinted helm backed up this theory. Nodding to his guards to remain alert, he motioned for Jörgen to approach.

Jörgen told the freed thrall to take his leave, thanking him for his service, and then turned and knelt before King Harald. Joe's deep voice reverberated through the chamber as he said, "My Lord, Jörgen of the Björnings humbly presents to you in this coffin the body of his dear friend Ivarr, a son of your people. He asks that you summon Ivarr's father or other family, so that he might repay them for their son's death."

Harald Bloodbeard, after a lengthy pause of contemplation, blew out a long sigh. "By Heithrún's teats, Jörgen of the Björnings, must ye be so dramatic? Guards, fetch this man a drink! He sounds like he needs one. Looks it too! Stand up, Jörgen – might as well, since you're as tall kneeling as most men standing! Talk to me straight; I'm a King o' the North, not some Achaean prince propped up by ceremony. Tell me where you come from, and why you should want to 'repay' Ivarr's family for anything."

"Apologies, Lord," said Joe, rising to his feet again, so high that his eyes were level with the king's atop his throne. "Jörgen... *I* come from a battle to the south. Ivarr and I fought as volunteers alongside the Geatlings. We took an Imperial village. As for what I wish to repay... No disrespect, my Lord, but I would rather tell that to Ivarr's family."

King Harald snorted. "Good answer. Better than I hoped for, since I already know exactly what happened. Jarl Thorsten sent a message by raven explaining the whole bloody thing. And what a mess! You're lucky I don't like Thorsten, the stuck-up little man, so I won't even consider his request to put you in chains. Hell, I'd throw you a feast instead, if you wanted it! So... alright then, Bull. Guards! Go fetch Ingi, father of Ivarr. Bring him here to see his son and hear what Jörgen has to say."

Jörgen nodded in thanks as the guards left the room, their scale mail hauberks clattering. The King and Joe sat and stood, respectively, watching each other in silence until they returned. It did not take long. Ingi's arrival was announced by an anguished wail that drove like a steel knife into Joe's heart.

"Ivarr! *IVAAAAAARR!*" cried the old man as he stumbled over and fell to his knees beside the open coffin. "Oh, my son! My son..."

Jörgen turned to him and bowed his head, waiting for the grey-haired fisherman – clad in naught but filthy rags – to finish pouring out his grief. This didn't take long either, for he soon wheeled on Joe. Apparently the guards had told him what Joe had said about repaying him.

"You... You're the one they call Jörgen?" Ingi said, swallowing his tears. "Tell me what happened. Tell me who killed my boy!"

There was a lust for vengeance in his voice, and in his old grey eyes... as expected from a man of the North. Jörgen had to swallow as well, in order to answer him. At first he couldn't get the words out, but then he took a deep breath and tried again.

"I did," he said.

Ingi reacted in an instant. With another loud wail of grief, this time mixed with rage, he leapt up and threw himself at Joe. He was smaller than Jörgen, of course – most people were – and he was frail. Perhaps Ivarr had gotten his strength from his mother's side. The old man's rain of blows barely even caused the giant Lone Bull to budge. But while they may not have hurt his body, each strike from the weak old fists sent a spasm of pain through Joe's heart.

"WHY?" choked Ingi, now leaning against Jörgen's sturdy form, almost sliding to his knees again as he tried to catch his breath. "Why? Why? WHYYYYY?"

Joe's jaw was clenched tight as he replied, "Alas, Jörgen cannot say. I'm sorry. But to say it might dishonor his memory, and Jörgen could not bear to do that to Ivarr, my brother! Those who hear Jörgen in this hall today... Let them say that Ivarr son of Ingi died a hero, in battle against the Empire, rather than by accident... at the hands of a friend."

Jörgen tried to go on, but a surge of emotion got the best of him, and his throat tied itself into a knot. Through blurred eyes, he saw old Ingi, father of Ivarr, push himself back to his feet.

"That's not good enough!" the old man spat, his face contorted with sorrow and anger. "That's-"

"*I KNOW!*" Jörgen bellowed, his voice echoing off the walls of the cliffside cave and frightening away a flock of resting birds outside. "I... know. Jörgen will repay you for your son's death however he can. Sadly, he has little to give in return for a life he held so valuable. Only this."

Joe unfastened his sword-belt and dropped to his knees, presenting the weapon to Ingi. The old man's eyes went so wide they looked like they might burst out. It was the most beautiful sword anyone in the room had ever beheld, except perhaps King Harald, who had been on so many daring raids against the Empire.

The guards all craned their necks for a better look at Skera's great golden hilt, which ran up the sides of the blade to form a foregrip. The designs on the pommel and crosspiece, decorated with dragons and runes and the hammer of Thor, were so intricate and perfect that they looked beyond human skill to make – perhaps the handiwork of elves or dwarves... or of men in the days of legend, when gods walked among mortals and true heroes strode the land.

"This is Skera," Joe said. "Or so Jörgen named her. Jörgen took her from an Imperial knight-captain that the Wolfpack captured some years ago. He in turn claimed to have taken it from the tomb of a mighty Northern king of a long-forgotten tribe, who was buried with treasure beyond count, but this blade alone sat atop the sarcophagus.

"When the Wolfpack captured the knight, every Wolf wanted his sword, but they also wanted a share of the ransom gold, and they knew this blade was worth two shares easily. So Jörgen forwent all his shares twice, that he might keep it. The blade must be wrought of deepsilver, for seldom has it required sharpening. It's worth a king's ransom, some might say... but still Jörgen knows not if it is worthy weregild for his friend Ivarr."

Ingi was speechless as he took the blade, holding it with surprising ease, for deepsilver was as light as it was hard. "I... I... This is too much to be weregild for my son. Ivarr was the son of a fisherman..."

"Take it!" Joe insisted. "Jörgen never wishes to see it again. In fact, in this moment Jörgen swears that never again will he draw a sword to harm another man. He will never again even carry a sword! His armor also is yours! Jörgen is done with fighting. Perhaps 'Joe' will wander ascetic, like his lost friend Stígander... until he finds a better path in life."

For a long while, Ingi looked like he was trying to think of some way to respond to that speech, but he couldn't find the words. It was such an impassioned declaration that the old man knew he could only forgive Jörgen for the accidental slaying. He wrapped his arms around the sheathed sword and merely nodded. It was the best he could do. Jörgen looked relieved, but only slightly. His eyes still burned with grief.

Then King Harald Bloodbeard gave a low grunt. "Mmm, yes. Well. He's right, Joe. Friend or no friend, that's far too great a sword to be weregild for a fisherman's son turned outlaw, bandit, and mercenary. Ivarr's man-price would not be one tenth that much, and Ingi has no more sons and no use for such a blade anyway. But Ingi: I will give you ten gold pieces for the sword now, plus another gold piece every month for a year, and a new house on the main shore town – a better home for an infirm old man than these cold, wet cliffs. And I will have the skalds sing songs for years of your son's heroic death fighting the Southron Empire, as Jörgen said. Sound fair?"

Ingi looked around the room with blank eyes, as if this were all simply too much to take in, but eventually he licked his lips and managed to reply: "I... Yes, yes... Of course, my Lord... my gracious King... I... Can I have a new fishing boat too?"

Harald chuckled, carefully taking the sword with a reverential bow of his head when Ingi handed it to him. "Done. You can go, Jörgen. When you finish your 'ascetic wandering' and decide you do want to fight some more after all, I just want you to know there's a spot on my longship for a warrior like you. That'll be all. Dismissed."

Later, Jörgen could barely recall leaving Wurmbreath Fjord. He went about the rest of his actions there in a daze, shedding his armor for a simple cloak and taking only a hunting bow and a wood axe for his weapons. Then, on foot and carrying few provisions, he left alone. He didn't seek out Hjordis or anyone else he knew. He just pointed his feet in the direction that felt the best in his gut, and started walking.

Part 3: Let the Rainbow Remind You

The next several months of Jörgen's life passed less eventfully, and he was thankful for that. For the first few moons, he wandered the North, visiting villages he'd never seen, meeting people he'd never met, and seeing sights that were new to his eyes. But living alone on the road was hard, and he grew weary of it. Perhaps that was Stígander's way, but Joe began to think it wasn't his.

So, at the next habitation that struck his fancy, he stopped. It turned out to be a small farm, operated by one lonely old man. Joe was running low on provisions, and though he hated to take advantage of the unwritten laws of hospitality that governed all men of the North, he had little choice. So he stopped in at the farm and listened to the old man – who only gave his name as 'Bert' – tell his story while Joe ate a bowl of his stew.

"It'll be hard going without my son," his host said wearily, with heavy heart and heavy eyes. "He died fightin' against the Empire. Signed up with the Chunni horde, if you can believe it, just because they were the only ones fightin' at the time. I begged him not to; told him there was no need for us to get involved. The Empire's never done us wrong, not directly. But off he went, and less than a year later, one Chunni rider – a dirty little horseman who didn't even seem to care – he came by my house to let me know my boy was dead. Didn't even give me any of his possessions. He was all I had left..."

Joe placed one enormous hand on the old farmer's shoulder. "I will stay and help you, for as long as needed."

"What...?" the old man said incredulously. "But I can see you're no farmer. You've got a warrior's walk, and a warrior's scars. Why would you want to help here? I've got almost nothing left..."

Joe's beard parted in a wide, bright smile – one of precious few in the last three months. "Think nothing of it, friend. You gave Jörgen soup, so he will fix your farm. Jörgen always pays his debts."

And for the next two moons, he did just that. He helped repair the buildings, harvest the crops, feed the animals, carry goods to town to sell, and carry supplies back. It turned out to be far more work than his life on the road had been, but also far more rewarding. It felt good to work the earth, feel satisfaction at a hard day's labor, and most of all: to use his hands to *build* something, rather than only using them to destroy.

But it was not destined to last.

It was grey that day, the sky overcast with dismal clouds that stubbornly refused to give up their precious rain. Jörgen was on his way back from town, carrying some much-needed supplies, when he saw the column of smoke just beginning to rise from the farmhouse, somehow both whiter and blacker than the grey clouds above. Joe immediately dropped his goods and took off at a run.

He was entirely unprepared for what happened next. As he ran down the dirt road leading to the farmhouse, a great black shape emerged to his left and pounced. It hit him like a charging bull – an even bigger one than Joe himself – knocking all the wind from his lungs and throwing him to the earth so hard that his heavy shoulder left a rut in the dirt.

Joe quickly turned over and shielded his face with his arms. He saw a shadow swinging down from above and almost instinctively recognized it as a battleaxe. Or something like a battleaxe – a twisted and misshapen facsimile of one. Even so, his attacker was no bull or other beast. It was armed.

Just as instinctively as he'd recognized the threat, Joe rolled out of the way to one side, and he heard the weapon land with a soft thud in the ground, right where he'd been lying. He pushed himself quickly to his feet and turned to face his foe as it struggled to pull its axe free. Joe had planned to retaliate while his enemy was distracted, but the sight of the attacker's true form froze him in place.

In all his travels, Jörgen had never seen anything like it. It bore the shape of a man, but everything about it was *wrong*. Its skin was a sickly dark grey-green, pitch-black in places, like the color of a long-dead corpse. Its teeth stood out startlingly in contrast, yet its eyes looked like mere pinpricks of deathly light. Where the whites of its eyes should have been was dark black, fading into a pale yellow iris that almost glowed, and its teeth were a tangle of crooked fangs that jutted out so badly that it couldn't properly close its mouth. Its hair was the color of rotten straw, wiry and tangled, fashioned into long knots that dangled down its back. Its entire form was covered in scarred, twisted musculature and little else, save a loincloth and bits of bone and human ears dangling from strings. And worse than all of this... it was even bigger and taller than Jörgen himself.

The abomination opened its lopsided maw and let out a howl unlike that of any man or beast, full of fury so primal that Jörgen felt his heart start pounding against his chest. He resisted the urge to turn on his heels and run as fast as his legs could carry him. Instead, he summoned up the courage to dive straight in, grabbing the haft of the creature's great axe before it could bring the weapon around again.

Both combatants struggled for the axe, pulling it back and forth, each trying to trip the other and throw them off balance. Jörgen quickly realized he was losing. This monster's strength was beyond any man he'd ever fought. So, Joe kicked his foot up into the creature's groin as hard as his muscles could propel it.

The monster didn't even flinch. In fact, Joe almost thought he saw its mouth muscles tense up into a mockery of a grin. For it took advantage of Joe's move to push him to the ground as he stood awkwardly on one foot.

Jörgen felt his back hit the dirt, and then the weight of the beast pressed upon his arms as it bore down against the axe they both still held between them. The monster leaned in close, opening its eyes and mouth wide and letting out another bellowing howl, spittle flying from its maw into Joe's face.

Joe reached over, grabbed a clump of dirt from the ground, and dashed it into the demon's eyes. The timbre of its howling changed suddenly as it shook its head, temporarily blinded. Joe felt its strength ebb just slightly, and he took the opportunity to shove hard against the axe and push the creature off him. Then he jumped to his feet and kicked the struggling monster in the throat. It gasped and released the axe.

Once the weapon was in his hands, Joe brought it up and then back down, right at the abomination's head. But the beast brought up its arm, and the weapon struck that instead. It went right through, severing the wrist, but the creature didn't even seem to care. It rose to its feet and lunged at Joe in a mad frenzy, foam flying from its lips. Joe twisted the axe around and smashed the butt of its handle into the oncoming monster's forehead. There was a loud crack... but it was from the axe handle splitting, not the monster's skull.

The beast kept coming. It grabbed Joe's arm and bit his wrist with its twisted teeth. It was Jörgen's turn to howl. But not from pain. He channeled the pain into rage, letting out a war cry that rivaled even the monster's bellowing. Then he took the splintered axe haft and rammed it into the side of the creature's throat. Black blood poured out, staining the ground and the side of Jörgen's trousers like ink. Even then, it took a moment for those fangs to finally release his arm.

With one last spasm of twitching, the monster finally fell to the earth, dead. Still pumped up in the moment, Jörgen made sure it was over by striking the neck once more, this time with the blade of the axe. The severed head rolled away to one side. Only then did Joe allow himself a moment to catch his breath.

But he didn't wait long. Then he dropped the broken weapon and instead took a long knife that the monster had sheathed in one of the trophy-covered ropes it had tangled around its body. Joe drew the weapon and ran toward the burning farmhouse. Silhouetted against the rising flames, he saw yet more of the huge alien creatures, wielding terrifying weapons forged from black volcanic stone and rusty metal.

But he was surprised to find that he wasn't the only one fighting them. A flash of steel shone out in the darkness, cutting one of the monsters across the stomach, spilling its guts. As it fell, Joe saw its killer: an Imperial knight. He wore a suit of finely-crafted chain armor, with steel plates on his gauntlets and boots, and a steel great helm. Over top of it all flowed a grey tabard bearing a simple four-pointed white star, stained with splatters of blood, and bound at the waist by a red sash.

One of the abominations leapt upon the knight from behind, wrapping its twisted muscular arm around his throat. The knight stumbled back, flailing his sword ineffectually over his shoulder. The Lone Bull charged in.

"Turn around!" Jörgen shouted, using the Imperial tongue, and fortunately the knight immediately followed the order, twisting his body so that Joe could strike the monster clinging to his back.

The beast barely had time to glance in Joe's direction before the long knife sank into its eye socket. It immediately released the knight, falling limp to the ground. Joe pulled his long knife back out and looked around, prepared for another attack. Beside him, after giving a nod of thanks, the knight did the same.

But there was no need, for the other monsters had no desire to fight them. Their yellow and reddish eyes exchanged quick glances, and then they turned and fled. Some dropped sacks of loot or even weapons so they could run faster.

"Go, demons!" Jörgen shouted at their backs, pounding his chest with one fist. "Go back and tell your masters you were no match for Jörgen the Lone Bull and…"

He glanced at the knight beside him, but the Imperial only shook his helmed head. Joe shrugged and lowered his arms. The knight then slid the great helm from his head. Joe was surprised at how young he looked. He had the complexion of a southern Achaean, with dark hair and brown eyes. His features were as handsome as a statue's, with an aquiline nose, high cheekbones, and a chiseled jaw so clean shaven it looked like a young boy's.

"My name is Sir Willem of Whitehorn," he said. "I apologize for not saying it before, but I did not wish it shouted at those orcs… not because I fear them, but because I do not spread tales of my deeds. I am but a humble servant of Astra. And I humbly thank you for your aid. I owe you my life."

"You owe me nothing," said Joe. "Jörgen never asks that anyone repay a good deed. Do a good deed for another instead – someone who needs it."

The knight paused a long moment, giving Jörgen a quizzical look. "A noble philosophy. I'd never thought of that. I will do so."

"You are welcome, Star Knight."

Sir Willem chuckled. "I'm surprised you speak Imperial so well."

"A wise friend of mine once said, it is good to learn as much as you can about your enemies. But the Empire is no longer my enemy. You have nothing to fear from Jörgen."

"I don't serve the Empire anyway. I am a knight-errant – a masterless wanderer."

"Good," Joe said with a smile, "I like wanderers." He started looking around then, peering right over the knight's head – since he stood about a head taller. "An old man lives on this farm…" Jörgen said. "Have you seen…"

His voice trailed off when he spotted a shape leaning against a fence in the distance. When he saw it move, he ran to help. Old Bert was barely alive, his clothes and the fence behind him stained with blood. Joe moved to help him, but the farmer waved him back.

"I'm… done…" he choked out, barely able to breathe. "Jörgen… the farm… is yours… The village folk… know you now. They'll… understand… Take care… of Flare…"

He started coughing then, and Joe held him steady until he stopped. But when the coughing stopped, so did the breathing. Bert did not move again.

"May you join your son now," said Jörgen, by way of a prayer, "in the halls of your ancestors."

"I'm sorry…" said Sir Willem, as Joe closed the dead man's eyes and rose back to his feet. "Who is Flare?"

"The mule," Joe replied, scanning the farm. "It looks like all of the other animals were taken or killed by these monsters."

"At least they didn't take your friend here. It's better this way, if what I've read is true. Orcs do horrific things to their captives."

Joe turned to face him, his expression grim. "These were really them then? Orcs? Real orcs?"

"Yes," replied the knight, "one of the Chaos Races, created by the giants to battle the Noble Races favored by the gods. Most of them dwell deep in the Jagged Edge; they seldom attack this far out…"

Jörgen thought of the words of Nick Wolf, and his nostrils flared. He looked at the destruction all around them, and then down at the twisted monsters lying dead on the earth, staining it black with their blood. One had a broken jaw, and Joe noticed that not a single tooth in its gaping mouth was flat. Every crooked tooth was sharp, for tearing meat.

Joe shook his head. "So, these creatures are raiders, gathering meat to bring to their families in the mountains?"

"Not according to the Venatori – the Empire's monster-hunters, who have been fighting them since before recorded time. They say the Chaos Races have no families. They are born from great breeding pits full of disgusting concoctions into which prisoners are thrown... or sometimes the prisoners are hung in cages over the pit and bled out slowly. The stronger the prisoners who are fed to the pit, the stronger the orcs and goblins that emerge from it."

Joe picked up a weapon that one of the monsters had left behind. The sword, if one could call it that, was little more than a great hunk of metal with a handle carved into it, along with as many jutting spikes and cutting edges as could be sharpened. He tried to give it a few swings, but it was awkward and unbalanced. He dropped it back into the dirt, where it embedded itself at an angle, standing lopsided. It looked hideous, unnatural, like the orcs themselves.

"They make nothing of beauty," Willem said. "They create no art, only savage weapons. They have no women, no children. For such things are weak, and they cannot abide weakness. They feel no positive emotions. No joy, no love. Only hate and fear."

Joe frowned at him. "How can you know this? Some imperials might say such things of us men of the North."

"But these are not men. Not even animals. A mockery of life."

Joe just frowned even more deeply and nodded, grunting. He still had his doubts.

After a moment's pause, the knight said, "So... What are you going to do now, good Jörgen? Repair this farm–"

Joe cut him off. "I will tell you what Jörgen is going to do."

He strode over to the woodshed and picked up the large, double-bit axe there, testing its weight and grip. He pulled on the axe-head to make sure it was tightly attached. Then, satisfied, he swung it in an arc, noisily cutting the air, before letting it rest on his shoulder.

"Jörgen," he said, "is coming with you. He wishes to see the Armies of Chaos for himself."

Sir Willem broke into a smile. "I was hoping you'd say that. I have been wandering for many months now, traveling alone as a knight-errant, in search of wisdom in the name of Astra. You, Jörgen, are not quite like any Nordling I've met. I'd be honored to travel with you to the edge of the world, to spill the blood of the chaos races."

So the Nordling and the Achaean set to work repairing parts of the farm and putting out fires, and Sir Willem penned a note on some parchment for Joe, in which Joe declared his ownership of the farm, and they left the note on the door of the farmhouse. Willem's horse had been killed by orcs when he arrived, so he transferred his saddlebags to the mule named Flare, which Joe also loaded up with other supplies. Then they buried the old farmer and the knight's horse, and they left the farm together.

Jörgen and Sir Willem traveled north, staying off the main roads, keeping their eyes peeled for more signs of attacks by the minions of chaos. They saw nothing. To their right rose the towering Jagged Edge mountains, so tall they seemed to stretch into infinity, with the endless trees called the Immortal Wood spread out like a dark blanket over their feet.

There was no guessing how far away those peaks might lie. The Edge was as wide as many nations and filled with its own empires and cities and networks of caves. Even now, thousands of orcs, ogres, and goblins might be spilling forth from breeding pits there, preparing to overrun the unsuspecting North as they struggled against the Achaean Empire.

"Jörgen is done fighting men," Joe remarked as he and the knight walked, and he sharpened his wood-axe. "See this axe? 'Tis a far nobler weapon than a sword. With an axe, a man can cut wood for the fire. With a hammer, he can craft and build. With a spear or bow, he can hunt food for his family. That's why these are the weapons of the common people – because in times of peace, they are tools. But what can a sword do? It's a luxury of nobles, made only for one purpose: killing men. And Jörgen is done with it. *I am done with it.*"

Sir Willem gazed at him with something like wonder. "Truly, my goddess must have led me to you... You almost inspire me to give up my own sword, if it did not bear the symbol of my faith. Perhaps if I can find her a worthy resting place..."

Joe shrugged. "You give too much credit. Jörgen is far more foolish than wise. He has done many reckless things, regrettable things, and certainly would not wish that any follow in his footsteps. Keep your sword, and may you do far more good with it than Jörgen did with his own blade, Skera."

"All wisdom must be earned," replied the knight, "and it takes wisdom to recognize one's foolishness."

Joe pondered this for a moment, rubbing his temples, and then he burst out with a laugh. "Then let us stop at the next mead-hall and share a foolish number of drinks! And see if that leads to wisdom too. All this sober talk of wisdom is giving Jörgen a headache."

"Alas, I don't drink. I took an oath..."

"Then I shall have to drink enough for both of us!"

Sir Willem smiled and nodded, and so they carried out their plan. A few locals in the mead-hall gave Sir Willem hostile looks, but Jörgen vouched for him, either using his reputation or his fists to convince them to leave the knight alone. Joe drank and laughed at Willem's tales of his travels, no matter how dull. All of this set the journey back nearly a full day, but as two wayward souls seeking wisdom in unlikely places, they were in no particular hurry.

As they drew closer to Endibraut Hall, signs of human life became more and more scarce. They found themselves in the midst of the wilderness, with only a few overgrown trails visible amidst the rocky fields of the highlands. The Jagged Edge seemed none too distant now, and the black forests of the North were close enough to touch. They dared not head through the woods directly, however, for fear of angering the forest's unseen guardians: elves, trolls, and other fabled creatures of the Northern wilds.

At length, they spotted Endibraut Hall, keeping its lonely vigil atop a rocky foothill of the Jagged Edge: an outermost sign of Mankind's dominion, daring invaders to attack it. The settlement was surrounded by a ring of rough stone walls topped with wooden battlements. To their surprise, they saw that the tall gates were flung wide, and a group of men and women stood at the entrance, exchanging words. And based on their gestures, they did not appear to be kind words.

Sir Willem glanced at Joe. "They don't seem to know we're here. Do they even have sentries in place?"

Jörgen shook his head in bewilderment. "Strange. What's going on? Perhaps we should make ourselves known."

"I agree," replied the knight. "I just hope that my presence doesn't add to the commotion…"

Jörgen led the way, his hand raised. Sir Willem walked slightly behind him, hoping not to catch too much attention until Joe vouched for him. He wondered if they would both end up having to hide behind the poor pack mule, Flare, to avoid a hail of arrows. He hoped it wouldn't come to that. Yet still, no one in the fortress hailed them. As they drew closer, they could hear the raised voices of the men and women standing in the gateway. They were arguing.

At last, Jörgen could take the suspense no longer, and with both hands raised, he bellowed in his tremendous voice: "Hail, fellows of Endibraut Hall! I am Jörgen, the Lone Bull of the Björnburg! And this is my companion, Willem of Whitehorn, a knight-errant of Astra! We come to join you!"

One particularly large, rotund man – as great in girth as he was in stature – turned and barked angrily at some of the soldiers gathered in the fortress behind him: "Dammit, Milo! I told you to keep some ploughin' watchmen on the walls! Get some archers up there, before I load your worthless arse into a catapult!"

A dark-haired woman in a raven-feather cloak threw back her head and laughed. "Ha! Do you hear that, Nick? No archers! We probably could have taken the fort ourselves!"

As they talked, Joe and Willem continued to move forward, until finally the great round man – clearly with plenty of muscle under all his healthy layer of insulating blubber, despite his beard being nearly as white as snow – swung around a great long-axe and waved it at them. A violet banner hung from the weapon's haft, bearing the silver reindeer emblem of the Skridar tribesmen.

"Hold, wanderers!" the fat man shouted. "I've heard of this Jörgen the Lone Bull, but he'll come no closer with an Imperial knight in his company!"

"An *Achaean* knight! I do not serve the Crown!" Sir Willem called back – using the common tongue of Northrim, though he was no expert at it. "I fight only for what is right, and your cause is good! I will lend my sword, if you will have me."

The great white-haired man spat on the ground and then planted the butt of his flagpole-axe where it landed. "Well, we *won't* have you! So maybe you should be gone while we're still willing to let you walk away alive!"

"Ignore the fat man, Jörgen!" called out a familiar voice to Joe's weary ears. "Come on up! Any friend of Jörgen's is a friend of all the North!"

"Wolfman!" Joe laughed, his beard parting in a beaming smile. "Nick Wolf, who fought with the Geatling army in their march up the Rime?"

"The very same!" replied the wolf-headed Nick, waving him forward with one great, painted arm.

"He's not the boss of this fort!" retorted old white-beard, stamping his flag-axe again. "I am Olaf the Strong, former war-leader of the Skridar, and Endibraut Hall belongs to us and our allies! Archers, loose a warning arrow at their feet! ... *Archers!*"

But no arrow came, so Joe and Willem exchanged a shrug and continued walking, until they stood right behind Nicklas and the dark-haired woman. Nick looked much more approachable without his dark green face-paint, though somehow his eyes seemed to shine even greener as he clapped Joe's hand in his. His arms were still covered in markings, and he still wore the wolf-skin helm on his head, with a green cape hanging down his back, decorated with the silver wolf head emblem of the Wulfing tribe.

The raven-haired woman was equally painted, Joe noticed, with some tattoos even climbing up her neck and onto her scalp, which was shaved bald on one side to show the inking. The rest of her head was covered in an untamed, short black mane that seemed to point in every direction. Her blue eyes were equally wild. She wore little on her muscular form other than her ink, some strips of cloth, several sheathed blades, and many scars... and a torn blue Frost-Raven banner dangling from her belt.

She caught Jörgen looking at her and gave him a wink. "You can look, big bull, but don't touch, unless you want to lose a finger. I'm Caiside, of the Frost Ravens."

"I'd say don't let Cais scare you," said Nick, "but actually she's terrifying with that spear and those knives. She's a berserker too. So's the rest of our group here."

"That's right," said Cais, turning her blazing blue eyes back on the men assembled behind the walls, "we're *all* berserkers, and you should *all* be scared of us! Now let us inside the damn walls, before you make us lose our tempers! You don't want us to lose our tempers..."

"I never let a bare-chested madman – *or* woman – on my longship," bellowed Olaf the Strong, "and I'm not about to let one into my fort! You animals can't be trusted any more than this Southron knight!"

"*It is not your fort,*" came a voice as loud and clear as an eagle's cry, from somewhere within the crowd inside the walls.

The speaker was the most surprising sight thus far at this fortress full of surprises. Joe's eyes went wide as soon as he saw him, and then almost shut again at the gleaming light that seemed to radiate from every golden part of his body. It was a Ljosalfar – a Light Elf – one of the ancient race that dwelled deep within the Immortal Wood. His skin was pale and his eyes a bright light blue, but everything else about him was gold: his long flowing hair, his armor, and the narrow banner dangling from his elegant weapon: a long spear with a curved, sword-like head.

"I am Eledér, Justiciar of Mimameidr," he said. "You warriors have a right to be proud of the work you do here, helping fight back the Armies of Chaos. But do you know why your lands were not overrun by Jötnar forces centuries ago? Because my people – the Alfar – have been fighting them for all that time, and longer. In order to reach your lands, the orcs and goblins and ogres must first travel through *our* forests. And I can assure you, very few of them slip through alive."

Caiside blew out an impatient sigh. "Get to the point, elf."

Eledér shot her a sharp look, and even the fierce berserker woman took a step back. Though average in height, somehow the Light-Elf seemed taller than everyone in sight. There was an otherworldly aura about him, as if he could ascend into the heavens at any moment, should he choose... or perhaps fade through the veil into the Spirit Realm, and then walk back again.

"The point," said the elf, resting a gloved hand on the hilt of his sword, "is that my people have an interest in keeping this fort in working order. It has a key strategic position on the border of the mountains you call the Jagged Edge. We certainly would prefer if you continue to occupy it... but if you cannot work out your differences and keep the defenses properly manned... then the Alfar may be forced to step in."

"Is that a threat?" Nick asked, his green eyes narrowing.

"Not yet," replied Eledér.

"Well, there, you see?" proclaimed Olaf the Strong. "We should close the gates now! Better to have a stable Endibraut Hall under the control of me and my allies than–"

"Or under the control of Nick!" retorted Cais, and she slammed the point of her spear deep into the earth at the bottom of the wooden gate, to hold it open. "Or perhaps Joe here, who is a well-known hero of the North!"

Joe looked around between them and put up his hands. He could hardly believe what he was witnessing. Here was this legendary hall of heroes – the fortress at the edge of Northrim, the first line of defense against the armies who wished to end all the world – and the gates were standing wide open, defended by nothing but self-centered squabbling rabble.

"Jörgen is no leader..." Joe began, but Olaf cut him off with another great belly-laugh.

"*Hahaha!* Some hero of the North, traveling with an Imperial knight!"

"*Achaean* knight," corrected Sir Willem. "I told you, I am *not* here on behalf of the Empire."

"What's that around your waist then? That red sash, with a hint of gold on the edges... looks more like the material of a flag to me! The flag of the Empire!"

The berserkers wheeled on the knight too then, and faster than anyone could blink, Cais reached out and tore the sash from Sir Willem's waist. As soon as the cloth was unfurled – and revealed to indeed be a red Imperial banner adorned with a golden crown and a Legionary eagle – Sir Willem's sword came halfway out of its sheath. He stopped himself from drawing it completely, but stood his ground with fire in his dark eyes.

"That is not a flag of war!" Willem said. "But I swore a holy oath never to let anyone take it from me. So give it back, and we can talk about this like reasonable–"

Olaf laughed again, resting one hand atop his armored belly. "Oh, this is rich! A hilarious jest, to be sure. But I've had enough now, thanks. Milo, close the gates!"

"Not a chance!" shouted another berserker, who slammed his spear into the ground next to Caiside's, to further jam the door. It was quickly joined by several more.

"This is bordering on an act of war now!" Olaf bellowed.

"We've spent too long squabbling," said Eledér the elf. "End this now, mortals, one way or another, and *seal the gates.*"

"Let in everyone but this damn Imperial!" said Cais, pointing at Sir Willem, with the flag still dangling from her fingers.

The knight quickly snatched his banner and stuffed it into a bag hanging from Flare. Cais reached for one of her long knives. Olaf saw this and lowered his poleaxe, pointing it at her. Eledér brandished his golden glaive in an acrobatic display. Nick unslung both of his axes...

And Jörgen was nowhere to be seen. He found he could no longer take it. He was sick of seeing men and women and elves and dwarves and all other noble beings always at each other's throats. He'd seen enough of it, taken part in enough of it. He didn't want to get caught in another petty fight, lose his temper, and end up with someone else's blood on his hands...

So, while they were still shouting, he had simply walked away. He wandered several feet off and climbed atop a small rise near the edge of the rocky hill upon which Endibraut Hall rested. He could see a long way from here... and he saw someone approaching from the mountains to the east. It was a man... but there was something very strange about him. He seemed to be a fair distance away, walking in the shadow of black clouds that loomed on the midday horizon... and yet he looked as if he were closer.

Then Joe realized why.

He was huge.

No, not just huge: enormous. He stood as tall as the great Northrim pines on either side of him. He was a Jötunn, a Giant... and the black shapes behind his feet, kicking up a cloud of dust that followed in his wake... they were an army. Joe could only guess they were orcs, ogres, goblins, hobgoblins, and who knew what else. The Chaos Races.

They were here.

Joe wheeled to tell the others just as they were drawing their weapons on each other. He saw them readying to kill one another, and he felt rage well up inside him – the same rage that had killed his best friend. Taking a deep breath, Joe interrupted the fight with a shout:

"*GIANT! A giant is coming!* And the Army of Chaos behind him!"

For half a second, they could only stare at him in stunned silence. Some of them swallowed, looking ashamed. Then Olaf the Strong let out a furious roar.

"*Whaaaaat!?*" the great man shouted, looking back up at the battlements above him. "Milo, what in the name of Hel!? *Didn't you see them!?*"

"I was w-watching the fight!" Milo called back. "W-we all were!"

Nick Wolf's eyes narrowed yet again. "Get these gates closed! *Now!*"

The great doors made a grinding sound, but barely budged, and they heard Milo shout, "We can't! They're jammed! The spears..."

Caiside ran to her spear and grabbed it, trying to pull it loose. But she couldn't budge it. "It's stuck under the damn gate now! Pull it back open some!"

"No time for gates!" called Jörgen. "They'll be here in minutes! Everyone, *prepare to fight!*"

As soon as he said this, a heavy stone as large as man came hurtling through the air, thrown by the giant in the distance. It missed the fortress and landed in the dirt, leaving a small crater and a cloud of dust and dirt, but the effect was immediate: the warriors of Endibraut Hall assembled for battle.

Olaf sent the archers to the battlements and called the strongest warriors to form a line at the edge of the hill, their brightly-painted shields held tightly together. Behind them gathered the berserkers, led by Nick Wolf. Then followed the other warriors of the Hall, from tribes all over the North and beyond. In addition to Eledér, Jörgen spotted at least one wood-elf and two dwarves, and of course the Achaean knight Sir Willem, who looked very much the part now that he had retrieved his shining helm and kite shield from Flare. These defenders of Endibraut Hall were an even more motley assortment than the mercenaries and volunteers Joe had seen in the Geatling army. And most were outcasts and outsiders, even outlaws, not unlike himself.

Then, as suddenly as the first thunderclap of an unexpected storm, the forces of Chaos arrived. Most of the monsters wore little armor, and all of them ran as fast as the wind, taking great long strides with legs at least as long as a man's – every hideous creature in the horde was at least man-sized, and most were larger. Jörgen had heard goblins described as small, but these were tall, lanky things, only appearing shorter than the rest because they tended to run with a hunched posture.

Jörgen had seen orcs now, but he was unprepared for the sight of the other Chaos Races. The goblins had long ears and noses, wiry and twisted muscles, and beady black eyes with points of light glowing dimly in the center. The ogres were like orcs but nearly twice as tall and with twice as many teeth – some with tusks longer than a great boar's. And most terrifying of all were the creatures that Joe could not identify: deformed things covered in fur or scales or even feathers, with beaks and tusks and fangs and claws of all kinds. Some of these Chaos Beasts moved upright and carried weapons, while others ran on all fours and were even used as mounts by the orcs and goblins.

Even worse than the sight of such an army was their smell and the sound of their horrid roaring and hissing and braying. Their presence was overwhelming to all the senses, and as they came within range of the archers atop the fortress, Joe could see the fear in the eyes of the other Northmen around him. He doubted that a horde of demons from the depths of Hel could be more terrifying than this Army of Chaos. And darkness seemed to follow them – the clouds in the sky had thickened, blotting out the sun.

Joe tried to bolster the courage of his comrades: "Let's see who can kill the most! They will NOT take this hill!"

A shout arose from the assembled warriors, and though it was quickly drowned out by the cacophony of roars from the Chaos monsters, Joe saw some of the earlier fear fade to be replaced by determination. They tightened their lines and dug their feet in, ready for the worst.

First came a hail of missiles fired mostly by goblin archers at the back of the horde. But they were poorly-made weapons and short ranged, and for every volley the goblins sent, the Northern archers loosed one of their own, which flew far truer and deadlier. The goblins took heavy losses and might have broken and fled if the ogres had not been behind them, stomping their enormous feet and pushing them forward.

The monsters reached the hill. Part of the hillside was rocky and impassable, so they were forced to go around to a narrow slope... where the defenders of Endibraut Hall stood waiting. Yet even the ascent of the hillside barely slowed the charging orcs and goblins. They made the climb in a few long strides and hit the shield-wall running.

The defenders wavered, but every time a breach was made in the row of shields, a berserker or two advanced from behind to fill it and push back the orcs. Nick and Cais were the first ones out, terrifying even the children of Chaos with their sheer ferocity and imperviousness to all pain. Swords, axes, and spears sang through the air and began hacking orcs and goblins limb from limb.

But Joe's sights were elsewhere.

He couldn't take his eyes off the Jötunn.

Never before had he seen a creature so terrifying and awe-inspiring. It stood taller than the fortress walls of Endibraut, and it even wore armor: a hauberk of scale mail fashioned from what looked like broken shields, both human and orc-made. And it carried a "short" sword as long as two men at least, with a quality blade forged of fine steel.

Most terrifying of all, however, was what seemed most normal about it: its features were entirely human, not deformed in the slightest like those of its minions. Indeed, its face looked almost handsome behind its red beard. Yet also ancient – its features shriveled and severe, weathered by time, like a time-worn colossus carved from stone centuries ago.

Suddenly, the Ljosalfar Justiciar, Eledér, was standing beside Jörgen. He shone there like a visitor from the gods, like a vision sent by Freyr to aid Joe in his time of need. In his clear Elven voice that cut through the din around them, he said:

"That is a Hill Giant - the least of all the Jötnar. Their godlike cousins who live in their empire of Jötunheim would make this one look like a babe. And yet, 'tis strange to see any giant this far from home, for they risk the wrath of the gods for interfering with the mortal world directly..."

"Hrmm..." Joe growled under his breath. "So, if we hold out long enough, Thor himself will fly down on his chariot and slay this one?"

"I doubt it. And by the time they notice a giant is loose upon the world, it may be too late for us. We'll have to take him down ourselves. Then his army will break."

Joe glanced at the Alfar, into his otherworldly blue-green eyes. "Take him down together? Jörgen would be honored. Does the Elf-Lord have a plan?"

"I do. The enemy forces are all on that side of the hill, so we'll run straight down the rocks instead, and charge the Jötunn. You go after one leg with your axe, I will go after the other with my glaive, and when he topples, we will both go for the throat."

"Glaive?"

The Ljosalfar twirled his long, gleaming weapon, and the light that reflected from it glittered on his golden armor. "My spear. It has a blade as long as a sword's. My people favor it. It is something like your people's *atgeir*."

"Well then," said Joe, gripping his simple but hefty double-bit wood-axe. "What are we waiting for?"

The elf gave a smile, which was at once both handsome and strangely fierce, and in those blazing eyes Jörgen sensed decades of battle experience. Alfar were immortal, and Joe had no way of knowing how long Eledér had walked this earth. His features were strong and severe, even more timeless than the giant's. It was likely he had been killing the minions of Chaos for a lifetime before Joe was even born.

Jörgen was an experienced climber and made his way quickly down the rock-face, but he was no match for the elf. Joe went down backwards, searching for handholds and footholds, while Eledér simply ran – almost danced – from one tiny outcropping to the next, hardly ever touching the stones with more than the toes of his boots. His armor could not be true deepgold, Joe thought, to weigh so little.

Still, the light-elf did not have to wait long for Joe to catch up. Once they both had their feet on the ground, they took off at a run, straight toward the giant. No one seemed to have spotted them – the army was still entirely concentrated on the sloped hillside, and not a single orc or ogre or goblin stood directly between them and the towering Jötunn.

Never noticing the two tiny foes dashing through the grass toward him, the giant was taken completely by surprise when he felt a sharp pain in each of his knees. In his right leg, he felt a blade jab precisely into his tendons and then twist and slice, while his left leg was assaulted by a shower of heavy blows, as Joe chopped away at it like he was felling a tree.

The giant looked down and let out a rumbling growl that Jörgen felt shake the very air around him. With alarming speed, its great trunk-like leg lashed out, kicking Joe in the chest. The blow would have knocked every ounce of wind from most men, but Joe retained his strength enough to grasp tightly to the straps on the giant's armored boot.

Meanwhile, the Jötunn turned his attention to Eledér, swinging his tremendous sword down at the elf. Eledér took a step back, dodging the blade, but it cut right through the handle of his glaive, breaking the haft in two. Undaunted, Eledér sprinted right up the side of the giant's boot and grabbed the weapon's blade where it was impaled in the monster's knee, pulling it free.

Hanging tight to either of the giant's boots, both Joe and Eledér swung their weapons with their free hands – putting all the strength they could into their blow – and slashed deep into the back of the giant's knees. With a long, echoing groan that made both of the battling armies pause... the Jötunn crashed to the earth. First, he fell to his knees – knocking Joe and Eledér to the ground – and then his upper body followed, crushing a few goblins and an ogre in the back of the enemy lines.

Joe looked past the giant's feet at Eledér on the opposite side. He was pleased to see the elf uninjured.

"Go for the throat!" Eledér shouted.

Jörgen did as he was told, running around the fallen giant's arm and cutting down a pair of goblins on his way to the head. As the second goblin fell in a burst of black blood, Joe grabbed its crooked spear. But when he got to the giant's head, it was already rising back to its feet.

Joe saw the Jötunn lift its arms high in the air and then put them down again, pushing itself back up. He then saw Eledér standing in front of him, where the other side of the giant's head had just been lying. The elf had his broken spear raised to strike, but he hadn't reached his target in time either.

A voice as deep as the abyss – so deep and loud it made even Jörgen's seem like a mewling kitten in comparison – came from high above their heads:

"You think you can fell a son of Ymir so easily?"

The Jötunn's great hand came swinging through the air, slamming into Eledér and sending him flying. The golden elf struck the rocky hillside like a catapult stone. He crashed into a heap in the shadow of the hill and didn't move again.

The Jötunn barked out a command in some guttural tongue Jörgen had never heard before, and his army's rearguard of hulking ogres stumbled over themselves in their rush to obey. They were heading for Eledér, probably to finish him off. Joe ran to stop them.

But then the giant's hand swung again, and wrapped its fingers around him. Joe felt the entirely novel sensation of being lifted bodily into the air, almost as if he had learned to fly and simply leapt up to join the birds. Except for one difference: the crushing pressure of the giant's fingers, which had his entire body in their grasp.

His arms were being squeezed hard against his sides. The giant's thumb was pressing the arm holding his wood axe tight against his chest. Joe's other arm was pinned straight down under the giant's four fingers, where it held the stolen goblin spear near Joe's uselessly dangling legs.

The giant brought Jörgen up for a good look, holding him right in front of his eyes. For a second, Joe could only stare into those huge grey eyes – each one as big as his head. They were not the eyes of a dullard or a simple monster, like those of the Chaos Races. No, there was cunning behind these eyes, keener than most men's.

And, strangely... a spark of recognition. Or something like it. The giant's expression changed slightly, its eyes narrowing as it studied Joe's face.

Yet the monster didn't say a word. He just kept squeezing Jörgen tighter and tighter, crushing the wind from his lungs until his ribs began to snap. And Joe saw him bringing the other hand around now... the hand that still held the colossal sword. It brought the blade to rest against the giant's forearm, as if preparing to slice horizontally and carve off Joe's head.

Joe had only one choice: he had to be stronger than a giant.

Taking as deep a breath as he could muster, the Lone Bull called upon all his rage. He roared at the top of his crushed lungs and pushed out with his axe-hand, straining against the Jötunn's thumb. The giant paused for a split second, holding its blade still as its eyes went wide in surprise. It was all the time Joe needed. He forced the huge thumb back, further and further – the muscles of his arm bulging as thick as the giant's fingers – until he heard the finger bone snap. The giant roared in pain, spraying Jörgen with spittle. Its sword moved, sliding toward Joe's head, but Joe ducked just in time, and chopped away at the giant's other fingers with his wood-axe.

Jörgen felt the world begin to move again. He looked around. The giant had rotated him sideways, so that he was looking straight down at the goblins and ogres watching from below. He looked 'up,' to see where the giant was taking him... and saw a gaping maw, surrounded by huge yellow teeth. The Jötunn was going to eat him... or at least bite his head off.

Joe took another swing at the fingers with his axe, and then pushed, loosening their grip enough to wriggle his other arm free. Then he dropped his axe, reached up to the top of the giant's hand, and grabbed a wad of hair there... and then pulled himself up. He heard the giant's teeth gnash upon the empty air below him as he steadied himself into a crouched position atop its hairy hand.

Fortunately, the Jötunn had closed its eyes before biting, so it didn't see him until it was too late. The only thing it had time to see was Jörgen's black goblin spear headed straight into one of its eyes. Joe drove it in as deeply as he could, with all the strength of both his arms and legs. The Jötunn let out the most horrifying wail thus far, outdoing all its previous sounds in volume. The noise echoed off the white faces of the distant Jagged Edge mountains.

Joe felt himself falling... and then realized it was the giant who was falling. He turned around just in time to see the ground rising up to meet him, and he jumped, landing with a roll in the dirt. The ground beneath him shook as the giant followed him down, toppling onto the earth in the same spot he had fallen before, crushing again the same ogre, which had only just struggled to its feet again.

Joe coughed and sputtered, wheezing for air, trying to regain his strength before the Army of Chaos closed in on him. He struggled up to his knees and looked around, feeling dizzy. When he could see clearly, what he saw amazed him.

The forces of Chaos were in full retreat. Orcs, goblins, and even ogres rushed past him, with panic evident in their wide black eyes. They stumbled around Joe, giving him the widest berth they possibly could, as if he might reach out and destroy them with a single swing of his arm at any moment. Joe was enveloped by a cloud of dust as the monsters stampeded around him.

When the dust settled, it was over. Joe gazed around at the ruins of the Army of Chaos. He saw dead orcs and goblins in piles at the foot of the hill, where the heroes defending Endibraut Hall had cut them down, never allowing them anywhere near the fort. He saw Eledér standing near the rocky cliffside, with one foot atop an ogre's corpse. The elf gave him a nod. And then Joe saw the giant... the body of the Jötunn he'd slain with his own two hands.

Then another sound echoed off the snow-covered Jagged Edge mountains, but it was no bellow of rage or pain. It was a united shout of joy, as the Northmen cheered in victory. Joe smiled. It was a good sound.

Putting one foot in front of the other, he headed toward the hill, trying to ignore how painful it was to breathe with his bruised and probably cracked ribs. Many of the Northern warriors ran to meet him, showering him with praise and clapping him on the back. Nick Wolf grabbed Jörgen and helped him balance, for he was still weak from the fight.

Nick looked over his injuries and smiled. "You'll be okay. By the gods, you killed a giant and lived to tell the tale! Everyone, let's hear it for Joe the Giant-Slayer!"

The roaring cheers filled the air again, and the army parted to let Joe and Nick through, up toward the fortress gates. Caiside approached and slid under Joe's other arm, giving him another wink. Apparently, she didn't mind him touching her now.

They made their way to the gates, which were still stuck open. Olaf the Strong was waiting there, covered in black blood and laughing with joy over their triumph. But his face fell when he saw Nick.

"Hey!" he shouted. "Release the hero! He's allowed in the fort now, and we'll throw him a feast fit for a king, but *you* are still forbidden. I saw the way you berserkers fought out there... One of your number even started growing fur and fangs! He ran off into the woods when the fight was over, and thank the gods he hasn't come back! If you think I'm letting you animals–"

"That's a lie!" said Cais, sliding out from under Joe's arm and drawing two of her knives. "I've had enough of this; I'm gonna carve up this loudmouthed ham!"

But to Joe's surprise, Sir Willem himself stepped in front of her and raised his shield. "Halt, berserker! Olaf is right! Whatever dark magic fuels your rage, it cannot be trusted!"

But Olaf just let out another belly laugh behind him. "Wise words, Imperial! But don't think that by taking my side, that means I'll let you into my fort..."

"Again!" interrupted the clarion voice of Eledér, who had just made his way up the hill to join them. "Again, this is not *your* fort, fat one! Nor does it belong to anyone here. If anything, you've only proven you *cannot* defend it! Were it not for Jörgen's heroism, this surprise attack would have crushed this hall to splinters. My people should take charge here, secure this position for good!"

Joe heard Nick give a distinctly wolf-like growl right next to his ear and say, "If you try to deny the North its proudest hall of heroes, elf, then you will answer to me!"

Joe heard weapons being drawn. He felt Nick's arm move, reaching for his axe. And then Jörgen felt a fury rise within him even greater than the rage he'd summoned to fight the Jötunn. It was the anger of righteous fury, the same anger that had killed Ivarr.

"*STOP!*" he roared, and everyone did exactly as they were told, freezing in place and staring at him.

First, Jörgen slid his hand off Nick's shoulder and grabbed the berserker's green cape in both hands, tearing it in half with one mighty pull. Then he marched up to Eledér and grabbed his broken glaive, ripping the golden banner right off it. The Ljosalfar simply stared at him, betraying no emotion. Joe went next to stand between Caiside and Sir Willem. He reached out and grabbed the sashes at their waists, one in each hand, tearing them free. Cais looked furious, and raised her weapon…

"Hold it, Caiside!" Nick shouted, and something in his tone actually made her stop. "This man just killed a giant, and probably saved all our lives!"

"Yes," said Eledér calmly. "Let him finish."

Finally, Jörgen approached Olaf. The man who looked so huge next to his own comrades suddenly seemed small next to the taller and very determined Jörgen the Lone Bull. To everyone's surprise, Olaf didn't even budge as Joe snatched the weapon from his hands and ripped off its purple-and-silver reindeer flag.

Then Joe stepped back, out into the center of the wide ring of onlookers gathering all around him. He glanced at them briefly, left and right… and then started rending each of the flags with his bare hands. Several warriors took a step forward, but each one was stopped either by his comrades or by the look of fury in Jörgen's eyes and the size of his rippling muscles as he shredded the colorful banners.

"These pieces of cloth…" he said between breaths as he rent and tore, "stand for tribes out *there*, far away from where we stand now! You left them behind to fight here, for a higher cause! But you cannot let go…"

He was about to say more, but something caught his eye, as he glanced down at the bits of flag already piled up at his feet. He saw their many, myriad colors… and he stopped, dropping what was left of the banners in his hands. Then, reaching down, he plucked one strip of cloth of each color from the pile: one red, from Sir Willem's Imperial flag; one gold, from Eledér's finely-woven Elven pennant; one green, from Nick's Wulfing cape; one blue, from Caiside's Frost-Raven sash… and one violet, from Olaf's Skridar banner.

"Give me a spear," Jörgen said.

Nick nodded to one of his berserkers, who tossed him a broken pike. Nick caught it and carried it to Jörgen, passing it to him almost reverently. Joe took the spear and began tying each of the long strips of cloth to it, one next to another: red, gold, green, blue, and purple. Then he held the spear aloft sideways, so that all of the colored streamers dangled beside each other.

"What does this look like to you?" asked Jörgen.... not like a grand proclamation, but in a curious voice, as if he were simply talking with a friend.

After a few seconds, Sir Willem of Whitehorn swallowed and answered: "A rainbow."

Nick's eyes lit up then, looking even more reverential than before as he said, "The Bifröst. The rainbow of the Bifröst Bridge."

An onlooker in the crowd shouted, "Could this be a sign from the gods!?"

Nick's bare chest heaved as he turned to the assembled warriors, exclaiming, "It *is* a sign! Look, all of you! The gods speak to us! They have given us a symbol of our holy purpose – a *new* flag, under which we can fight the forces of Chaos, together as one! United under the Bifröst, whose blazing holy fire keeps the Jötnar and their minions from entering Asgard!"

Joe actually let out a laugh, and so infectious was it that a few warriors in the crowd echoed the sound. "The Bifröst Banner. A new flag..."

"We will be the Brotherhood of the Bifröst Banner," said Nick Wolf, "defenders of Endibraut Hall!"

"Nick..." Caid said, sneering and scratching the shaven and tattooed side of her head, "are you losing your mind? Surely you don't buy this goat-cheese about brotherhood and holy purpose?"

Olaf snorted. "Took the words right out of my mouth, Frost-Raven."

"I believe it!" exclaimed Sir Willem, stepping into the open ring to join Joe and Nick. "Since I met him, Jörgen has spoken with great wisdom, such that I believe the gods brought me to him. And now I see that I was right. The gods *speak through him!* And Astra teaches that the gods of the North are as noble in purpose as those of Achaea, all allies against evil. Just as we are today!"

"Impressive," said Eledér the elf, striding up alongside them. "Such divine inspiration – such unity of purpose – I did not think existed among mortal men. This is a cause that I, and all of the Alfar, can proudly support."

Hearing these words spoken in that lordly Elven voice seemed to shake Joe out of a daze. He blinked and swallowed, as if he were slowly waking up from a dream, and only just now realizing what was happening. He still wasn't certain *how* or *why* it was happening. Had he started all of this? All he'd done was the same thing he always did: act without thinking, just as he'd done when he accidentally killed Ivarr. He was amazed that his rending of all those flags hadn't simply started a war. Instead, it seemed to be starting a movement. All because he'd looked down at the torn flags and seen something familiar...

After a moment of seemingly difficult thought, white-bearded Olaf the Strong puffed out his cheeks and blew a long sigh, and then threw his hands in the air and smiled. "Welp! I know when I'm beat! I reckon you're our leader now, Joe..."

"No!" Jörgen interrupted him, raising his hand. "Joe is *no one's* leader. He never has been. Jörgen fights *alongside* his comrades, not in front or behind."

"Jörgen," said Sir Willem, "look at what you've done here today. You have forged a peace between more than half a dozen warring peoples, saved this fort, slain a giant! There is no better leader."

Joe took a deep breath and blew it out through his nose, like a snorting bull. "Perhaps. But Jörgen will have no titles. I am Jörgen – even Joe, if you prefer. Nothing more. We are all equals here – brothers and sisters."

Caiside gave a satisfied snort. "Works for me."

Olaf threw out his arms. "Well, why are we just standing around out here then? Let's go in and have a feast! In honor of the Brotherhood of the Bifröst Banner! And Jörgen the Lone Bull, Giant-Slayer! *SKÁL!*"

"*SKÁL!*" returned Nicklas, and the cheer was echoed by every warrior present.

"*SKÁL! SKÁL! SKÁL!*"

They waved for Jörgen to enter the fortress first. He shrugged his great shoulders, hefted his banner of shredded cloth, and marched inside. The others fell into step behind him, breaking out into a marching chant as they set to work getting the gates closed and hanging new banners made from the scraps Joe had left in a pile behind him. They feasted well that night, each telling tales of the battle that would only grow more exaggerated with each new telling. And there would be many more tales told of that night, of the founding of the Brotherhood of the Bifröst Banner.

Thus ends this tale of an orphan boy who dreamed of the glory of the wars of men, but found that glory lacking, and so lay down his sword and sought a nobler struggle. Thus ends the tale of how Jörgen the Lone Bull, Outlaw of the Wolfpack, became Joe the Giant-Slayer, founder of the Bifröst Brotherhood – which still guards the realms of men from the forces of Chaos to this day. The man himself lives on as well, and I hope to bring you many more tales of his exploits in time, as we walk the world together.

- Dagfari Firebeard

Continue your journey through the world of Wulfgard!

ALSO AVAILABLE:

WULFGARD:

THE TOMB OF ANKHU

A Novella by Maegan A. Stebbins

An ancient mummy, a curse, and a forgotten tomb – though the loyal Medjai of Kemhet ever strive to protect their land's many secrets, a powerful warlock seeks to awaken the greatest evil the Southern Realms of Wulfgard have ever known, one who wielded power so great the gods themselves descended to curse him and seal him away: Pharaoh Ankhu the Endless. While a small group of Medjai race against time to stop the warlock from unleashing and attempting to steal the mummy's unspeakable power, one of the warlock's own rebellious slaves, Djedar Rath, may become the key to sealing Ankhu away in his tomb forever.

Wulfgard:

Into the North

A Graphic Novel by Justin R. R. Stebbins

In Northrim, a Wanderer stumbles down from the Jagged Edge after a long journey, and runs into a werewolf. In the Imperial capital, a young elven thief finds herself caught by demons and assassins hunting for a set of mysterious ancient artifacts. In the city of Rimegard, a princess struggles to hide a terrifying secret. And in the darkness beneath the world, a clan of dwarves wage war with demonic dark elves. Soon, all their fates are destined to intertwine. This volume of comics introduces their stories, comprising the first few chapters of a much larger tale.

For more Wulfgard books, comics, and stories,
please visit us online at:

WWW.WULFGARD.NET